RATION OF LIES

Maggie Sullivan Mystery #8

by
M. Ruth Myers

Independently published

Cover design by Cheri Lasota
Formatting by Karen Perkins

ACKNOWLEDGMENTS

Words cannot begin to express my gratitude to the following individuals whose input made this a better book:

Charles Potter, vintage car connoisseur, for sharing his knowledge of 1930s DeSotos, in particular the size of the trunk on Maggie's car and the workings of its lock

Retired Dayton police sergeant **Stephen Grismer**, secretary-treasurer of the Dayton Police History Foundation, Inc. for patiently answering my questions

Keiko and David Hergesheimer for their knowledge of Japanese culture and our long years of friendship.

Any inaccuracies are entirely my own.

ALSO BY THIS AUTHOR

Maggie Sullivan Mysteries

No Game for a Dame
Tough Cookie
Don't Dare a Dame
Shamus in a Skirt
Maximum Moxie
Dames Fight Harder
Uncivil Defense

Other Novels

The Whiskey Tide
A Touch of Magic

For ages 9-12:

The Great Leandro's Treasure

Ration of Lies

April 1944

CHAPTER ONE

Should I put on my prissy little black hat like a proper funeral goer or buy a live goldfish? Which was a truer tribute to the man with whom I'd scraped more knees and committed more childhood high jinks than I could count?

A rap on my office door spared me a decision. There was more resolve behind the knock than would-be clients usually showed.

"Yeah, come on in." I sat up, tossing the hat aside.

The girl who came in halted halfway between the door and my desk. She couldn't have been more than sixteen or seventeen. Black hair in a Victory Roll framed a determined yet wary face. An attractive face.

A Japanese face.

She held a handful of twenties before her like a shield.

"I'm American, born to American parents. I need a detective. Am I welcome or are you going to give me the bum's rush?"

Bubbling emotions I couldn't identify choked me.

1

News accounts of Japanese marching innocent Westerners to their deaths in Bataan, and of bloody battles raging in the Pacific shot through my brain. Struggling in beside those were memories of nuns from my school days telling us God made people of every color and loved them all. We hadn't been at war then, though.

I found my voice.

"Walking around with a wad of cash like that's asking for trouble. Especially a kid like you." I wondered whether she could hear my anger.

"Money talks. I needed you to know I can pay."

"Sorry. I have to be somewhere in twenty minutes."

"Just give me one — no, two — of them." Coming forward, she thumped the cash onto my desk, then extended her hand. "I'm Daisy Hashimoto."

I shook it awkwardly. She was composed and I was off balance. I didn't like the equation. With a back as straight as a telephone pole, she perched on the edge of the chair in front of my desk. She crossed her hands on her knees.

"My brother is missing. Nine days ago, there was a fire at the place where he worked, Kirby Printing. We haven't heard from him, no one has heard from him, since. We don't know if he's dead or missing or…The police came to see us. They told us someone was seen running away.

"If my brother had anything to do with the fire —

he wouldn't, but if he did — our family wants him to own up to it. If he's innocent, that's almost as bad. Maybe worse. Since he's disappeared, they'll suspect him. But what if the person running wasn't him? Or what if he saw something? What if he's hiding because he's scared? He could be in danger!"

Her rush of words came to an end as she ran out of breath.

I shook my head. "I'm sorry—"

"Please!"

All at once she registered my black dress. Her gaze jumped to the hat resting half on my phone. "Oh. You're going to a funeral." She jumped to her feet. "Forgive me for intruding. I'll come back tomorrow, when…when you don't have other things on your mind." She turned to go.

"Wait. You forgot your money."

"I'll leave it until you decide. Since you think it's unsafe for a kid like me to carry around." She took a step. "Oh, by the way, there's plenty in my bank account if that doesn't cover your fee. You can check."

She sailed a business card back toward my desk. I caught it as the door closed behind her. For several seconds, I sat trying to decide whether I felt outraged or ever so slightly amused by her cheekiness over the money. She was fast on her feet for a girl that young. Then again, I'd been out on my own when I wasn't much older, and I'd been quicker with a comeback than was sometimes prudent.

I went to the window and watched her come out of my building and start up Patterson, past businesses displaying big V-for-Victory signs in their windows. In contrast to when she stood in my office, she walked with head bowed and shoulders drawn protectively together. Several passersby ducked glances at her. One woman veered pointedly to the edge of the sidewalk. For the first time, I realized the girl who'd sat before me was wearing the uniform of the same girls-only Catholic high school I had attended.

She was American, she had announced almost fiercely, the first words out of her mouth because she knew they were vital. Yes, on the one hand, Daisy Hashimoto was as American as I was. On the other hand, I, with my blue eyes and light-brown curls held back behind tortoise-shell combs, could walk down the street unnoticed, except for occasional wolf whistles at my legs. Daisy, with her exotic eyes and golden skin, attracted attention. She represented the enemy. Her looks, however unfairly, engendered mistrust, nervousness, and for some, even hatred.

It was time to put on my hat. I took one last look as the girl disappeared around the corner, protected by nothing except, perhaps, her Catholic-school uniform.

CHAPTER TWO

Wee Willie wasn't in the shiny walnut casket in front of the altar. Like all the men dying in battles in Europe and on remote Pacific islands, he was buried near where he fell. The only part of him that had come home was his dog tags. His widow, Maire, who had followed the two of us everywhere when we were kids, clutched them as fiercely as her mother, seated next to her, clutched her rosary.

In the row behind, I watched their shoulders shake with sobs. My own handkerchief was damp from furtive dabs I'd made at trickling tears. From first grade onward, Willie and I had run the streets of our neighborhood together and gotten into scrapes together. As adults, after he'd finished his letter-carrier route for the day, he'd occupied the same stool at Finn's pub, nursing his half pint of stout and kidding me about anything he could think of when I came through the door.

"Wonder what that's about?" murmured Seamus Hanlon, a tall, silver-haired policeman who sat to my right. Sounds of a commotion were filtering in from the vestibule. A few heads turned.

5

A frowning young priest hurried out and five minutes later the Mass began. I sat too numb with grief to hear the words. Then the box that didn't contain Willie any more than life had been able to contain his high spirits made its way out to the cemetery where his parents and grandmother lay and was consigned to the ground. As everyone was turning away, Maire broke free of her children and mother and darted over to seize my hands.

"You'll come to the house now, won't you? For his send-off?" Her little face, red and puffy from crying, was pleading. "Please, Maggie! I don't think I can get through it without you. It will be…seeing you will help me hear his voice telling me I can do it."

I didn't want to do it, but I said I would. It was something I could do for Willie. But when I got to the little house where they'd lived with their four children, I could hardly squeeze inside. There was no getting close enough to Maire to murmur reassurance. The best I could do was catch her eye and blow her a kiss. I treated myself to a couple of servings of the liquid condolence available on a side table.

"Did you hear a goldfish turned up in the holy water?" one of the men standing there said to another.

"Just like Willie himself did that one time."

They laughed.

"Shame on you for laughing," sputtered a woman who appeared to be attached to one of them. "It's - it's blasphemy, is what it was!"

"It's not like the goldfish died in it," said the first man.

I turned away with a grin. Drifting to a window, I stood looking out, thinking about other stunts Willie had pulled, and then about Daisy Hashimoto and whether I wanted to help her.

No, not wanted to. Whether I should.

Willie hadn't died anywhere near the Pacific, where enemy soldiers who looked like Daisy committed atrocities. Daisy had been born in this country. She couldn't be blamed for what people she'd never met were doing. Still...

"You okay?"

It was Seamus, his crest of snowy hair turned silver in the light from the window. One of my father's two close friends, Seamus' gaunt face and battered features had been a fixture in my life for as long as I could remember. From the days when he'd read to me on the back steps, and then taught me to do it myself, there'd been a bond between us.

"Yeah, more or less. What do you know about that fire a week or two back? The one at a printing place."

Seamus frowned. "Strange thing to be thinking about right now."

"Beats thinking about Wee Willie."

"He was good one, funny little runt." Seamus rubbed the corner of his jaw in thought. "A fire...about a week ago, you said?"

"Yeah. The place is called Kirby Printing. I

remember seeing something about it in the paper, but I didn't pay attention."

Seamus made a chirping sound with his tongue and eyetooth as he reviewed things he'd read and heard. He was well past the age when he could retire and collect his police pension, and had a bad knee from an injury in the line of duty. Before the attack on Pearl Harbor, he'd been ready to put in his retirement papers, but instead he'd stayed on in a desk job so that younger men could patrol the streets or join the military.

"I think I know the fire you're talking about. As near as I recall, it wasn't a very big one. Could have been a lot worse with all that paper around. Still, fast as it got put out, two people died in it."

Daisy hadn't told me that part.

"I think I heard that several witnesses saw a man running away who could have started it. Don't believe they've caught him, though."

Before we could discuss it further, Maire squeezed through knots of mourners, past murmurs of sympathy, and flung her arms around my neck.

"Oh, Maggie, the goldfish! That was you, wasn't it?" she whispered in my ear. "Just like Willie did with that grumpy old neighbor of ours! He would have loved it!"

"Maire…" Her mother was bearing down on us like a locomotive. "People are waiting to talk to you." She gave me a look made of granite. She thought I was a bad influence on her daughter.

"Okay, Ma."

Maire started meekly after her. Then she spun and gave my neck another hard squeeze.

"You won't stop coming to see me now, will you, Maggie?"

"I'll be over to see you real soon, Maire. I promise."

Seamus had slipped off to go back to work. Maybe he hadn't asked me to drive him because he thought I'd had too much liquid comfort. I wondered whether there was anything else he hadn't had the chance to tell me about the fire at Kirby Printing.

Through the crowd in the little front room, I spotted a nun who'd taught Willie and me in grade school sitting alone in a corner. I went over to speak to her before heading out. Sadness seamed her face.

"Such a little devil, he was." She wiped at a tear. "But never did I see a boy as fast to take up for an underdog."

An underdog like Daisy Hashimoto, I thought, and wished I hadn't.

The kindly old nun had clearly comforted herself a few glasses more than I had. I persuaded her to let me walk with her to her bus stop, and then to one farther along the line to clear both our heads.

Backtracking, I got into my car and drove to the gravel parking lot near my office where I usually parked it. From there I walked to Finn's Pub. Willie had brought me to Finn's for the first time after my Dad's funeral. It had been the closest thing I had to a home ever since. The stool that Willie had occupied was draped in black. A small white card bearing Willie's name and the years of his birth and death sat on the black covering.

"It just seemed like the right thing to do," said Rose, the owner's wife, as she drew me a Guinness.

***

I don't know what drew me to the printing plant where the fire had occurred the night Daisy's brother vanished. Yet I found myself there after leaving Finn's and having a sandwich and thinking about times with Willie and Maire more than I wanted.

I had no intention of taking the girl's case. The kid just couldn't accept the idea her brother was guilty of something. Loyalty probably played a role in that, but mostly she hadn't seen enough of human nature yet. I had to hand it to her for guts, though, the way she'd strolled in to see me when she was fully aware how I might react. I knew a thing or two about pretending confidence when you were scared all the way to the soles of your feet.

Kirby Printing was small, probably a quarter the size of giant McCall's several streets away. It was brick and three stories high, but judging by the window outlines

I could make out around its blackout curtains, the lower floor was high-ceilinged, with a single floor above it. Two darkened buildings flanked it. One looked like it might be a warehouse. The other, judging by its fancier doorway, probably housed commercial offices of some kind. From the front, I didn't see any sign of fire damage.

I drove around the block to the back of the building, hunting the delivery entrance. It proved to be a long swath of beaten earth and cinders that was nearly as wide as the building itself. Halfway down on one side of a drive, I could make out the shape of a tree and lumps that must be bushes. At the entry from the street, half-dozen houses sat to either side. They were dark, their occupants in bed. I did a U-turn and pulled my DeSoto to the curb and parked, so I could have a better look.

As might be expected, a large bay door for trucks to pull up to and load or unload faced the street. It stood open, and with the night shift hard at work inside, the lights were on. Some kind of overhang shielded the illumination from planes overhead, but at ground level, I could see occasional movement in the printing plant.

As any Peeping Tom will tell you, it's easier to see things in a lighted room if you're outside in the dark than it is vice-versa. I wondered how anyone inside the plant had been able to make out the features of someone outside well enough to identify him.

Maybe if I got a better look inside it would answer my question. It was uncommonly balmy weather for April, so I got out of my car and crossed the street.

Truck tires had beaten the edge of the lane where I walked almost into concrete. The cork soles on my shoes were noiseless. When I got to the halfway point, where the tree was, I could make out a stack of cartons inside the open bay door, but not much beyond that. I discovered, however, that what I'd mistaken for bushes from across the street were actually four picnic tables. They made the place feel oddly welcoming.

That impression was shattered as a man hurtled into view from around the corner and pounced on a youth in a cap who'd been somewhere in the shadows next to the door.

"If you think you're going to swipe something, sonny, you've got another think coming."

"I was coming to ask if you had any odd jobs!"

The boy tried to pull away. Something in the fluid movement, the way the chin went up and the sound of the voice was familiar. Unless the amount of liquor I'd consumed after Willie's funeral had clouded my judgment, the "boy" was Daisy Hashimoto.

CHAPTER THREE

"Fine, you can tell it to the police," said the man who was possibly a night watchman.

"Hey, wait!" My yell as I trotted forward was enough to make the watchman pause. "If that's my brother — yeah, I see it is — I'll save you the trouble of smacking his ears off." I came to a stop with my hands on my hips and leaned forward toward Daisy. "When Mom gets through with you, you won't be able to sit for a week."

Her mouth fell open. Her eyes had widened.

"He's your brother?" The watchman looked as startled as Daisy was, but also suspicious. He still had Daisy by the arm.

"Much as I hate to claim him, yes." Grabbing her by the same arm, I jerked her toward me. "It's the second time he's sneaked out and gone around pestering places for work. Believe you me, there's not going to be a third time." Careful not to dislodge her cap, I cuffed Daisy none too gently on the ear.

"Ow!" She glared at me.

"He don't look much like you," said the watchman. "He looks kind of—"

"Dad was Greek, rest his soul." I crossed myself. "Butchie takes after that side." It took digging my fingers into her arm and giving her a shove to turn Daisy away. "Hey, he didn't damage anything, did he?" I called over my shoulder.

"No…but if he comes around here again I'm calling the cops." The watchman pointed a finger.

I nodded vigorously.

Daisy tried to pull free as soon as we started to walk. "What are—?"

"Quiet!" I hissed. I gave her a shake. "Wait till we're out of earshot."

When we reached the street, I flung her arm free, struggling to control my anger.

"Don't you have an ounce of sense? You're violating the curfew on unaccompanied minors. Not to mention it's dumb for a woman to be wandering around on her own this time of night."

"Gee, don't you suppose maybe that's why I dressed like a boy? How'd you turn up back there? Have you been following me?"

"I was having a look at the place because in a weak-minded moment I thought I might possibly, foolishly, consider doing what you asked me to do."

"Does that mean you will?"

"It depends on whether you give me straight answers and how much you annoy me. Get in the car."

I indicated the DeSoto and started toward it. She lagged behind with wariness, which under other circumstances I might have applauded.

"Why? Where are you going to take me?"

"A place we can talk. A café."

Maybe the part about annoying me had made an impression. She got in.

***

Blind Andy wasn't really blind. He could make out shapes and smears of bright color. His small café was open eleven a.m. to two a.m. six days a week, and the java was always hot, never bitter.

"Hey, Ginger Rogers, it's been a while since you've come in. How you doin'?" he greeted as I entered with Daisy sticking close to my side.

"Working too hard for the money I make."

It was a line I'd borrowed from him. He chuckled.

We settled in at a table wedged into a corner at one end of the counter. The counter, with its stools, was favored by most customers. Only two were currently occupied, one by a woman reading a newspaper, and one by a man who was shoveling macaroni and cheese with peas on the side into his mouth faster than a hummingbird moved its wings.

"Okay, I told you what I was doing there in the back of the printing place. I want to know why you turned up there. And don't get cute."

Daisy flicked the edge of the tabletop with her thumbnail. Her eyes were downcast.

"Tosh and some woman left notes for each other under the top of one of those picnic tables. Where it wasn't nailed on tight to the legs underneath. I thought there was a chance there'd be one there, and...and I don't know what."

"Tosh is your brother, I take it?"

She nodded.

"You thought he might have been to the picnic tables since he disappeared? Left a message?"

"I don't *know*. It was all I could think of to do. The way you acted, I didn't think you were likely to help." Her eyes swung up to mine in accusation. "I thought I'd better look there myself. I could get out tonight. I can't always."

I sat back while Andy set down coffee for me and a glass of cider for Daisy. It gave me time to process what she'd just told me.

"Do you know who the woman is?"

She shook her head.

"Would your parents know?"

"I don't think so. They would have said something, called if they knew who she was, or asked me if I knew her name."

"And you didn't tell them."

"No." She'd been watching me intently. Now she picked at the varnish coating the table. "They've got enough to worry about, with him disappearing, and…I wasn't sure how they'd take it.

"And before you ask, I didn't tell the police when they came to the house, either. It doesn't take much of a brain to know they think Tosh started the fire to…to interfere with war production."

Daisy certainly wasn't short on brains. My guess was she had some to spare. She was watching me shrewdly.

I folded my arms and leaned forward some.

"You also didn't tell me two people had died in that fire."

"You didn't give me time."

She had me there. One corner of her mouth stirred with satisfaction.

"Let's go." I left change sufficient to cover our drinks plus a tip and slid my purse onto my shoulder.

"Where?"

"I'm taking you home."

***

We rode in silence for several minutes. In the passenger seat of the DeSoto, Daisy fidgeted. I figured it did her good to fidget.

"You seem to think the woman your brother left notes for was someone who worked there, at Kirby Printing," I said finally.

In the dim light, I caught her shrug.

"It stands to reason. Who else would know about those picnic tables?"

"He could have told someone."

"Okay, then how did they manage to hang around the picnic tables and pull a note out of wherever they left them without being noticed? Maybe you missed the fact they have a watchman at night. Somebody who didn't work there would attract attention walking in during the day, wouldn't they? Why risk that? And where else would he have met someone? If she was a girl who'd been at Heart Mountain or come through Cincinnati with us, someone we know would have mentioned it. Teasing or nosey, you know? And there aren't any Nisei women — Nisei means Japanese-Americans — working there, just men."

Her reasoning was good, I had to hand her that.

She and her parents and one set of grandparents lived with a family taking part in a project hatched by a local church coalition. Working with the Cincinnati field office of the War Relocation Administration, the coalition found housing and jobs for some of the American citizens of Japanese ancestry currently held in internment camps. The house was a little way out on Fifth Street in a decent neighborhood of mostly wooden houses. The dwellings were two-story, and probably ranged from four to six bedrooms upstairs, not grand but comfortable.

"My parents are out, if you're thinking of marching

me in to them and watching them read me the riot act," Daisy said. "It's just me and my grandparents and the Browns there. That's why I was able to sneak out."

Sure enough, as we neared the address she'd given me, a barn-like white house, I saw that a very dim porch light burned under the roof of a roomy front porch. But something else drew my eye as well. Across the street from the house, someone at the wheel of a nondescript black car that was parked there ducked down so as not to be seen.

CHAPTER FOUR

"Hey, you missed the place. Back up," said Daisy as we passed.

"Sit still and don't look around. We're coming back."

To my relief, she clamped her mouth shut and waited.

"Would you recognize the cars your neighbors drive?" I asked as I turned at the corner.

"Maybe. What's going on?"

"I think someone might be watching your house. Or they could be watching one next door, or they could be waiting for someone."

Daisy twisted around in her seat, but of course she couldn't see anything.

"So, what are we going to do?"

"I'm going to circle the block so we go past again. I want you to slouch some — not enough to look like you're hiding. Just lean against the door maybe, with your head turned enough you can get a good look without the driver noticing. The corner house that's two doors past yours has the lights off, so once you've gotten a look at the car, I'll pull in there, all the way up the drive, and let you out. You stick to the shadows and cut across the lawn to the street we're on now. I'll be waiting and we'll decide what to do."

"Yeah, okay."

I thought I heard her teeth chatter a time or two, but I couldn't be sure. Neither of us felt inclined to chat as I finished the final two legs of the block and started up Fifth Street again. Daisy lounged with outward casualness against the window on her side of the car, the cap pulled low on her forehead. I was glad of the cap, glad of her boy's garb. Unless the occupant of the black car was keeping an eye out for her brother.

We rolled past without slowing our pace. Again, whoever sat in the car in question sank down. At the corner house, I pulled in as planned. Daisy threw the door wide as she got out, and finished with a jaunty wave. If the driver of the black car was paying any attention to us, it would look like someone getting off a night shift or coming back from something equally innocent. Around the corner, well out of sight, I waited only briefly before Daisy emerged from the darkness next to a hedge.

"I don't know if I've seen it around here or not," she said as she got in. "It's just a car. There's nothing about it to make it stand out. The house where it's parked, though, those people keep theirs in the garage. They don't drive it very often, but it's squatty." Her hands shaped a fluid description. "I think it's gray.

And the people on one side of us have a car so old I'm surprised it doesn't have a crank on the front to get it started."

She described a few other cars, but admitted they weren't something she usually noticed. All the same, it reassured me that I wasn't jumping to conclusions. People didn't scoot down to avoid being seen in a neighborhood where they belonged.

"Is it…could it be the police, do you think? And does this mean you're going to help?"

"No, it's not the police, and I haven't made up my mind on the other." I started the engine. "Is there a back way into the place you live?"

"Doesn't every place have a back door? If you're asking can I get in that way, sure. It's how I sneak in and out."

I remembered now that she'd said something about going to Kirby Printing tonight because she didn't know when she'd get another chance. Weariness from the effort of Willie's funeral and of dealing with this kid on top of it began to overtake me.

"Sneak? I thought you said your parents had gone somewhere."

"Yeah, to a meeting some of the Japanese-Americans and some of the church people have every month. But you didn't suppose they went off and left me alone, did you? The Browns are there with their five kids, and my grandparents. But my grandparents fall asleep early and Grandma snores like an avalanche. I've cleaned out one end of the attic so I can study up there where it's quiet, and sleep there sometimes now that it's warm enough. Raise one of the windows, climb down a trellis, it's a piece of cake."

"Okay, I'll drive into the alley and you tell me which house to stop at. When you're inside…" My brain was running out of gas. "You can't flick the light to let me know you're safe inside, can you?" I muttered. "Not when we're supposed to have curtains closed."

Daisy was signaling for me to stop.

"How about I stick my head out and whistle?" she asked as she opened the car door. "I'm a good whistler. Tosh taught me. He's fantastic, trills and double notes and such."

"Okay." It was better than anything I could think of. I killed the engine, the better to hear her signal, as well as any other cars approaching. "Do more than a couple of notes, though, so I know it's not some guy walking along out front and whistling on the way home. And raise up your window so I don't miss it."

Leaning back against the frame of my own open window, I savored the smell of the spring night. I watched Daisy glide like a shadow halfway across the back yard, at which point darkness swallowed her. I strained for sounds, for hints of anything amiss. All that met my ears were notes from early-season insects, and far away, the wavering wail of a screech owl.

Then, through the black velvet world that surrounded me, came a clear and spirited rendition of *"I'm a Yankee Doodle Dandy."*

As I reluctantly admired Daisy's wit as well as her skill, a muscular arm caught me from behind, jerking my head back in a choke-hold through the window opening. I grabbed for the Smith & Wesson I'd placed on the passenger seat when Daisy got out, but I couldn't reach it. With my breath being cut off and panic threatening, I fumbled for the handle that opened the car door, yanked it, and pushed with my feet.

The unexpected opening of the door broke my assailant's hold. He stumbled backward, scrambling to keep his footing. I landed flat on my back with just enough presence of mind to tuck my knees to my chest and go into a backward somersault. I staggered up.

He swung at me. I blocked it. And just like that, he turned and ran, a man at least half a foot taller than me and solidly built. Then, suddenly, there was only the sound of something dragging on gravel.

Daisy's whistling had stopped.

***

By the time I parked the DeSoto and went up the walk to the pretty white house that had been my home for seven years now, all I wanted was to curl up in the quiet of my room and nurse my bruises and let sleep blot out all memory of Wee Willie's funeral. Opening the front door blasted me with a reminder such refuge was a thing of the past.

Music blared from a radio in a room upstairs. Two girls in bathrobes ran past me, chattering, bound for the extra shower Mrs. Z had installed in the basement to supplement the single bathroom we all shared.

America's war effort had brought a desperate need for housing for defense workers, especially women. Mrs. Z, our jewel of a landlady, had answered the local appeal by wedging three new beds into the room at the foot of the stairs where visitors once waited. She'd added two more in the laundry room and extras in three of the bedrooms. The house once occupied by twelve of us who knew each other and had to be in by a set time each night, now had a constantly changing cast that came and went at all hours.

By the time I reached the top of the stairs, my temples throbbed with every beat of the music. Not only was it up to full volume, but the door to the room that housed it stood wide open. A party appeared to be under way, and spilling into the hall.

Three or four months ago a blonde at least four inches taller than I was had moved there with another girl. She stood in the doorway braying laughter almost as loud as the radio.

"Hey." I stepped in front of her. "Could you turn it down a little, please, and close the door? Some people up here are trying to sleep."

"So?" She was waving a cup, which I suspected held more than water, in time with the music. "People sleep all hours. Gotta get used to a little noise."

"A little noise is what we'd get with your door closed and your radio down, oh, halfway."

"You gonna make me? I've got a right—"

I slammed her back against the wall, my hands on her shoulders, my thumbs at her neck.

"Why, yes, I will make you, since asking politely doesn't seem to work."

"Let — me — go!" Her eyes were bulging. She seemed to have trouble speaking because of my thumbs.

"Now I'm going to tell you this one last time. Close the door. Turn the radio down. If you don't do that by the time I count five, I will drag you down these stairs by your bleached-blonde hair and throw you out the front door, making sure your chin hits when you land. Got that?"

I let her go with a shove that propelled her back into the arms of startled party goers. Someone slammed the door.

"You're crazy!" she yelled from the other side. "You're gonna pay for this!"

The radio was squelched a few seconds later.

Three girls, one a teacher who had lived at Mrs. Z's

since before the war, were in line for the bathroom with towels on their arms. Esther, the teacher, nodded approval as I walked by. The other two stared. Going into my room, I closed the door, heaved a sigh of relief that the day was over, and fell onto my bed fully clothed.

Sound from the radio down the hall was muted now. My own thoughts weren't.

I lay remembering Wee Willie, pint-sized enough to be a jockey, walking up to a kid who towered over him and telling him to give back another kid's new marbles. They'd both ended up with cut lips. I remembered the joy in his eyes the day he married Maire, him eighteen and her sixteen.

Those scenes melted into the sound of pride in Daisy Hashimoto's voice as she told me she'd been born in this country…the defiance when she told me the wad of cash she'd pressed into my hands was hers, and had been honestly earned.

How did a high school kid earn that kind of money?

Why did a driver who didn't want to be seen park his car and watch her house?

Why had someone attacked me while I sat watching her?

CHAPTER FIVE

Daylight screamed its way under the curtains. I squinted awake. A look at my Baby Ben told me I hadn't set my alarm. Since I didn't have any appointments scheduled, the oversight didn't matter. As a bonus, the house was blissfully silent. I lay for a while soaking in the peacefulness. When I finally made my way to the bathroom, there was no one else waiting to get in. I ran back for my towel and soap and had a fast bath.

At McCrory's lunch counter, the breakfast shift had seen three waitresses come and go in the past year. None held a candle to the constantly darting woman who'd worked there for eight years before them. My oatmeal, when I finally got it, was lukewarm and lumpy. I consoled myself with the fact I at least had milk and a smidgen of brown sugar with which to anoint it.

Although I scanned the stories in the newspaper folded beside me, my mind kept jumping to the attack in the alley last night. Why had somebody jumped me? And how had that somebody managed to sneak up?

My attacker had been male, sizable enough his footsteps in the gravel alley should have been easy to hear as he approached. Either he was stealthy as a cat or he'd already been in position back there, the most obvious reason being to keep an eye on Daisy's house.

A car in front, a stakeout behind — I didn't like the feel of it. Especially since I was almost positive the car in front wasn't a cop car.

I tried to recapture other details from the previous night. What had I heard or smelled or seen from the few seconds prior to being grabbed around the neck to when my attacker was fleeing?

Night sounds...Daisy whistling...Brylcreem. Looking back, I thought I recalled a faint whiff of Brylcreem. If so, it told me absolutely nothing. Half the male population, if not more, used the product to hold their hair.

Afterward, when I blocked his punch and my assailant fled, there'd been a crunch or two of gravel. Footsteps then, and fast ones, which meant he was running. Then...

The footsteps had ended abruptly. A ribbon of sound had followed. Not car tires, more like a rake handle dragging through gravel. A gate opening? I frowned in thought.

"You want more hot water?"

The waitress was getting impatient for me to move on. I complied. I couldn't quite place what the whirring sound reminded me of. It would come to me.

Most of my mind had already moved on to Daisy's determination to learn what became of her brother. He might have started a fire that killed two people. It might have been sabotage. It might have been motivated by some other reason. There was even a chance it had been an accident, or the more remote one, that he was innocent.

Whatever the case, I knew the pain it caused a family not to know what had happened when one of its children vanished. My brother, Geroid, had hopped a freight when I was nine, and my mother and father had never stopped grieving. Ger hadn't been much of a brother to me — Wee Willie had been that as well as a friend. Still, it ate at me after all these years, wondering what had happened to him. Had he died in that first year, or even month, crushed when he miscalculated jumping on or off a train? Had he met with foul play? Had he fallen in with a bad crowd, or maybe found work somewhere out West and grown up and married and had a family? Sometimes I wondered if he was wearing a uniform now, and fighting somewhere.

Daisy Hashimoto's family was Japanese, which made me uneasy, but they were human beings. Conscience told me they deserved to have someone take at least an initial peek at their son's disappearance; someone approaching it with a different perspective than that brought by the police. Resignation rumbling in the back of my throat, I crossed Main Street to Market House where the Dayton Police housed their detective division and a few other specialized units.

***

Lt. Freeze led investigations into homicides and suspicious deaths. I wasn't sure whether the two deaths in the fire at the printing place were being looked at as homicides, but it seemed like the most efficient way to start. Freeze's eyes narrowed as he watched me swing along toward him in my blue-and-white gabardine dress and a tiny blue hat with a curlicue feather.

"What?" he said as I stopped at his desk.

"Such lack of trust in a single word."

"Yeah, well, I recognize that expression you're wearing. You want something."

I sat down in front of his desk. He rubbed out the Old Gold which, lighted or not, generally hung from his lips. Freeze was lean and grizzled and would win an award for being in the dark about how to deal with women.

"Two people died last week in a fire at a place called Kirby Printing. Did those land in your lap?"

Leaning back in his chair, Freeze gave me a long look.

"Who wants to know?"

"Me." I gave a sunny smile.

He snorted.

"Cute."

Until a year ago, we'd regarded each other with seething animosity. He broadcast his opinion that I solved cases by batting my eyelashes rather than with digging and shoe leather. I thought, and still did, that he was too quick to dismiss ideas that didn't originate with him, and overlooked possibilities at the very fringes of things. A particularly nasty case where we decided we could be allies rather than adversaries had changed things between us, though we still were wary of sharing what we knew.

"Okay, truth is somebody's trying to hire me to have a closer look at what happened there. I haven't decided yet whether I'll say yes. It seemed smart to get the lay of the land first, before I jump in."

Freeze glanced at two detectives working on something unrelated to his cases in another corner of the room. The detective unit handled robberies, burglaries and numerous other matters, so the homicide squad was an unofficial designation. Freeze toyed with a pencil. His gaze slid two desks sideways to a peach-fuzz kid who'd been promoted from street duty after the draft claimed two seasoned detectives. The kid had been assigned to help Freeze, but his lack of aptitude was matched by his failure to acquire any in the year he'd been here.

"Tell you what." Freeze sat up. He unwrapped a

stick of gum and put half in his mouth. "I'll answer your question and maybe tell you a thing or two more. In return, you do me a favor."

"What's the favor?"

"Talk Boike into coming back to work."

It was my turn to sit up.

"Boike's back?"

"Yeah, he got injured. Sent back and discharged. He's okay now, but he's spouting nonsense about not thinking he could do this job right anymore."

I tried to digest it. Boike was a boxy blond who'd been Freeze's right-hand man until Uncle Sam sent him greetings a year and a half ago. I liked Boike. He'd never said much, mainly because Freeze expected men who worked with him to open their mouths only when he authorized it. Get him alone, though, and it was clear he was sharp, and even had a dry sense of humor. His absence was one of the factors that had led to better relations between Freeze and me. Freeze had even admitted he missed having Boike around to discuss the minutiae necessary for solving cases.

"Freeze, maybe he's seen too much—"

"It's not shell shock or anything like that, if that's what you're thinking. He's just deaf in one ear now. Got some cuts on his jaw, is all."

"You've seen him?"

"Yeah, he stopped by couple of days ago. I think maybe he misses the place, which is why I think he should be nudged to come back. He's good at this work."

"You ever tell him that?"

He gave me a baleful look.

"What makes you think I could interest him in it if you can't?"

"He didn't work for you. It would just be pal-to-pal. Besides…" He grimaced at having to say it. "You've got a way with you, the way you kind of weasel around so people don't see what you're doing."

"Such flattery. You ought to put that weaseling part on a Valentine's card."

"You want information or not? You know it can't be good for him just sitting around."

It was the first semi-persuasive thing I'd heard him say. I crossed my arms.

"How do I know I'm not getting the very short end of this stick?"

Freeze hunched forward, glancing to make sure Dotson, the peach-fuzz kid, was still on the phone and scribbling away. He was useful at office work, Freeze had acknowledged, except for the couple of times he'd gotten addresses wrong.

"That question you asked, are we looking at those two deaths as homicides? We won't know until the fire department tells us whether the fire was started on purpose or not. If it was, then we'll have to determine why."

"What about you? Anything suggest one way or another?"

"Besides the watchman and two other people who work there saying they saw Hashimoto running away when it happened?" He glanced toward his young assistant. "Dots. You take that evidence from the fire back yet?"

"Yes, sir."

Freeze grunted. Reaching into a desk drawer he brought out a Manilla folder. He shuffled half a dozen pages of typed information out of the way and brought out a photo.

"These belonged to the man seen fleeing. He's a Jap. One of the bunch the Church Federation brought in. His fingerprints are on them. The optometrist who made them confirmed it was Hashimoto's prescription."

I was staring at an eight-by-ten photograph of wire-rimmed spectacles. The left lens was cracked, the numerous lines suggesting it had been stepped on or hit.

"Who's looking to hire you? The printing place? Their insurance company?"

"I don't want to say until I decide."

"Suit yourself." Returning the folder to the drawer, Freeze raised his voice. "Dotson! Is she at home? What about the sister? Let's roll then."

He stood and shrugged into his jacket.

"Don't forget your end of the bargain." He jabbed a finger in my direction. "If I don't see Boike back in this office with his badge and his card in his pocket, it's gonna be a cold day in Hades before you worm information from me again."

"Hey, wait a minute." I sprang up. "I never promised I'd get him to come back to work. As a matter of fact, I never promised anything. I'll talk to him. Period. I'll see what I can do."

"You'd better." He bent and scribbled. "Here." He shoved the square of paper at me, and I snatched it just in time to keep it from hitting me in the chest.

It was an address.

CHAPTER SIX

I found the fire investigator in the Fire and Signal Building on the corner of Main and Monument. He was in his fifties, solidly built, and wore his uniform well.

"I'd say eighty-five, maybe ninety percent certain that it was arson," he said when I'd introduced myself and handed him one of my business cards. "Flammable solvent had been splashed around in a big arc where cartons of paper were stored. It's solvent they use there, for cleaning machines, so that complicates things."

We were in his office, him behind a battered desk and me in front of it. He squinted his eyes shut hard and then opened them again as if to clear them from something that stung. "You didn't tell me who you were working for. This has to do with insurance on one side or the other, I guess?"

"Someone wants me to have a look at what happened. Before I decide, I want to know how much of a can of worms that would be."

"Well. There's a lot of worms, I can tell you that."

"Do you mind naming a few?"

"One's the two men who died. They'd come in to repair a press. They were mostly done and taking a break, sitting on the floor back there leaning against the other side of some of those stacked-up cartons with their lunch boxes open. One of them could have started a cigarette, but they wouldn't have. They were longtime employees. They knew the dangers posed by working around that much paper. The fire didn't spread much, but the area where it happened went up fast. Those two fellows didn't have a chance."

He gave that hard squint again, his nose wrinkling with it. I wondered if it was an attempt to rid his eyes of permanent discomfort brought about by all the fire and smoke he'd been exposed to through the years. Or maybe the horrors he'd witnesses in their aftermaths. Neither of us spoke for a time.

"So, one of them could have started the fire accidentally."

"One chance in a thousand, but maybe."

"Except you found solvent spilled in an arc."

"The pattern where it had been, yes. But the can it was in could have leaked. And the two victims had been using some. They'd stowed the rags they used away properly, but they'd have had some on their overalls, and most likely on the bandanas they wiped their foreheads with and stuffed in their pockets."

I saw the dilemma the fire's uncertain origin made

for Freeze. If the fire had started accidentally, the police had no part in this. If it had been started deliberately, which seemed more likely, then he and young Dotson would be hunting the perpetrator. They'd be trying to solve two homicides, or maybe something termed manslaughter or accidental homicide or some such. That got into legal waters where I couldn't swim.

I was fine at fishing, though.

"The police say there wasn't any sign of violence to the victims, apart from the fire," I said and held my breath.

The fire investigator squinted again.

"That's right." He went into details that I would gladly have skipped about how the two men had died.

"What about evidence? Anything that might point to whoever started it — if somebody did?"

He got up and took down a cardboard box from the top of a filing cabinet.

"Right here. Two others who've done their share of this kind of work are due in about twenty minutes to review it all again and see if we have any new ideas, so I happen to have it handy."

Setting the box on his desk, he undid the wrapping on two metal shapes. After several seconds, I realized they were the twisted shells of lunch buckets.

"Like I said, they were taking a break. One had a Thermos. It got blown to bits. That's how bad it was. We found a chunk. It's in that little envelope."

It was hard to look at the remains of the lunch buckets with their story of how quickly lives had been snuffed out.

"Not exactly something I'd called evidence," I said.

"No, except that it tells us why they were sitting where they were."

"There was nothing that seemed odd back there? Nothing that didn't belong to the victims?" I'd never had a case involving a fire before. I didn't know the questions to ask.

He undid the string on a small Manilla envelope and tipped its contents carefully out on his desk blotter.

"Just this little lump of metal, but it was clear over by the stairs, well away from the worst of the fire. It had gone underneath them — the stairs. We'd never have spotted it if we hadn't had men down combing the place on their hands and knees."

"Any idea what it is?" I bent over the distorted thumb-sized shape, so close to it my nose was almost touching. All I could make out was that there might be traces of white enamel on one side, and a black line straight enough it could be intentional.

"No. It could be something from a machine. A logo, a number. Or it could be a clasp off something. Whatever it was, it could have come off before the fire. Days ago, weeks, a year even. It could have been lying somewhere else down there, or on the stairs, and gotten kicked in the confusion."

I sighed. A nipple of metal stuck out on the back of

the side that didn't have enamel. Whatever it might have been, I was stumped.

"If the fire had damaged the stairs worse, it might have melted beyond anything recognizable," the investigator was saying. "Probably not important, but you never know."

I straightened. Something else he'd said was registering.

"The stairs. You said they weren't burned as badly. Why? I thought fires traveled up."

"Well, for one thing, it was an open staircase, so it didn't have much extension. Plus, one of the upstairs workers brought a fire extinguisher and knocked down what got to the stairs pretty quickly. And like I said, the fire was mostly where we found the solvent. It made a real nasty jump to where we found those two men. It didn't get started good on the stairs. Odd why it went there at all, but fire's funny that way."

"What about the eyeglasses? Why aren't they with the rest of the evidence?"

His expression clouded.

"There's fire department turf and police turf. And in this case, somebody else who gets to claim whatever turf they want."

***

Pesky questions began to gang up at the back of my brain as I returned to my office. They were small, none of the magnitude to raise red flags. But pearls began with a grain of sand, a wall started with a couple of bricks. Taken together, the things that were bothering me argued that the theory Tosh Hashimoto had started the fire and run from the scene needed a closer look than it was currently getting.

How could he have poured flammable solvent around without being noticed? People were working not far from where the fire started. They'd been moving around, and certainly able to see if they glanced up.

When the arsonist dropped the match, or whatever he'd used to ignite the solvent, wouldn't his hands have been burned? They would have had solvent on them, just like the clothes of the two men who burned to death.

Finally, there was the question that had bothered me from the moment I heard there were witnesses: How could anyone inside a well-lighted building have made out the features of a figure running away in the dark?

Was I thinking of taking the case?

Yeah, I was. Digging around a little, at least.

God alone knew why.

The problem was, the girl who wanted to hire me was a minor. She still lived with her parents. They might not be pleased that their daughter had gallivanted around trying to hire me to help with what they might see as a family matter. That sentiment might be even stronger because of what people like them had been through, being moved from their homes into internment camps and then, along with well over a hundred other Japanese-Americans who had come to Dayton last fall, relocated in unfamiliar communities.

Even under the best of circumstances, waltzing up to their doorstep and introducing myself and telling them their daughter had come to see me because their son was in a spot of trouble wouldn't have been the smartest tactic if I hoped they'd be receptive. Here, I was keenly aware, I might also be walking into cultural differences.

What I needed was guidance from somebody who understood those differences. Maybe even someone who already knew the family. I let my chair swivel side to side as I thought.

I needed to talk to someone from the group that had brought the Japanese to Dayton. The group had broached the idea to civic leaders, then lined up jobs and housing for the new arrivals. Church Alliance? Alliance of Churches? What had Freeze called it?

I couldn't find a listing for it in the phone book, and I didn't want to call the detective squad room about it. The policewoman who headed up the Women's Bureau and had worked with the church group on other matters, was out. The lone clerk holding the fort there didn't know the group's name.

With a groan, I reached for the phone to call a woman who was very rich and involved in most innovative civic improvements. She was bound to know the name of the group and someone to contact there. She was also bound to stick her nose into why I needed the information and want to tag along.

Before I finished dialing, another idea struck. I pressed the hook and dialed the *Dayton Daily News* photo department instead.

"Here I thought you'd be out adding artistic flare to the humble news photo," I said when Ione Jenkins came to the phone.

"They're starting to call me Miss One Shot already. There is no scope for creativity when shooting City Council or Kiwanis, or Girl Scouts. Well, the Girl Scouts at least tie knots and do other interesting things, so I might do two or three shots of them. Otherwise there's no point weighting myself down with the number of film carriers Matt did. I tried it the first two days and my shoulder may never recover. Now I try to make it back here mid-morning and mid-afternoon to drop what I've shot and reload."

More accustomed to taking more creative pictures to accompany articles she wrote for national magazines, Ione had stepped into her husband's job in the newspaper's photo department. They were both my pals.

"Have you heard from Jenkins?" He'd left for basic training a few days earlier.

"I got my first letter yesterday. He says he's the only one in his platoon whose feet aren't sore."

"Hey, that church group that brought the Japanese workers up here, do you happen to know its name? Maybe somebody in it?"

"The Church Federation. The man who used to be in charge here got moved to Cincinnati. I'm not sure who his replacement is. Any church secretary will know, or know where to point you.

"Got to dash. I'm souping prints."

CHAPTER SEVEN

By the time I'd tracked down someone to talk to at the Church Federation and made an appointment for that afternoon, it was time for lunch. I walked a few blocks over to buy a copy of the noon edition and then to the Arcade to get a sandwich.

The kid who'd been selling me papers for seven or eight years now was named Heebs. He was a happy-go-lucky towhead with a little gap between his front teeth when he grinned, which was most of the time. Today, though, instead of greeting me with his usual wisecrack, he just said, "Hiya, Maggie." This morning I hadn't noticed it. Now I did.

"You okay, Heebs? You're awfully quiet today."

"Doing great, Sis." He pulled his breezy manner back into place. "But I've been thinking…" He paused to sell a paper to someone else and dip into his carrier's bag for another copy. "I've been thinking, you could make some nice change on the side if you posed for some pinup shots and sold copies. Nothing real trashy, just hike your skirt to show those great gams."

I started to laugh.

"I'm serious, Sis. GIs are buying those pictures like hot cakes. We'd make a killing."

"Ah. You're going to be my agent. Is that it?"

"Well, sure. 'Cause…" He peered politely around. "…we both know I'm better at sales than you."

He paused to peddle two papers in quick succession. I turned away smiling. For as long as I'd known him, Heebs had been on his own, sleeping in doorways and getting food whenever and wherever he could. He could hatch more schemes than anyone I'd ever known. When I could, I came up with odd jobs for him to help him out. Last year, I'd barely managed to come up with one that got him away from an idea he had about lying about his age to enlist in the Army.

When he'd seen to a couple more customers, he called out to me.

"You take care of yourself, Sis."

I looked back and waved. "Yeah, you too, Heebs."

If he was in some kind of jam, I was pretty sure he'd come and see me. I got a sandwich and took it and the newspaper back to my office to see what had happened since breakfast time.

***

The man I finally reached from the Church Federation met me in a room at the back of a huge brick church overlooking the Great Miami. Spires and arches and a dozen big stained-glass windows decorated it. My middle-aged host was round at the hemisphere without being fat. He peered at me through tortoise-shell glasses with eyes that were guarded but kind. His name was Willard King.

"You told me on the phone that you're a private detective, and that this has something to do with one of our Nisei families?"

He observed me intently as we took our seats on either side of his desk.

"I'm not here to make trouble for anyone or ask about anyone. I'm here for advice."

His shoulders relaxed enough to see it.

"Go on."

"Day before yesterday a girl came into my office. She wants to hire me to help her brother, who she thinks might be in some kind of trouble. She brought a wad of cash to pay for my services, but I have a feeling she didn't consult with her parents first. Her name is Daisy Hashimoto."

"Ah. Daisy." His voice gave a turn that suggested a held-back sigh. His lips curved slightly.

"I'm guessing you're feeling glad you're not her father."

He chuckled. "Something like that."

King had been sitting up. Now he eased back a little. His index fingers formed a steeple like the one on the roof outside. He rested his elbows on the arms of his chair.

"Daisy is a remarkable young woman. I won't call her a girl, because the word doesn't seem appropriate. In many ways, she's mature for her age. She's intelligent. Acutely observant. I hesitate to use the word 'genius,' but she's highly gifted in certain areas. She already holds some kind of patent. Perhaps more than one."

"*Patent?*" I wasn't sure I'd heard him correctly. I associated patents with men like the Wright Brothers and engineering whiz Charles Kettering.

"I don't know the particulars. She apparently developed something several years ago, back in San Francisco. Before the Japanese were rounded up and sent to camps.

"That has nothing to do with her brother, of course. It's just to explain that because of the business dealings she's had, I think Daisy's used to being viewed as an adult." He paused. "I assume this has something to do with the fire at the place where Tosh — her brother — worked?"

"Yes. But I told you I wasn't here to ask questions, and I'm not. From the little I've learned, I think Daisy could be right that whatever happened that night, and to her brother, merits a closer look. I can't, in conscience, do that without making sure her parents agree. I want to talk to them. I was hoping for your advice on how best to approach them, so I don't offend them because of, um…"

"Differences in our two cultures?"

"Yes."

"*In conscience*. How refreshing," murmured the man behind the desk. He smiled. "Daisy's parents are thoroughly American, I assure you. Mrs. Hashimoto came here as a babe in arms. Dr. Hashimoto arrived with his parents when he was a toddler, I believe. I expect they'll react like any other parents whose child has taken it upon herself to talk to a stranger about a family matter."

I winced. He laughed.

"Exactly."

"Would you be willing to call ahead and prepare them somehow? I thought perhaps if you told them you'd met me…"

"Yes. They will appreciate that you've made the effort to approach them with some sensitivity rather than simply turning up on their doorstep. You're wanting to see them as soon as possible, I expect?"

"Yes."

"They're both at work right now, but Dr. Hashimoto is just down at St. Elizabeth's, assigned to the laboratory. I'll stop by and see him. If he agrees, would half past seven tonight be agreeable?"

"It would be perfect. Thank you."

King stood up. Gracious as he'd been, he probably had a dozen other tasks awaiting him. We shook hands.

"Would you like to have me there when you talk to

them? I could meet you there," he offered as we started out.

"If you can spare the time, I'd be grateful."

Despite his assurance the Hashimotos were like any other family, I'd feel better having someone who could act as a buffer if I made a misstep. As the door at the back of the church opened into the outside world again, King's kindly eyes gave a twinkle.

"And you were right. As challenging as I find my own two daughters at times, I tremble at the thought of having to keep one step ahead of a child like Daisy."

CHAPTER EIGHT

What with Wee Willie's funeral the previous day and my running around today, I was behind on the background checks that I did week-to-week for regular clients. For the next several hours, I worked my way through the stack of them waiting on my desk. I was down to one where I'd have to talk to people in person, not on the telephone, when Daisy showed up again just as she'd said she would.

This time I noticed her uniform as she helped herself to the chair in front of me.

"I forgot to say thanks last night for getting me out of that jam with the watchman," she said. "So, thanks. Have you decided?"

"Hello to you, too, Daisy. Nice to see you again."

She gave a martyred snort.

"If you're inquiring whether I've decided to have a look at Tosh's disappearance, I'll let you know after I talk to your parents this evening. Mr. King from the Church Federation was kind enough to pave the way for me. He just called to confirm that they're expecting me."

Daisy's mouth flew open and stopped. She couldn't

decide whether to be indignant or pleased she was one step closer to getting what she wanted. Somewhere in the midst of it, civility inserted itself.

"They can hardly see straight, they're so worried." Her voice was low. "I wanted to spare them."

"I understand. But they needed to know."

"Are you going to tell them about last night?"

"Not unless you really annoy me."

She had been slumping. Now she came erect in her chair.

"What kind of answer is that?"

"My kind."

Her lip curled just enough to show disdain. "And cautionary?"

I grinned. "Glad to see Julienne still drums vocabulary into its students. Look. If it will smooth your feathers any, there are a couple of things about the night of the fire and people claiming they saw your brother that bother me." A lift of my hand forestalled her question. "They may come to nothing, but I think they're worth checking.

"Now, why don't you tell me about the man who tried to strangle me, or maybe just scare me, last night in the alley?"

"What? When?" She was startled enough to forget she disliked me, as I had hoped she would be.

"Right after you went inside. Right after you began whistling."

"How did…? Did you get out of your *car*?"

She showed every sign she was about to light into me with a lecture on safety just as I'd done her.

"No, I did not."

"Then how—?"

"We'd put our windows down, remember? The man reached in."

"You saw him?"

"No."

"Then how do you know it was a man?"

"By his size. By the way he moved running away."

"It wasn't Tosh, if that's what you're thinking."

"How do you know?"

"He wouldn't. He wouldn't come near the house. He'd be afraid it would get us in trouble."

"What if he was the one in trouble?"

Her mouth quivered once before she controlled it.

"He wouldn't then, either. I don't think. It's...a matter of honor. And he wouldn't hurt anyone!"

I studied her for a couple of minutes. She believed every word she was saying.

"What about some fellow who's sweet on you. Could someone be playing Sir Lancelot, trying to protect you?"

"Are you *nuts*? Of course not. I haven't met a single boy here or anywhere else that I'd give the time of day!"

Which wouldn't necessarily prevent one having the sort of crush on her that would make him fiercely protective.

"Okay, then scoot. I've got things to do before I talk to your parents."

"'Scoot.'" Her disdain returned full blown. She shouldered her school bag and left.

***

I walked to a drugstore and then to McCrory's in hopes one place or the other had received a shipment of shampoo. Neither had. When I'd gotten around a bowl of vegetable soup and the four crackers served with it, I headed to Mrs. Z's to freshen up before presenting myself to the Hashimotos.

On the door to my room, I found a felt flower peering from the little corduroy pocket now tacked to each door. If you'd had a phone call or someone wanted to see you, a slip of paper with the pertinent information appeared in the pocket. A flower meant Mrs. Z wanted to see you. I put my purse in a bureau drawer and went downstairs.

There was no response when I knocked on the door of our landlady's cozy apartment. I was turning to go when she peeked out the door to the kitchen at the rear of the house. She was wiping her hands on a tea towel.

"Oh, I've interrupted your dinner. I saw the flower on my door. I'll come back later."

"No, now is fine. The burners are off. Go on in."

I opened the door as cautiously as possible. Mrs. Z

had a fat yellow tom cat who loved to bite ankles almost as much as he loved to escape. Butterball was curled up in a chair and stirred himself only enough to hiss.

"Sit down, Margaret."

I did. I had a feeling whatever I was about to hear wasn't going to be pleasant. That hunch was confirmed as Mrs. Z seated herself in a chair across from me and clasped her hands in her lap.

"Margaret, one of the girls in Room 4 came to me with a very upsetting accusation. She says you tried to choke her to death last night—"

"The big blonde."

"Yes. It seems quite outlandish, but given the type of work you do…I felt I must ask, Margaret. Did you?"

Several seconds passed before I responded.

"I shoved her up against the wall. I did not try to choke her." Though there might have been a second or two when I'd tried to give the impression I might.

Lines of concern appeared on Mrs. Z's forehead. "I assume she had provoked you in some way?"

"She had her radio playing full blast with the door open. There were a bunch in her room yelling and whooping it up and having a party. I asked if she'd turn the music down and close the door. When she smarted off and refused, I put it to her more forcefully." I let my breath out. In retrospect, I wasn't especially proud of my behavior. "In case she didn't tell you, I also threatened to drag her down the stairs and throw her outside."

Mrs. Z grew more distressed with every word of my account.

"She said you were quite drunk, that she could smell it on your breath."

"I'd seen my closest childhood friend buried that afternoon. So, yes, I'd had a few. I'm surprised she could smell it, given how freely they were passing their bottle around."

With that, the tide turned in my favor. My landlady's chin hardened. She expressly forbade liquor in our rooms. Knowing my actions had dragged her into all this unpleasantness made me feel lousy.

"Look, I'm sorry I've put you through this. I'll go apologize—"

"No. Don't. There's not a speck of quality to her. I can't take the measure of someone before I decide whether or not to rent to them like I did with you and Jolene and Genevieve and all of you who knew each other. There's such pressure to provide housing. When there's a vacancy, I have girls at the door — men, too — before I can even put an ad in the paper. Turning someone down if I'm not outright fearful of what they might do or that they might have a disease seems unpatriotic."

"I understand. I'll try not to lose my temper again."

"That's all then. I'm sure you have things to do. If

her music is too loud again, come tell me. I'll see to her myself. And, Margaret," she added, causing me to pause at the door and look back. "You've always been one of my best renters. I should hate to lose you. But if there is…another altercation like this, I may have to ask you to leave."

CHAPTER NINE

Sufficiently contrite, I arrived five minutes early at the house where the Hashimotos were staying. The car that had been parked across the street last night was nowhere in evidence. Just in front of me, Willard King, the man from the Church Federation, was getting out of a tan Dodge that had seen better days.

"I don't believe I mentioned the Hashimotos have another son, Haruto," he said as we went up the sidewalk. "He's with the 442nd. It's an all-Nisei U.S. Army unit," he added. "Nisei are second-generation Japanese-Americans, those born to parents who had already become American citizens."

"Like Daisy and her brothers."

"Yes. Some of us involved in the local project, on both sides, have come to use the term loosely to mean all those brought to Dayton, save for the very few elderly couples like Daisy's grandparents. You may meet them. They're Mrs. Hashimoto's parents."

A frazzled-looking woman who wore an apron and smelled of dish soap greeted us. She and her husband and five children were one of the families who had agreed to share their homes with relocated Japanese families. Just inside the door, beside a low bench, a dozen pairs of adult shoes were lined up neatly behind a jumble of smaller ones.

"They're all in there." The woman who'd greeted us waved toward a room on the left and scurried off.

Absorbing the novel experience of running around in my socks, I followed Willard King through a pocket door into what until recently must have been a living room. Now, despite several decorative folding screens, it served as the entire living space for Daisy and her family. A sofa and upholstered chair from the room's original furnishings were pushed against one wall and surrounded by an odd assortment of trunks and baskets, a low table, and assorted lamps. A profusion of graceful Japanese brush paintings such as I'd seen once in a museum decorated the walls.

Two photographs in silver frames sat on the fireplace mantel. One showed a young Japanese-American in an Army uniform. The other showed three teenagers laughing and looking obediently at the camera as they stood with arms around each other in front of a roomy four-door Buick so well polished the camera had captured its gleam. Daisy was in the middle. The boy who was now in uniform stood to her left. On her right was a boy whose good looks were accentuated by a pair of black-rimmed glasses that framed a glint of wry humor. He was the tallest of the three, and wore his fedora tipped back at an angle. He must be Tosh.

Daisy's mother greeted me with a smile and offered her hand.

"We're grateful you came to speak to us about Daisy's...initiative, Miss Sullivan."

Her voice, like her handshake, was firm and had a bell-like clarity. With my eyes closed I wouldn't have known her skin color. Daisy's father gave a slight bow over my hand as he introduced himself. He then gave the names of two other Japanese-American men in suits standing somewhat behind him.

"My wife and I invited them as representatives of our community here in Dayton since the matter involving our son reflects on all. I hope you don't object."

"I don't. I understand."

"Please, have a seat on the sofa," his wife said. "The chair is for you, Mr. King."

I felt as if I were taking part in some diplomatic meeting. Perhaps I was. Mrs. Hashimoto settled next to me on the sofa. Except for an elderly couple who had remained on a low bench at the back of the room, everyone else now knelt and sat on their haunches. To say the space was crowded would have been understatement.

"It never would have occurred to us to take the step that Daisy took, seeking help from someone outside the family."

Her father sent her a look of gentle reproval. Daisy, kneeling next to the old woman, looked down at her hands. She and the old woman both wore loose-fitting trousers.

"Mr. King says you are well thought of, and knowledgeable in your line of work. Do you really believe Tosh may be innocent of any wrongdoing?"

I took a moment, forming my answer.

"Whether or not he's innocent remains to be seen. I do think there are some discrepancies in the reports that identified him as the one seen running away the night of the fire."

Next to me, Daisy's mother made an almost inaudible sound of relief and of hope.

"Such as?" Dr. Hashimoto asked.

I went through the bit about looking from a lighted room into darkness. At the back, the old woman said something to Daisy in a low sing-song voice. Daisy replied, whispering. Explaining what I'd said, perhaps?

"Also, I don't see how he could have left his workstation and gone back to where the fire started without someone noticing."

For several moments, no one spoke as I concluded what now appeared to me my very short list.

"That wasn't his shift!" Daisy burst out. "No one would even have recognized him! How could they say he was the one who ran? How could we have missed that?"

Her grandmother hissed her to silence.

"She's right," said one of the men with Dr. Hashimoto. "None of the Nisei worked that shift. I made the arrangements there and at several other places. They preferred that all the Nisei work during the day."

To offset her scolding, Daisy's grandmother now was stroking the girl's shoulder. Daisy pressed her cheek to the old woman's hand. Dr. Hashimoto was nodding thoughtfully.

"Such a small detail," he murmured. "Of course, it shines an unpleasant spotlight on the question of why Tosh was there — if he was. But it also strengthens what you said, that someone would surely have noticed. Perhaps they would have given no heed to a colleague moving around, but they most certainly would have noticed a stranger!"

"Yet the police, to judge by the questions they asked us when they came here, are absolutely certain Tosh is the one who was seen — that he started that fire." His wife's voice was harsher than it had been earlier. A look passed between the couple.

"Have you spoken to the police? Do you know if they're even considering anyone else?" asked Daisy's father.

"Yes, I've spoken to them, but I don't know who they've talked to, or if they have other suspects. As much as I'd like to know, and to find out what sort of evidence they've collected, I can't just ask and get an answer. It doesn't work like that. They did tell me three people had identified Tosh, and that they'd found his glasses at the scene."

"Not the ones he wore! Look. Look!" Indignation brought him to his feet. "Those are the glasses Tosh wore. Black frames. Always!" He gestured at the photograph on the mantel. "The ones the police showed us had wire frames. They looked like a pair he had years ago, but why would Tosh have kept them? And even if — *if* — he did, what were they doing there?"

CHAPTER TEN

"They woke us up around five the next morning. They asked if we had a son named Tosh, and if he worked at Kirby Printing." Dr. Hashimoto's anger, or maybe just frustration, started to surface. "They told us there'd been a fire there, and asked if our son wore glasses. When we said yes, they asked the name of the optometrist he'd gone to. They said they needed to check the prescription for the lenses in a pair they'd found."

"We were terrified!" said his wife. "We thought…we didn't know what to think. That maybe he'd gone there to pick up something he'd left in his desk and been caught in the fire. That he'd been so badly burned—" She pressed her hand to her mouth.

"We were afraid he was dead, and they needed the lens information to confirm his identity," her husband said harshly. "We gave them the optometrist's name, of course. Then they showed us a pair of glasses, the ones with wire, and asked if we recognized them."

"I started to cry."

"I tried to explain. That he'd had a pair similar once,

but wore different ones now. They didn't listen then, and they haven't when they've been back since. It's clear they think the fire was started. Why look for any reason other than sabotage? Especially when you can so conveniently blame it on a Japanese."

I'd walked into a windmill. I picked my way through with words.

"The Dayton police aren't lazy, and they're not vindictive, either. They do sometimes fail to see the importance of a detail."

That was particularly true of Freeze, who, unless he could lure Boike back or could magically cause an experienced man to join his team, was just about the entire brains of the homicide unit at the moment. Freeze wasn't a bad cop. In fact, in the past few years I'd come to realize he was pretty smart. But when an idea didn't originate with him, he was too fast to dismiss it.

"But you do? About the glasses?" pressed Dr. Hashimoto.

"Yes."

"Another of the small discrepancies you spoke of in the beginning."

"Yes."

Daisy's parents shared a quick communication with their eyes.

"Does that mean you'll help us, then?"

"I'm willing to spend a few days asking a few more

questions. If you answer a couple for me first."

He glanced at the two men representing the resettled Americans as if to gauge their reaction before he spoke. "Yes. Of course."

I hated to ask what I needed to next, especially in front of people who weren't part of the family. There was no other way. I sought the tranquility of the brush paintings before I spoke.

"First of all, I want to stress that I ask questions like I'm about to ask you of anyone who comes to me for help. It helps me see where the police might be forming an altogether wrong idea, so I can gather facts to the contrary. With that in mind…" I drew breath. "Can you think of anything — something Tosh wrote, people he associated with — that would make them think your son might engage in sabotage?"

"Absolutely none!" said his mother. Her voice broke. "He's completely loyal to this country! He…he said he was shamed that we shared blood with people who launched such a cowardly attack in Hawaii and are doing the things they're doing now. Oh, when they forced us all into camps, he was angry, of course. What person wouldn't be? But…"

"He would never do something like this," finished his father. "Start a fire knowing people could be hurt? Tosh is kind. He knows right from wrong."

"Tosh good boy." That was one of the grandparents.

The two Japanese-American guests had been

conferring in low tones. One seemed to disagree with something, but finally shrugged.

"He is exemplary," the one who prevailed told me now. He turned to Dr. Hashimoto. "If your family wishes to retain her, we have no objection. We think it can only benefit all concerned. If she can remove this…cloud of suspicion, it will be a great relief."

***

Coming up the stairs to my third-floor office the following morning, I turned the whole scene from the previous evening over in my mind. The most startling event had been when the old woman, Daisy's grandmother, suddenly spoke. Her broken English contrasted sharply with the flawless speech of younger family members.

"I pay. I put name on hiring. Anyone want be angry, be angry with old lady, emm? Daisy be my…emm…my agent."

She hugged the girl next to her, who appeared as caught off guard as everyone else had been. Dr. Hashimoto had turned for a quick conference with his wife. Then both spoke to the grandmother in Japanese, apparently concurring.

The scene in my head evaporated at sight of Freeze standing outside my office door. His face was half lost in a haze of smoke from his Old Gold.

The blue cloud didn't bode well for a friendly visit.

Once upon a time such a cloud had almost always engulfed the good lieutenant. These days it only appeared when he was in a foul mood. As I drew near, he stabbed what was left of his glowing cigarette into a cigarette stand filled with sand whose sole role in life was to suffer such abuse.

"YOU went to talk to the fire investigator." He crossed his arms as if to keep from throttling me.

"That's right, and he was considerably more pleasant than you are this morning."

Unlocking my door, I sailed inside with him stalking after me. I tossed the paper I hadn't finished onto the desk and pulled out my chair. Freeze leaned across my desk as I sat down. He balanced on his knuckles.

"You told me yesterday you weren't working for anyone."

"Which I wasn't."

"You told the fire investigator you were representing someone on the insurance claim."

"Nonsense. He may have jumped to that conclusion. I didn't tell him that."

A gust of irritation escaped Freeze and he pivoted to stalk across the room and back.

"You're something, you know that? You slice the truth so thin I could read that newspaper through it. No matter what you told him, you had no right going there sticking your nose in a police investigation."

"I was sticking my nose into what occurred at a fire. I had as much right to know as anyone else who pays their taxes, and I certainly learned a lot more there than I did from you. Oh, and by the way, while I wasn't working for anyone yesterday, as of about twelve hours ago, I am now."

"Who?" Freeze scowled.

"The Hashimoto family."

"What? You're working for a bunch of—"

"American citizens who happen to be Japanese? Yes. So, since you're here anyway, I have some questions."

"Have you talked to Boike yet?"

"I will. If you give me a fairer shake than you did yesterday."

His jaw worked once or twice, but he sat down.

"Why haven't the papers said you're hunting a young Nisei man for questioning?"

Mrs. Z saved all her newspapers for the war effort. Paper was used in ammunition. After getting home from my meeting with the Hashimotos, I'd gone through back issues and read everything I could find about the fire. After the first few days, apart from obituaries for the two men killed in it, there hadn't been much.

Freeze took a cigarette out and twirled it restlessly but didn't light it.

"The powers that be don't want the city stirred up. So far there's been no hostility toward them. The American Japs. Other places that tried employment-release projects like this one, mostly out West, have had problems. Factories need workers. So do other places. Beyond that, you need to ask the newspapers."

"And you honestly don't know where Tosh Hashimoto is, or what happened to him?"

He shook his head.

"Seems like a lot of effort and expense making a long-distance call to California to check on the glasses you found."

I had a hunch I knew the reason behind it. I hoped I was wrong. Freeze didn't respond.

"Why are you making a big deal over them when the Hashimotos have told you repeatedly that those weren't the glasses he wore?"

Freeze stared at me for a minute. He rose abruptly. "It doesn't work. The two of us. We're on opposite sides too often."

He clapped his hat on his head and walked toward the door.

I wasn't sure what he meant by "the two of us." It was true, though, that interaction between us could only be cordial when we were both on the same side in a case.

Halfway out the door, he paused. He didn't look back.

"We don't call all the shots the way we did before the war. If you want any more information out of me, have that talk with Boike."

CHAPTER ELEVEN

I spun my desk chair in a complete circle, lost in thought. Reading between the lines was an art, and subject to error, but doing that with what Freeze had said about not calling the shots confirmed my theory on the long-distance call to the optometrist. With the country at war, the Dayton police were in constant contact with officials at Patterson Field as well as the FBI. The fingerprints of military secrecy decorated that long-distance phone call. Clearly sabotage was the favored explanation for the fire, and the only one those in authority were pursuing.

Could a printing facility, and a small one at that, be important enough to target for sabotage?

The best way to determine that was with the item already at the top of my list for untangling what had happened the night of Tosh Hashimoto's disappearance. I picked up the phone and spun the dial to the numbers for Kirby Printing.

The secretary guarding the phone of Walter Kirby, the president, wasn't keen to let me have an appointment when I told her it was about the fire.

Assurances that I wasn't with the press didn't help. Telling her in my friendliest voice that I'd hate to leave my phone off the hook so other calls couldn't get through proved more persuasive. In testier tones than became a first-rate secretary, she said Mr. Kirby could see me at eleven.

That didn't leave time enough to go see Boike, which was fine by me. I was glad he was back, but if he'd been discharged, meaning the Army didn't think he was up to further service, I was afraid I'd find him in worse shape than Freeze let on.

Instead, I got out a lined yellow tablet and started a list of other things I wanted to check on and questions to answer. The Hashimotos had given me names of two or three friends Tosh did things with, but I suspected Daisy might know more. That became Number One on the list, getting those names and talking to those individuals. Number Two might overlap. It was talking to other Nisei men where he'd been staying.

Beneath my list of things to do, I wrote the word GLASSES in big, fat letters and drew a circle around it.

Why would Tosh keep a pair of glasses he no longer wore?

Why, especially, would he bring them with him through several forced relocations?

What did it tell about what had happened to him

that the glasses were found on the ground, with one lens shattered?

It was possible he'd kept the glasses as a spare pair. It was possible he'd broken his good ones and was wearing the old ones that particular day. It was possible that in fleeing he'd stumbled, and they'd fallen off.

It was also possible that his part in the incident was being stitched up a little too neatly.

Having handed myself more questions than answers, I turned my attention to the paperwork on my desk until it was time to meet Walter Kirby.

***

The front entrance to the printing firm gave a considerably different view from the one in back. Six feet or so inside the door, a long counter with a lift-up gate barred further entry. At one end, a small board displaying samples of wedding invitations and business cards proclaimed bygone days of civilian life. Behind the counter and three desks, the open archway in a wall let in the thump and clatter of machines.

When I gave my name and said I was expected, a clerk picked up a telephone. A few minutes later, a quietly stunning woman with chestnut hair wound in a Victory Roll that stopped just above her ears, came down a narrow staircase set against one wall.

"Miss Sullivan? I'm Mr. Kirby's secretary. If you'll

follow me." Her absence of small talk suggested she hadn't forgiven the tactics I'd used on the phone. She managed politeness, though, as she ushered me into Kirby's office, a comfortable-looking space with a green-shaded desk lamp and a plant in the window.

"Some days I think I spend more time on this fire business than on the work we're supposed to be doing here," Kirby said, shaking the hand I offered.

His handshake was exhausted. It tried to be strong, but managed for just a few seconds.

"My secretary didn't say who you were with, just that I should see you. If you've come for paperwork on the insurance—"

"I'm a private detective, Mr. Kirby. It's there on the card."

I'd handed him one when we exchanged introductions. He'd looked at it. Apparently, the information hadn't registered. I wasn't sure it did this time either. His eyes glided over it and that was that.

"Oh, yes. Of course."

Kirby was fiftyish with regular features and straight black hair that swept back from his forehead. I discarded my initial impression of exhaustion. He wore the same dazed expression as people who'd walked away from something horrific, a fatal accident, a shooting, something whose magnitude was too great for them to process.

"This has nothing to do with insurance." If that was

a concern to him, I'd allay it — and look there more closely. "I'm not here to make trouble for anyone. The family of Tosh Hashimoto has asked me to look into his disappearance the night of the fire. Why he might have come here, if he did. Who reported seeing him, why they believed it was him, what was happening in here at the time. That sort of thing."

"Good."

For a moment, I wondered if he'd understood what I said.

"He was a nice young man. Very bright. Mannerly. I can't believe...the police, the authorities all seem to think that he started the fire. They seem set on the idea it was sabotage. I like to believe what we do here helps in the war effort. But training manuals? Instruction diagrams? Surely a place that makes gun parts or airplane wings would be a likelier target."

The dullness in his eyes had receded. Bewilderment replaced it.

"You won't object to my asking questions here, then?"

His head shook slightly. "But what other explanation is there? The police — at first — kept asking about the men who were killed..."

His mind was starting to drift. I wasn't sure how much longer I could keep his attention.

"If Tosh or anyone else had a grudge against the victims, you mean?"

"Yes."

"And?"

"The two who died weren't even supposed to be here."

"What do you mean?"

"An old press, one that we put into service again when we added a second shift, broke down a month ago. We'd finally found a part we needed and it came in. That afternoon, late. Those two…" His features quivered, close to crumpling with emotion. He managed to master it. "I asked them if they'd come back after their regular shift. Go home, have supper, relax a few hours and then come back to make the repair. If they hadn't, they'd still be alive. I killed them."

"The person who started the fire killed them. It may have been Tosh Hashimoto. It may have been someone else. Either way, I want to find out."

"Good."

The phone beside him rang. He jumped, then picked it up and listened, looking more drained by the minute.

"Tell him I'll call him back. Oh, and Phyllis, will you check about that coated stock from…You did? Yes, yes. I remember now. Sorry."

Possibly no longer aware of my presence, Kirby pulled a lined tablet identical to the one I used for lists toward him. His list ran all the way to the bottom.

"Forgot to cross it off," he muttered. Lifting a fountain pen from its stand, he did so now, then looked at me again.

"The fire cost us dearly. We're insured, of course, but it won't cover the loss. Even that won't pay out until the fire department signs off on their paperwork. The heat damaged a belt on another machine, and we've just managed to track down a replacement. Meanwhile, we've had to turn over a contract we're halfway through, so we can keep up with the other ones. I don't know what I'd do if the bank hadn't let me borrow enough to cover salaries for two months."

He smoothed his hair even though not a strand was out of place. "Sorry. You're not here to hear my troubles."

"It's useful. I'm sorry you've had them. As much as I hate to, if I'm going to get to the bottom of what happened the night of the fire, I have to start by asking you things the police already have asked."

"Like who might harbor ill will toward me or the company?"

"Yes"

His head was shaking.

"I did something foolish a few years back, but I told my wife and we…she was more understanding than I deserved."

"By something foolish, you mean—"

"Another woman. Yes. She moved to a different

state. We've heard she married a man who's quite well-off."

His gaze flicked toward the clock on the wall, then the list. Something there stayed his attention and he suppressed a sigh.

"I'll be on my way," I said. "Thanks for your help. If there's a manager or personnel director you could tell I'm here, and that I'd like to walk around and talk to some employees?"

He looked at me blankly, then blinked.

"Yes. Yes, of course. I'll show you the way." He got to his feet. "If you think you might want to talk to my wife…"

"I do."

"Let me write the address." He turned over one of the business cards from the brass holder on his desk. "I'll call her to let her know it's all right to talk to you."

"Thanks."

He opened the door for me and told his secretary he'd be right back.

"I'm taking her over to talk to Gene. He's my manager," he added to me. "Gene Spooner. Gene's a brick. I couldn't have survived this past week without him."

"If you don't mind, I'd rather not have him or anyone else know it's the Hashimotos who hired me," I said.

"What shall—?"

"Just say I've been hired to provide an independent assessment."

"Independent. Yes. All right. Good."

CHAPTER TWELVE

Gene Spooner had bounce enough for himself as well as his boss. He was somewhere near fifty and not quite plump, with a head of thinning black hair, an inch-thick mustache exactly the width of his upper lip, and a ready laugh.

"A private detective. Well, well, well now. Detect away." He laughed and cocked his head to the side as if anticipating delight at his wit. "You run along, Walt. I'll see to it that Miss Sullivan gets whatever she needs. You look ready to drop."

The manager and I exchanged a few sentences of polite conversation.

"I'm afraid I'm a bit of a thick noodle sometimes," he said with an affable chuckle. "Who is it you're investigating for, and what are you hoping to learn that the police haven't?"

"Probably nothing." Since he seemed to like them, I gave a smile as sunny as the day outside. "It's just that what happened here is so complicated. It's just a precaution to make sure nothing was missed. I guess you could say I'm here to make sure all the *i's* were dotted."

Beneath his cheery exterior I saw frustration. He couldn't bring himself to say I hadn't told him anything on the off chance I had.

"Well, I expect you'd like a tour of the circus. I'll show you around and answer any questions you have along the way."

"You can probably answer one of them better than anyone else," I said as we left his office for an open room filled with desks and workers hunched over them. "Since you're the manager."

My hint of his importance smoothed his feathers. As soon as I left I'd have a beer to clear my mouth of the sticky-sweet taste left from talking to the man beside me.

"I'm sure you keep your finger on the pulse of the place. Any good manager would. So, you're in the best position to tell me about Tosh Hashimoto and how he got along with his coworkers."

"Hashimoto? He seemed like a fine young man. Just goes to show, doesn't it? How you can't judge a book by the cover."

We were starting a traipse through the open room. Kirby's office was at the end by the stairs I'd come up. Spooner's office sat at the edge of the open room and halfway down. Doors to two other small offices sat next to Spooner's. Beyond them, a hallway most likely led to restrooms and storage, and presumably to the back staircase mentioned by the fire investigator.

Before I could get a word in, Spooner stopped to

point out the personnel office next to his and to do a theatrical jig step to one side as we passed a freckle-faced blonde with a bow in her hair and an armload of papers.

"You're looking awfully chipper today, Portia. New beau?"

She blushed. "You're wearing my favorite, Mr. Spooner."

He chuckled as if she'd said something terribly clever.

"My tie," he whispered as we continued.

I noticed his bow tie for the first time. Over the years, especially when working at Rike's department store, I'd known other men who wore bow ties. Usually those ties were black or navy; maybe maroon or red for Christmas. I remembered one green one on St. Paddy's day.

Spooner's tie was black and white houndstooth. Neon signs demanded less attention. As I stared at it, wondering if I was expected to comment, he chuckled again.

"They're my little smile makers, my flashy ties. The employees like to guess which one I'll be wearing. My way of boosting morale. Every little bit helps, don't you think?"

His elbow nudged mine, pal to pal.

"Uh, right. Mr. Hashimoto?" I prompted.

"Yes, well, as I said, a likable fellow. Bit of a ladies' man."

"Meaning?"

"Oh, just that he seemed to enjoy talking to women. Some got a bit silly at the attention. Not that it ever affected his work. Excellent worker."

"Could he have been hunting information in his talk with them, do you think? About work you do here, or…?"

"No, no…that is, it never occurred…surely not." He chuckled and brushed his fingers open and closed a few times as if to dispense with the subject. "Probably just that his kind are chattier."

"All the same, could we go downstairs? I'd like to talk to the people he worked with before I do anything else, if you don't mind."

"Downstairs?" His surprise was clear. "He worked up here. At that desk there. He was one of our proofreaders."

All the more reason why he would have attracted attention down where the fire started, I thought.

"Hard job to fill. You want somebody who's had experience. That's why we were tickled to get him. I admit to being a holdout at first, when Walt proposed bringing in Japanese. It felt a bit odd, the idea of having them here when we're fighting people just like them."

"Except that the ones working here are Americans."

"Oh, of course. At any rate, it's turned out well. They fit right in. All of them.

"Keeping those commas in line, are you, Velma?"

We'd moved to an area where two long tables separated five desks from all the others. He bent over a gray-haired woman with short curls corralled by a hairnet. She hunched a shoulder and giggled silently as if his question was the funniest thing she'd heard all day. Her eyes remained fixed on the sheet of paper in front of her, where her left index finger moved methodically down lines of type.

"No, Mr. Hashimoto was well liked. I never heard of him having differences with anyone. Did you, ladies — and gent?"

Four women and one man worked in the proofreading section.

"No, Mr. Spooner," four voices chorused obediently.

One didn't respond. A brunette whose pale skin needed some color, tightened her jaw instead.

"There you go." Spooner gave a palm-up flourish. He might be taking Shakespeare's bit about all the world being a stage too literally. "If I hear anything elsewhere, I'll give you a call."

He started to move again, either to show me the layout below or to show me out, I suspected. I stayed put.

"Actually, I'd like to talk to the other proofreaders when they have a few minutes. Find out if he had interests he might have mentioned, friends, girls he went out with, things like that. When do they have a break?"

Spooner struggled to keep his joviality in place.

"The trouble is, you've caught us on a very bad day. I'm not sure they'll get one, or not more than five minutes. Too busy."

"It's a pretty full day for me, too. Monday will be better all around. Mr. Kirby sprang me on you today without any warning. I'll come back Monday. Half past ten?" I stuck out my hand.

The manager shook it without enthusiasm.

"Yes, all right."

He wasn't thrilled at the prospect of me returning. I didn't appreciate having to wait until Monday. The way I saw it, that made it a good compromise.

***

Responsibility drove me to give myself a raincheck on a palate-cleansing beer. Instead I returned to the office and telephoned Kirby's wife. As promised, her husband had already filled her in on what I was doing, and she agreed to see me at half past one.

I'd no sooner hung up than the phone rang, practically under my hand. Hoping it wasn't Kirby's wife calling back to plead a just-remembered appointment as a reason not to see me, I answered.

"Miss Sullivan, my name is Clarence Woods. I'm an attorney tying up the affairs of Lettie Gannon. I believe you helped her at one time?"

"Mrs. Gannon? Yes." She was a sweet little woman whose estranged son I'd located going on a year ago. "Does settling her affairs mean she's dead?"

"Oh, no. No. Forgive my poor choice of words. She's been staying with her son and his family in California, and she's decided to make the arrangement permanent. She's asked me to see to some matters here."

"I see."

"She's concerned about never paying you for your services."

"I told her it wasn't necessary."

She was a widow without much to live on, and judging by the heartbreak in her voice, not much to live for when I first met her. It was clear she'd scrimped to get together the small sum she'd offered as a down payment on finding her son. It had taken me a year and a half of writing letters, waiting for answers, and then writing more letters; of paying people I didn't know in distant cities to look up information in phone books and city directories. It had been intermittent work, and in the end, I didn't have the heart to bill her.

"She feels very strongly about reimbursing you," said the lawyer. "She's proposed doing so in a way that's, ah, highly unusual."

The words roused my curiosity.

"In any case, I need you to come by my office to sign some papers confirming I've presented the offer. Sooner rather than later, if you wouldn't mind."

"I have an hour free now."

"Unfortunately, I do not. Would half past four work?"

***

Walt Kirby's printing business provided the family a nice but modest brick bungalow with dormer windows in its second story. His wife didn't have much to add to what I'd already learned. Her husband had told her about his dalliance. He'd never strayed before, and she didn't think he would again. There was a sad serenity about her.

"I'm worried about my husband," she said in her soft voice. "The pressure he's under right now is eating him alive. We could lose the business because of this fire. A bank loan to repay, with interest. A press inoperable for goodness knows how long, with a contract and attendant revenue forfeited as a result. We've used most of our savings to get repairs under way while we wait for insurance.

"And, of course, there are the men who died. One had been with him since he started the business. Thank heavens he's had Gene Spooner to keep things going or I don't think he could have managed, he seems so...overwhelmed at times. Gene has a way of lightening his mood."

She laughed at my expression.

"Under his silly ties and that, Gene is very attentive

to what needs to be done. He has a talent for seeing solutions. Otherwise he'd never have managed to raise a child on his own, and a handicapped boy at that, while doing the work he does, I suppose. Anyway, I'm glad Walt has him. Doubly glad since Gene came into a bit of money a few years back and could have quit working."

The most productive part of our conversation came soon afterward, when we were shaking hands goodbye.

"Walt said you asked him who might harbor bad feelings toward the Japanese-American boy, or the business. One person who might overhear something like that is a retiree named Ethyl. She comes in on a volunteer basis three afternoons a week."

"What's Ethyl's last name?"

"White, I think. She worked there for years. Now she comes in to help with the filing. She pitched in when the place went crazy converting for war work and setting up the second shift. I was helping then too, so I got to know her. She's not a gossip. I didn't mean to suggest that. But she's one of those quiet people who gets overlooked, and she notices things."

CHAPTER THIRTEEN

Since I couldn't talk to employees at Kirby Printing until Monday, I had time on my hands before going to see the lawyer at half past four. His vagueness about a proposal had left me curious. Maybe the woman who owed me money wanted to set me up in business in California. Maybe I'd say yes if it came with a quiet room instead of the chatter and constant activity that now was part of life at Mrs. Z's.

Meanwhile, maybe I should use the time to go visit Boike.

I'd been avoiding the task, in part for legitimate reasons, but mostly out of dread. I doubted Freeze would out and out lie, but he might understate the extent of Boike's injuries. As much as he wanted Boike back, he might well be blind to the man's condition. Nevertheless, I'd promised Freeze I'd talk to his former assistant. Besides, I liked Boike. The least I could do was let him know I was glad he was back. I dug out the slip of paper containing his address.

Getting there took me angling up northwest of the

city. As I left the city limits and little patches too big to be yards and too small to be farms began to appear, I began to wonder if Boike might be staying with a woman he'd mentioned a couple of times who took in stray dogs. When the number I was hunting led me into a dirt drive, a chorus of barking confirmed it.

I slowed the car to miss a couple of bounding mutts and stopped in front of a frame house that had been ready for paint a few years back. As I debated whether to honk, a woman in bib overalls with a flowered apron over them came around the side of the house. Hushing the dogs, she put up a hand to shade her eyes.

"You need something?" she said in greeting. The words overflowed with the sound of Kentucky hills.

"I'm a friend of Boike's. I stopped by to say 'hi' and welcome him home. Is he around?"

She gave me a good once-over. Her gray hair was twisted up in a topknot.

"You got a name?"

"Maggie. Maggie Sullivan."

"I'll fetch him. You kin get out if you want. Dogs don't bite."

Despite the reassurance, I stayed where I was. A minute later Boike came slowly around the same direction the old woman had. He was still blond, still solid with the contours of a Frigidaire. I got out and sauntered toward him.

When I drew closer I realized he was missing the lower half of his left ear. Scar tissue stretched pudgy red fingers down to the edge of his mouth, his jaw, the back of his neck. Wondering if I should look away, or murmur some sort of sympathy, I said the first thing I could manage.

"Gee, since you can't wear an earring now, I guess I can quit worrying you'll run off to be a pirate."

I didn't really know Boike, apart from shared work, and wasn't sure how he would take it. His head pulled back in surprise. Then he started to chuckle. The unscarred side of his face drew up in a grin.

"Thanks for not trying to mollycoddle like everyone else does."

I ducked my head in awkward acknowledgment. Once when I'd had a stitched-up lip courtesy of men with brass knuckles, Wee Willie had teased me about it, lifting my spirits as sympathy wouldn't have.

"Good to see you, Boike. Glad to have you back."

We shook hands with the fierce kind of grip that said what words couldn't. He indicated the front steps.

"Want to sit for a while?" He positioned himself so I'd be on his undamaged side.

The woman in apron and overalls appeared again with two dogs trailing her.

"You two want beer or lemonade or anything?"

"Thanks, Mary Minerva. I'll get it if we do." Boike's head bobbed between us. "Mary Minerva Pike…Maggie Sullivan."

I wondered if she'd been around the corner listening protectively in case my reaction to his injuries upset him. Or maybe she thought I might be a girlfriend, and wanted to make up her mind whether I was good enough for him. We murmured hellos.

"I'll get back to it then," said Mary Minerva. Her tone was friendlier now. She confided as if I'd understand, "Worming."

I nodded politely. When I glanced at Boike he was chuckling silently.

"It's not as bad as it sounds," he said.

"Yeah, I'll bet.

"Want a beer?"

"That sounds good."

The screen door banged behind him. I sat enjoying the soft sounds around me. Squirrels in the trees. Two jays squabbling. At the corner of the porch away from where Mary Minerva had vanished, three kittens crawled out from under the porch to pounce and wrestle each other in the grass. Tiring of the game, one toddled over and pulled itself up the stairs. It stopped in surprise, or maybe with curiosity, upon seeing me. I picked up the handful of gray-and-white fur and stroked its small head with my index finger. It started to purr. I'd nearly forgotten how nice it was to be around a cat that didn't try to bite me.

At my back, the screen door banged again. Boike resumed his seat on the step and held out two bottles of beer, one dark, one lager.

"Take your pick."

I took the dark one.

"Here's to having old friends back," I said. Our bottles clinked. The kitten had taken up residence on my thigh, its needle-like claws holding my skirt and its eyes half closed. Boike and I drank some beer.

"I heard you and Freeze are an item these days," said Boike.

I swallowed the beer in my mouth faster than anticipated.

"News to me, unless grabbing a sandwich together a few times while we talked over a case and going to the picture show a couple of times makes you an item."

Amusement tugged at the side of his face I could see. After I'd known him a couple of years, I'd begun to suspect a dry sense of humor lurked beneath his stolid expression. It was hard to say, though, since Freeze didn't like the men who worked under him to speak unless invited to.

"Mick Connelly got married, though."

"Yeah, he did." Through cowardice I'd pushed the one man I ever cared for into the arms of someone else and then regretted it. "What about you? Do you have a girl I never heard about?"

Boike snorted.

"Did I have a private life when I worked with Freeze, you mean? Not much of one. I spent some time with Corrine Vanhorn before I went over. We wrote back and forth. Then I got a letter from her saying she was going to marry her stepbrother." He killed the rest of his beer. "Freeze send you here to talk me into coming back?"

"That's what he wanted." Not needing a spot on my skirt from a kitten whose urinary discipline wasn't what it should be yet, I set the little thing on the ground. "I told him I was all for seeing you to welcome you back, but I wasn't about to push you on what you should do."

"Thanks."

I prepared to dance across quicksand. "Boike, if what you saw overseas…if you've had your fill of blood and that, I'll be willing to tell him. Or you should. I think maybe he'd understand."

He gave me a startled look.

"It's not that a bit. The way I look now, I'd be no use as a detective."

"Why? It's not like you skulk around in disguises—"

"Come on, Maggie. It's hard enough getting people to open up about what they saw or heard and that. They'd be too scared even to talk to somebody who looks like I do."

"Horsefeathers. But okay, you could still do a desk job. It's your brain that matters.

"Look. I said I didn't come here to try and persuade you, and I didn't. Just stop by and visit with Freeze now and then. Once you were gone, he saw how much he'd depended on you. For chewing over ideas and just plain talking to. Have you met the kid he's stuck with as a replacement?"

"We got introduced when I went up there, is all."

"Dotson's a good kid, really, but he's no match for Freeze or the work. And he's young."

"We all had to go through that once, didn't we?"

"Yeah, okay." I knew defeat when I saw it. I finished my beer. Part of me wondered if I was wrong to push Boike as hard as I already had. He didn't deserve to be stared at and whispered about.

"What's eating Freeze about this case he's got now? The one where a Jap kid set a fire?" he asked after an interval.

"I think the War Office or FBI or someone like that might have a finger in. It probably doesn't help that I'm looking at it too and don't like a couple of pieces that don't fit."

"Ah."

Somewhere in back, a hen cackled her accomplishment at laying an egg. Mary Minerva spoke in soothing tones. Boike pressed the back of his hand to the scar on his cheek, which probably still hurt like sin. He sent me a sideways look.

"I like it, being out here with the dogs and no pressure, but I do miss exercising my brain sometimes. Since I'm not working for Freeze, if you'd ever like to toss those pieces that don't fit back and forth…"

"I'd like it a lot."

The offer surprised me, but I'd seen enough of Boike over the years to know he was good at analyzing, and coming at things from new angles. He was willing to look at a broad range of possibilities, even unlikely ones, whereas Freeze found it hard to consider anything beyond a few. Mindful of splinters, I leaned back against the porch and raised my face to the breeze and told the boxlike man beside me about the oddities of no one noticing Tosh inside the plant, and the glasses he didn't wear and lighted rooms versus darkness. Then, explaining my presence in the alley behind where the Hashimotos lived as an attempt to see the lay of the place and whether a fugitive son could get in and out undetected, I told him about the attack on me, and the thread of sound I couldn't quite identify.

By the time I finished, he was sitting erect, already deep in thought.

"What about a bicycle?" he suggested.

"A bicycle? Huh. Maybe." Footsteps ending abruptly, then that sound of something small moving on gravel.

"It would make sense. In fact, it's downright smart." He itemized raising blunt fingers. "It's more mobile than a car, and quieter. Harder to see because it's smaller and can stay close to walls or bushes. You're not dipping into your gas ration getting around. And if you don't have one — or even if you do — you can wait till dark, pick one up out of a yard, and take off. Leave it wherever you want, back where you got it or in a different yard."

His ideas kick started mine. "You wouldn't need a driver's license."

"And if it was a bike in that alley, you're looking for someone who plans," said Boike. "And you're looking for someone in probably better-than-average physical shape to duke it out with you the way it sounds like he did, and then hop on a bike and pedal away."

CHAPTER FOURTEEN

I talked so long with Boike that I barely had time to get back downtown and powder my nose before presenting myself at the office of Clarence Woods, Esq. He was a comfortable sort of lawyer. His rooms were done up several steps better than most one- and two-man operations that limped along on a shoestring, but well below the lavish furnishings of high-price firms. The man matched the office. He had thinning gray hair, a benign expression, and a pair of half-moon spectacles that he wore on the tip of his nose.

As soon as I was seated in front of his desk, he got down to business.

"I expect you see some unusual things in your line of work, Miss Sullivan. I don't mind admitting that what Lettie Gannon has tasked me with falls into that same category for me."

I put on my best Bright Girl look while wondering what was unusual about presenting me with some sort of paper to sign indicating I'd been paid in full for my work in behalf of Lettie Gannon or that I'd been offered payment and declined.

Wood took off his specs and frowned at them and put them back on.

"Lettie says at the time you were hunting her son you were unmarried. Is that still the case?"

The oddness of his question put me on guard.

"Yes, why?"

"And you have no family? Children, or a parent who lives with you…?"

"No. What does that have to do—?"

"Well, then, I doubt this will interest you, but Lottie insisted I offer the option. Her son has done very well for himself, finds actors for films or something like that. The blythe way she makes long-distance calls to me certainly underscores the fact that he's well-off. He's had an addition put on his house, so she has her own apartment. She gets on with his wife and adores being with her grandchildren. The sum of it all is that she doesn't plan to return to Dayton.

"Therefore, she wants me to give you two options: Receive a check for five hundred dollars, which she believes is about the amount she would owe you, or…" His eyes closed and he drew a breath. "…she'll sell you her house here in Dayton for an additional nine hundred dollars."

His words might as well have been gibberish. At that exact moment, they were gibberish.

A house? Out of the sky blue, someone was offering to sell me a house for nine hundred dollars? Was the man across from me mad? Was the sweet old lady I'd done work for in odd minutes, with no real expectation I'd ever be paid, mad?

The lawyer's voice was continuing, distant and watery, as if through a bad phone connection.

"In essence, the latter would be saying the sale price of the house is fourteen hundred dollars, and crediting you with five hundred of that. I assure you, the house is worth a good deal more. I advised her against the whole idea."

"It…is extraordinary."

"Preposterous is more accurate. Defense workers are sleeping in cars and barber chairs; you're a single woman who presumably already has a roof over her head…But Lettie wouldn't budge. She said she'd seen something in your face whenever you came to see her, a longing for a corner of your own, she called it. I can't help thinking that being out in California with those movie people around her has made her a bit romantic.

"Be that as it may, I've outlined the two proposals. Have you any questions?"

"I don't believe so."

The house option was clearly impractical. Thanks to a steady stream of background checks for defense work I now did on top of my regular work, my savings account had never been fatter, but I knew for a fact there wasn't much over three hundred dollars in it. Three-fifty, max.

M. Ruth Myers

"Then if you'll just sign this document attesting that both choices have been presented to you."

Woods opened a file folder on his desk and slid a sheet of legalese toward me.

"Your signature goes there, on the top line." He pointed with the tip of a pencil and slid a pen toward me.

What would I do with a house?

Sit on the back stoop enjoying the sun and the quiet, the way you did with Boike, a voice at my elbow whispered. *Get a good night's sleep without people slamming doors and talking and playing the radio.*

"Once you've signed that you understand the choices, you'll need to put an X in front of one of the items listed below that," the lawyer continued. "The one marked RECEIVE PAYMENT or the one marked PURCHASE HOUSE. You'll sign again beneath the one you choose when money changes hands. If you choose the payment option, I can give you a check right now and save you another trip."

"How long do I have?"

"I beg your pardon?" He looked up, midway through the act of opening a drawer in his desk.

I signed my full name on the indicated upper line.

"How long do I have to make up my mind about the two choices?"

I was going to take the money, of course. Add a hefty sum to my savings. But having been blindsided by a possibility I'd never envisioned, I wanted time to think, even if it only amounted to flirting a little with a choice I knew I wouldn't make.

The lawyer's mouth had opened, but he didn't speak at first.

"Until Wednesday," he said at last. "You can have until five o'clock Wednesday."

***

Rattled beyond rational thought, I went downstairs and sat in my car. For years I'd rejected the notion of marrying and settling down to a house and kids. Never once had it crossed my mind I might be able to have a house without the other two. Now…Now the whole idea was too outlandish to process.

To steady myself, I needed to think about something familiar. Something I at least half understood.

The bicycle.

Boike's ideas about why an attacker might use one made sense. His comment about my assailant needing to be in good physical shape in order to pick a fight in an alley and then ride off had started me thinking. Prior to that conversation, I'd operated under the theory that whoever had been waiting back there, watching the place where Daisy and her family lived, was a teenager or a young man in his early twenties. Either somebody sweet on Daisy, or Tosh Hashimoto himself. Now I wasn't so sure.

Plenty of men in their thirties and even their forties

still were capable of using their fists and riding a bike, especially if they engaged in some kind of sports or did physical labor. But who? A common burglar who liked the anonymity and flexibility Boike had noted? I'd check to see if there'd been a rash of burglaries anywhere in the city, but having the perpetrator turn up at Daisy's house felt too coincidental. While the car parked in front with a driver who didn't want to be seen might be FBI, or someone of that ilk if they believed the sabotage angle. I couldn't see an agent of the swaggering set riding a bicycle. Nor could I see them attacking me, for that matter.

All my fine reasoning had brought me full circle, but at least I was once more capable of normal thought. I headed for Finn's hoping Seamus would be there. He was sparing with words, and even more so with advice, but maybe when I'd told him about my meeting with Clarence Woods, he'd ask why I hadn't just pounced on the offer of cash. The question would carry more weight coming from him than it did when I asked it myself.

When I entered the pub, though, luck went against me and then poured me a second serving.

"Has Seamus been in yet?" I asked as Rose bustled toward me. His usual stool at the bar was empty.

"No, and I've been watching for him too. But now that you're here, you'll do just as well."

"For what?"

"Managing that."

Her head indicated a table in the far corner. I looked and my breath caught. A man with brick-red hair sat with elbows propped on either side of a nearly empty glass as he stared down at it. Every line of him communicated unhappiness.

"Whatever it is about Connelly that needs managing isn't my responsibility." With effort, my voice came out steady.

Rose scowled. "He wouldn't be sitting there like that if it wasn't for you."

"Yeah, probably. Are you going to get me a Guinness or not?"

Mick Connelly had courted me patiently for more than five years. I'd resisted, fearful of failure, fearful of losing my independence, fearful I'd forget who I was if I played the role of somebody's wife. He deserved to be happy. He longed for a home and a family, and I'd urged him to find a woman willing to give him that. So, he had, and I'd regretted it every day since.

Finn appeared with my stout and with a look of sympathy slid it past Rose's elbow.

"He's been in here all afternoon," he said in a low voice. "Drinking whiskey along with his pints. I'm cutting him off, and I don't know how he'll take it."

Finn was a good man, and he thought the world of Connelly.

"Yeah, all right." Fortified by a hefty slug from the

glass in front of me, I made my way past tables filling with the after-work crowd.

Connelly swayed and gave a lopsided grin as I sat down.

"Maggie *mavourneen*, you're still as pretty as the day I met you 'n not a day older. I think you're a witch."

"Uh-huh. And Finn says it's time you went on your way." I steeled myself for the offer I was about to make. "Shall I call you a taxi or drive you home myself?"

"Can't go home," he said smugly. "M' day off, but Kathleen had some of her fancy friends coming over to play bridge and told me to get out of the house."

"They'll be gone now. It's going on six."

"Sergeants' wives." He waved his glass. "Thinks it will advance my career. Advance *her*, she means. Being an ordinary copper's wife isn't good enough for her." His laugh was bitter.

"You're drunk, Mick. Taxi...or me wasting my gas?"

He crossed his arms stubbornly and stretched out his legs.

"Stayin' right here, thanks. Tell Finn I want another."

I went back to the bar.

"Call his wife. They have a car."

With a glare, Rose opened a drawer and took out a spiral-bound notebook she used for phone numbers. She spun the telephone dial, then shoved the receiver toward me.

"I'm not talking to that woman."

I barely caught it in time as a sweet voice came through the wire.

"Connelly residence, Kathleen speaking."

"Kathleen, this is Maggie Sullivan, a friend of—"

"I know who you are." The temperature of the words had dropped thirty degrees.

"Mick's down here at Finn's, and he's drunk as a skunk. You need to come get him or talk him into taking a cab."

"The drunken lout can take a bus. Or crawl, for all I care!"

Thinking she'd hung up, I started to do the same. She spoke again.

"Tell that barman to get him up to the front door, so I don't have to parade through the whole place. I'll be there in ten minutes."

Slam.

The was no doubt she'd hung up this time. Or that, with me holding the receiver away from my ear, Rose had heard what she said.

Rose's eyes slid down the bar. "Finn looks pretty busy to me."

"I like parades," I said.

She gave a small, wicked grin, readmitting me to her good graces. I sipped my Guinness. As I neared the bottom of it, the pub door flew open and Connelly's pretty blonde wife marched in.

Whatever she said when she reached him was too muted to hear, but when she reached for his arm to yank him to his feet, he came without protest. Every eye in the place was fixed on her, some because she was a looker, others watching the drama. Patches of fury blotched her cheeks.

"How dare you embarrass me like this!" She snapped, too angry to realize she could be heard. "You're a disgrace to your uniform!"

She was being forced to zigzag to hold him upright.

"I'm not wearing m' uniform. It's m' day off, remember?" Connelly winked at the room in general.

CHAPTER FIFTEEN

Rose, possibly to atone for snapping at me, tried to persuade me to have a pint on the house, but I declined. With Wee Willie gone, and so many regulars replaced by newcomers, Finn's was no longer the cozy place it once had been.

I wasn't hungry, though, or interested in a picture show, and I didn't want to go back to Mrs. Z's. As if drawn by an invisible force, my car turned toward the little street off East Third where Lettie Gannon's house was located. A house that now sat empty. That she was offering to sell me.

Parking in front, I sat for a minute. It was just as I remembered. If it had been any smaller, it would have qualified as a kid's playhouse. Three unadorned steps led up to a front door with a window to the right of it. As near as I could recall, that single front room led back to a kitchen and bath and, presumably, somewhere a bedroom.

A rose bush climbed a trellis to the left of the door. Beneath the window, evidence of this year's daffodils and tulips remained amid budding stems of things I didn't recognize. I rolled down my window. The fragrance of freshly cut grass in a nearby yard drifted in.

Up and down the street, all was quiet. For most, it was the dinner hour, or washing-up time after. After sitting there for another five minutes or so, I decided to have a peek at the back yard. Even though I wasn't going to buy the place, I could at least enjoy the full excursion.

I went around the side and sat down on the back steps knowing I shouldn't. Clothesline. Shed. A gnarled old specimen that looked like it might be an apple tree. A tangle of vines. It was out of the question.

Banks made loans to people who wanted to buy houses, though, didn't they?

Before I could grow too attached to the idea, I stood up and dusted my skirt. I had things to do. I couldn't sit here mooning over some pipe dream about a tiny refuge to escape to at the end of the day.

***

Late Saturday morning, I paid a visit to a rambling wooden house where Tosh had lived with a dozen or so young Nisei men. A Japanese-American woman who could have been somebody's grandma was pushing a baby buggy up to a side door as I arrived. The baby buggy turned out to have groceries in it. The woman pushing it turned out to be a widow named Mrs. Morita, a combination cook and housemother for the place.

"Tosh is very fine young man," she said when I'd introduced myself. "Very fine." She bustled around putting groceries away. Her English wasn't as smooth as that of the Hashimotos and their two guests, but it trotted along. "All these boys are good boys. None of them would make trouble like police think." She closed a cupboard.

"I'd like to have a word with one of the ones he works with, a man named Zenzo."

"All at work now. Six day. Home at five, maybe. One boy…" She hummed a single note in thought. "…Kensuke, yes. I think is here. Hurt hand." She raised her hand to illustrate. "But maybe went to town. He was talking of."

She went out into a hallway and didn't object when I followed. When she called his name from the foot of the stairs, though, there was no response.

"Where's the bus stop?" As I trailed her back to the kitchen, I noticed a framed photograph of Tosh and some of the other young men on the wall. Tosh wore black-rimmed glasses.

"Not bus. Bicycle."

She pointed with a cleaver that would soon be the adversary of a cabbage in her other hand. The woman had been in constant motion since I arrived. Now both cleaver and woman paused just long enough to draw my attention to a sturdy shed in the back yard.

"How many use the bicycle?" Attention sharply focused, I peered out the window closest to the shed.

"Four." She held up four fingers. "Four bicycle. How many boys use?" She shrugged. "All, I think."

Whack. The cleaver split the cabbage and she began shredding it with quick, easy strokes. Though she seemed to cooperate, Mrs. Morita was too unconcerned for believability.

"Mrs. Morita, if Tosh were here, if he'd slipped in and was hiding somewhere in this house, would you know it?"

The chopping ceased. She turned.

"If he…" Did she pause to make sure she understood what I was asking, or to decide on an answer? "Yes." She nodded indignantly. "Yes, I would know, and I would say he couldn't. I would call Mr. Oto or Church Federation people."

I'd offended her, possibly on several levels. She went back to chopping. When I thanked her, she acknowledged it with the barest dip of her head.

I checked the shed in back. It held three bicycles but no potential riders. As I came back around for my car, though, I saw a Japanese-American youth pushing a bicycle up the drive. It was wobbling a good deal. The source of the wobble came from the fact he was gripping the handlebar with only one hand while attempting to steady it with the back of his other hand, which was heavily bandaged. I strolled to meet him.

"You wouldn't happen to be Ken...ah, sorry, I forget the rest. Would you?"

His smile was cautious.

"Kensuke? Yes. That's me. Why?"

"My name's Maggie Sullivan. The Hashimotos hired me to try and find out what became of Tosh and if he's okay. Here. I'll hold the bike." Suiting words to action, I handed him a business card.

The smile deepened as he read it. Interest enlivened his eyes as he looked up.

"You're the detective, huh? We'd heard rumors they hired one, but I thought they were just, you know, rumors. And there wasn't anything about it being a woman." He cocked his head. "You're not with the police, then?"

"No. Like I said, I'm trying to help his family. I really need to talk to someone who saw him day in and day out, so I'm glad you got back from town before I left."

"Ah, I never made it to town. Barely made it a block before I realized I couldn't take the handlebar pressing into my bandage. Guess I'll have to get by without Zane Grey for a while."

"What did you do to your hand?"

"I'm one of the ones working at a plant-growing place up north. I knocked a scythe off a bench and tried to catch it. Idiot, huh?"

"Or not a very good juggler."

He laughed.

"Want this in the shed?" I had continued to push the bike. "If you were headed for the library, and the one downtown's okay, it's on my own list of stops. I'll be glad to give you a lift."

"And grill me on the way? Tit for tat? Sure. I'll get the best of the deal. Tosh kept his nose clean. There's nothing I could let slip about him because there's nothing to hide."

"Something you think's unimportant might prove to be something that could get him out of some pretty bad trouble, though."

It gave him something to think about. We put the bike away in silence.

"I shouldn't have been such a smart-aleck over the ride," Kensuke said when we were settled in the DeSoto. "I'm sorry."

I flashed him a grin. "I've been known to smart off myself. Tell me about the bikes. Who owns them? Who rides them?"

"The bikes?" The question startled him. "I don't know where they came from. The people letting us use their house, or the Church Federation? Zenzo owns one, I think, but we all use it, same as the others.

"Who rides? We all do. Well, except one fellow who's kind of pudgy and has asthma or something. How are we going to get around except that or the bus? The places that employ us, or Church Federation people, take us back and forth to work, though. That's part of the deal."

I took him through the same questions I'd asked Mrs. Morita, and got more or less the same answers. When I asked about the possibility that Tosh was hiding somewhere in the house, he laughed.

"Are you kidding, lady? We sleep four to a room in bunk beds. I bet we hadn't been here two weeks before every one of us had combed every corner from the attic on down hunting somewhere we could have a little privacy."

"Do any of you think Tosh is getting a raw deal?"

"Sure, all of us. Zenzo especially. When the police came asking us questions, he was so mad I thought he might explode. Afterward, he said we ought to band together and stick up for Tosh — go on strike or something. He's kind of a firebrand."

Finally, something worth noting. And Zenzo owned a bicycle.

"He and Tosh were friends?"

"Not especially. I mean, we all get along, but he and Tosh were too different to be what I'd call friends. Tosh had his nose in a book all the time when he wasn't working. Zenzo likes to go out, have a good time. They worked at the same place, though, so that may have made them closer."

"What about Tosh? Did he ever go out?"

"No...well...The last month or so, maybe half a

dozen times. Not with us though."

"Any idea where?"

"To see his folks, maybe. Or I kind of thought he might have been seeing someone."

"A woman, you mean?"

"Yeah. 'Cause he'd come back in a really good mood. I asked him once if he had a girlfriend."

"What did he say?"

Kensuke frowned. "The thing is, he might have been kidding. When I asked him that, he laughed and said 'Yes, and she's some lady.'"

CHAPTER SIXTEEN

Kensuke — he told me to call him Ken — and I parted ways at the library. He went to find his Zane Grey westerns. I got my own books and ran some errands and thought. Was Tosh's laughing admission that he had a girlfriend confirmation of what Daisy had said about him exchanging notes with a woman? If not, then the fact he'd gone out at night in the weeks leading up to his disappearance was a bad sign.

One thing remained that I could do today to get a fuller picture of the landscape in which Tosh had disappeared. Like many plants and factories, Kirby Printing continued work on Saturdays. In their case, I knew, it was only half a day. There was ample time for me to find a parking place on the street from which I could watch employees leave through the front entrance.

Watching people leaving work can tell you things. How they move, who they appear to be chummy with, whether their coworkers give them a wide berth. Since I hadn't yet had anything approaching meaningful conversation with anyone except one Linotype operator, I didn't know what I was looking for yet. I was basing my actions on past experience in hopes something might catch my eye.

The three younger proofreaders came out together. The older one who giggled at Spooner's jokes formed a wing to the group, part of it and yet separate. The young man who checked schematics and diagrams followed them. He said something that made them all laugh and turn. With a wave, he split off in another direction.

Other upstairs workers were coming out too, mostly in groups and pairs. One was alone, her manner suggesting she liked it that way. The cloud of platinum blonde hair on her shoulders would have been enough to make her stand out, but she also had the kind of figure that drew wolf whistles. A lazy confidence in the way she walked telegraphed her certainty that she didn't need to sway her hips to get men's attention.

I tried to place her. Dimly I remembered seeing her in the rows of desks occupied by clerks and girls who worked in accounting or payroll, but my memory was only because of her hair. As I speculated whether she'd been born with her distinctive walk or cultivated it, a man who'd been lounging against the corner of a neighboring building suddenly sprang forward and caught her arm.

The man wore a jacket too casual for a salesman but too good for working around machines. He was tall, muscular through the shoulders, and had it not been for the anger in his face, he would have been handsome. The pair stepped into a space between the buildings where they began to have a set-to. The size and anger of the man made my scrutiny of departing workers fade in importance.

Still gripping the blonde by the arm, the man shook a finger in her face and said something. She replied. He reached in his pocket and thrust a scrap of paper toward her. She crumpled it, unread, and tossed it to the ground. He spoke again, shaking her hard enough that my hand crept toward the car door.

Planting her free hand on her hip, the blonde leaned toward the man. Whatever she said caused him to jerk back. She flung free of his grip and watched him run across the street dodging cars. The man jumped into the driver's seat of a boxy delivery truck, whose lettering was obscured by a passing bus as he drove off. By the time I caught a look at it in my rearview mirror, the delivery truck was too far away for me to read the lettering on it.

The blonde was ambling away.

***

Remembering my promise to Maire, I called her to see if I could stop by that evening.

"Oh, Maggie! I wish I could, but we're going to Ma's for dinner. At least it got her out of my house for the afternoon while she cooks. Tomorrow I'm sorting clothes at the parish, mostly so I can drag the kids there to see their friends. How about Monday night? Please?"

I said I would.

On Sunday afternoon, chafing at the fact I'd have to wait until Monday to learn anything more about what happened during the fire at Kirby Printing, I realized there was another place I might dig up a scrap or two: The night watchman. Freeze said he was one of the witnesses who'd identified Tosh running from the scene. In my opinion, he was the one who would have had the best view.

There was just one teeny problem. I'd stuck my nose in to break up the scrap he was having with Daisy. I'd blabbed away, spinning a tall tale, too.

I'd been in my funeral togs then, black dress, black hat, hair curling above my shoulders as it usually did. He'd be seeing me in the dark, though, so in hopes I could pull off a chat without being recognized, I put on a polka-dot skirt and the frilliest blouse I owned. Thwarted in my attempts to corral my hair in a Victory Roll, I settled on a sedate little bun at the back of my head.

There was no sight of a watchman when I parked at the front entrance to Kirby Printing. Assuming he circled the building at some point in his rounds, I settled down on the front steps where he'd be sure to see me and waited. Minutes ticked by. Finally, there were footsteps and the beam of a flashlight announced his arrival.

"Hi there." I jumped up, dusting my skirt. "Just the man I've been waiting to see. I'm a private investigator. Mr. Kirby or Mr. Spooner may have told you I'd been here?"

He stepped back, wary and shaking his head."

"I'm talking to everyone who works here about the fire," I said before he could speak. "What they can tell me about Tosh Hashimoto, what they saw the night of the fire and that. Since the plant doesn't operate Sundays, I thought you might not be as busy tonight. I can talk to you as you walk, if you like. Oh, and here's my card, in case you want to tell anyone I was here. You might remember something you want to tell me after I leave, too."

I made sure to show him both hands as I handed it to him in case he was worried I was about to stick a gun in his ribs and rob the till. He shone the flashlight beam on it and read, then squinted at me.

"I've seen you before."

I manufactured a laugh.

"Oh, I don't think so. We Sullivans practically have a whole page in the phone book, there are so many of us. I've been told there's a second or third cousin who looks a lot like me. Her family's on the outs with the rest of us though, so I've never met her. Her mother married some kind of foreigner, I think was the trouble."

"Well, sorry, I can't help you much. I've only been doing this the past week. I wasn't around when the fire happened."

Caught flatfooted in a couple of ways, I trotted a couple of steps to walk abreast with him.

"You're new? What happened to the watchman who was on duty that night?"

"Quit, I guess. Got so rattled by the whole thing that his nerves gave out. Took his pension and that was that. The company tacked up a notice saying the slot was open if any employees wanted to apply before they advertised, and I did."

"You already were working here?"

"That's right."

"Night or days?"

"Days."

"What can you tell me about Hashimoto?"

"Nothing." We had paused outside the bay door. It was closed tonight. He checked the lock. "I worked in there." He indicated the other side of the bay door. "Printer's devil. I might have seen him come through a few times, if he came down for something, but I couldn't have picked him out from the others."

My thoughts were tripping over themselves. A man who had identified Tosh and said he'd been running away from the fire had been so unhinged by the event that he retired? Because of the horror of what he'd seen? Because of guilt that he hadn't spotted the perpetrator in time to prevent it?

"What was the watchman's name? The one you replaced?"

"Seth Rowe. Lives on Tecumseh. His wife used to be my Sunday School teacher, but she died. I think his oldest daughter and her husband moved in to keep house and that."

We were walking again, and nearly back to the front.

"Well, thanks for talking to me. I appreciate it." I held out my hand, and as he shook it, I listened to the silence around us. "Since you already had a job, what was the appeal of night work? If you don't mind my asking."

For the first time, his face relaxed a little. He almost grinned.

"Easier work, pays a quarter more an hour, and since I'm home in the daytime to keep an eye on the kids, my wife can work. We've been trying to sock money away so we can buy a house when the war ends."

***

"Seth Rowe? Yes. Yes, he put in for his pension right after the fire. The police questioned him thoroughly before that, though, I assure you. Poor old fellow."

Gene Spooner seemed surprised that before we even set foot out of his office to talk to other employees, I'd asked about the change in night watchmen.

"Between you and me, I think all that pushing by the police contributed to his nerves giving way," he confided. "Not that they did anything out of line. It's just that he already was getting a little bit…odd, shall we say? But with men hard to find…The stress of all those questions on top of the fire itself simply did him in."

"How so?"

"Oh, shaky, jumped at the least little sound. Saw things in the shadows that weren't there. You say you're going over to see him this afternoon? I doubt you'll get much useful out of him, except that he saw Mr. Hashimoto running away. Now, we'd better be getting to asking those questions you want to ask."

He straightened his bow tie. Today's was a plaid in red, green and blue that just managed not to glow. With his showman's strut, he led the way out to the desk clusters filling the open area. I spotted the platinum blonde who'd had the argument Saturday. Spooner came to a stop in the proofreading section.

"Good morning, everyone. Pencils down, please. Did you all have nice weekends? How was that naughty concert, Madeline? The one you were talking about on the way out Friday?"

"Naughty, Mr. Spooner?" a snub-nosed proofreader asked with the fortitude of one who'd already heard enough silly jokes to last her a lifetime but expected another. "It was a harp concert."

"Goodness! Don't you know that harps are naked pianos?"

The gray-haired woman who'd laughed uproariously at some comment he'd made the last time accommodated again. The rest joined in politely. The lone male, keeping his head bent to his work, crossed his eyes.

"I'm sure you all remember Miss Sullivan." Spooner waved toward me as if introducing a stage act. "She wants to ask you a few more questions. I'll just toddle over there and leave you to it."

His toddle didn't take him quite out of ear range. The proofreaders knew it too, I suspected. He perched on the corner of a vacant desk and flipped through a sheaf of papers he found there, doing his best to pretend he wasn't straining to hear. My best course, I decided, and maybe my only one, might be to stir things up rather than being discreet.

"I'm not here to cause trouble for anyone," I began. "I'm here to gather some background. In part, it's because a question has been raised as to whether the man identified as running from the scene was, in fact, Tosh Hashimoto."

Spooner's feet hit the ground. The heads of all five proofreaders snapped up. Some of the faces around me were wide-eyed.

CHAPTER SEVENTEEN

Although my announcement sparked considerable interest, it led to little information. Even without the manager looking over their shoulders, with opportunity present to whisper something or scribble a note, the proofreaders all repeated the same things they'd said in response to Spooner's general question to them Friday: They didn't know of any resentments Tosh had harbored toward the printing company, or the country that had locked up people like him. Nor could they think of anyone who harbored ill feelings toward him. Tosh Hashimoto had been friendly and worked hard.

"He is — was — a lovely man," the brunette said firmly. I thought I detected dampness in her eyes.

"Why did you say 'was'?"

"Because he's not here anymore."

Maybe being a literalist helped you qualify as a proofreader.

When I asked the fourth girl what she'd made of Tosh, she shrugged.

"I replaced him. I never met him."

"That's where he sat then? That was his desk?"

"Yes," confirmed the snub-nosed girl. She had returned to her duties, touching her pencil to the margin in small jumps to track where she was.

"He didn't leave anything, if that's what you're thinking," said the brunette. "The police turned it inside out."

"The night proofreaders use our desks, too," added snub-nose. "Nobody leaves anything personal."

The lone male in their group checked charts and mechanical diagrams. He covered the one he was working on as I turned to him.

"What about you? Did you and Tosh talk much?"

"Some, I guess, probably more than he did with the girls. The two of us joked how we had to stick together because we were outnumbered up here." He stretched and grinned. "We ate lunch together."

"And talked about…?"

"Work, mostly. How the war was going. That felt awkward at first, but then it didn't because Tosh was just like one of us. Yeah, and we talked about movies. He liked movies. And he had a kid sister he bragged about, how smart she was."

Spooner had grown impatient and was approaching.

"Sorry to interrupt, but we'd better get moving if you want to talk to other people up here and go downstairs, too. Lots of things on my schedule today, I'm afraid."

His head-cocked laugh said he was sure I'd understand. We moved on.

I talked to women who performed tasks related to supplies, personnel and accounting. Spooner hovered not quite out of earshot while pretending not to listen. I wondered whether he was monitoring adherence to security safeguards or was simply being a good if slightly annoying manager. Actually, I favored the theory he was just nosey.

Most of those women said they'd never spoken to Tosh, though they knew him by sight. One volunteered that he was a good-looking rascal. Another said he'd helped her untangle why the numbers on a batch of orders weren't coming out right.

Finally, I got to the platinum blonde.

"Did you and your boyfriend make up okay?"

"I don't know what you're talking about."

"The one you argued with Saturday right after you got off work."

She tucked her head sideways to examine the ends of her hair.

"That creep's not my boyfriend. I met him at a party and he thought that gave him the right to make a pass at me. I told him to get lost. What's that have to do with the Jap and the fire?"

"Nothing. Just happened to see it."

"Then how about asking whatever you're here to ask. I've got work to do."

"Okay, what can you tell me about Tosh Hashimoto?"

She stared at me as though bored.

"He was stuck up."

***

"Stay back from the machines." Spooner put his mouth close to my ear in order to make himself heard above the clatter of Linotype machines and the noise of small presses.

I nodded. It wasn't my first time in a composing room. Hot lead poured. Bursts of steam spewed out as water cooled metal type. Compared with that, the moving parts of the presses seemed almost harmless.

In a near reverse of the work force upstairs, the sweating bodies here on ground level were almost entirely male. The two exceptions were both among the Linotype operators. A woman with iron-gray hair escaping the blue bandana covering her head managed the keys and levers of the machine that towered over her. Several slots away, an operator who was little more than a girl and wore glasses held together with tape seemed equally nimble.

The older woman and three men after her shook their heads and yelled above the noise that they didn't know Tosh, though one allowed he might have seen him walk through a time or two. As we started on, the eyes of the last man flicked to Spooner's retreating

129

figure, then met mine for an instant. Did he have something to tell me?

When we came to the young girl, Spooner shouted, as he had to the others, that I wanted to know whatever she could tell me about Tosh Hashimoto. She finished a line of type and wiped the back of her finger across her upper lip.

"He seemed real nice." Hills and hollers nestled her words. "Asked me about my glasses. About how I busted them." Her gaze fell and scurried away from mine. "Now if you'll excuse me, I need to get back to work."

Two of the men who worked with the presses were deaf, one from years of working among them most likely, the other ineligible for military service because of it. They read lips, or pretended to, but shook their heads at my slowly spoken questions. One pointed at three Nisei men pushing carts and carrying cartons in different parts of the room. The pressman moved his index and middle fingers in imitation of legs descending stairs and then walking.

"Mr. Hashimoto came down here and talked to them?"

He nodded.

Spooner was already leading the way toward the corner that appeared to be their base of operations. It was at the back of the room near the bay door.

Our route afforded a good view of the fire-damaged

back stairs. They were almost all the way to the rear, and the bottom three feet of them where charred and crumbling. The bottom step was gone completely, along with much of the handrail, which was the only thing enclosing the stairs on the side near the work area. Ropes with red rags affixed marked off the damaged area, and two sawhorses blocked the foot of the stairs. In case those warnings were too subtle, a hand-lettered sign warned DANGER! while another read KEEP OUT!

Because it was somewhat removed from the nearest machines, conversation in the corner where Spooner gathered the Nisei workers was marginally easier. I asked what they could tell me about Tosh and his interests.

"He isn't the one they saw at that fire," the smallest of the three burst out, almost before I was finished.

"Why do you say that?"

"Because he was a good guy." The one who spoke this time was built like a welterweight. He stood with legs apart and arms crossed, daring me to ask more questions.

"You're Zenzo," I guessed.

"That's right."

"You live the same place Tosh did?"

"So what?"

Spooner's smile was now as fixed as rigor mortis. He'd taken a step or two back, not in a pretense of bestowing privacy, but because these men made him nervous.

"So, you had more opportunity to know him than most," I said.

"He kept to himself."

"You rode to work and back with him. You must have talked now and then. About girls or where you were going that weekend or what you did when you weren't working."

"Or how we'd meet on some dark street corner to plan sabotage, which it's pretty clear everyone thinks the fire was about?" Zenzo punctuated his words with an angry wave. "Who'd be dumb enough to think burning down this place would damage the war effort?"

"We all know how to spell 'scapegoat,'" said the one who hadn't spoken.

"The cops just jumped on the first thing that made sense to them," said the scrawny one. "Someone set a fire. Some Japs work there. Gee, it must have been one of them. Not the bosses; they don't think like that," he added hastily, glancing at Spooner. "Sure, they'll go along with what the cops tell them. What else are they going to do?"

At last I was learning something, but not about Tosh. I was seeing resentments — anger, even — that simmered in part of the Nisei community. I wondered if Freeze knew. If I told him, I wondered whether he would, or could, do anything about it.

"I'm hoping I can find another explanation besides the easiest one. Which is why I need answers from people who knew Tosh. Even the tiniest little thing might help."

Zenzo's manner was still guarded, but he shifted his stance and his shoulders relaxed.

"Mostly we talked about things that had happened in the different relocation camps we were in before we came here. Funny things. Or things that happened where we live. Once we talked about movies; he liked movies. Other than that, we didn't have much in common. He was…he made me feel like I was a kid and he was a grownup sometimes. Always helping, always responsible. He was a pain in the butt, kind of. But he was a good guy."

The other two didn't add much. One said Tosh whistled. Spooner was giving me high signs that it was time to leave.

"Well, we both have things to do, don't we? I'll just see you to your car," he said brightly.

In his eagerness to escape the area where no one could hear his jokes and no one had commented on his bow tie, he failed to see the Linotype operator who had sought my eye do so again. This time the operator then looked pointedly through the open bay door.

He had something to tell me. And he wanted to do so outside.

I dipped my chin to indicate I understood. When we reached the front office, I still was scrambling for a way to arrange it. I also realized that since the fire had occurred at night, there was a whole additional shift of people I needed to talk to. The sight of Spooner's secretary hurrying toward us from the bottom of the front stairs tempted me to believe in saints again.

"Mr. Spooner, that call you were waiting on Friday just came through. I thought you'd want to take it."

"Ah, yes." He looked uncertainly at me. "I'm sorry. I have to take—"

"Of course." I waved a dismissive hand. "I'll just go around back and wait by those picnic tables. I forgot there's something else I need to arrange with you. I won't poke around at anything, Scouts' honor."

He was torn, but after only a second's hesitation he nodded. He dashed up the stairs. A well-behaved young woman would have continued out the front door. I'd seldom been accused of good behavior. Instead, I flashed a smile at one of the front office employees and continued through to the printing part of the operation again.

My pace, as I wove my way past Linotypes, composing tables and presses, was brisk enough to suggest I wasn't interested in anything or anyone in the room. Hopefully, it also gave sufficient time for the Linotype operator who'd caught my eye to notice that I was back and alone and headed outside.

***

The area just outside the bay door, where the watchman had scuffled with Daisy four nights earlier, was beaten bare by truck and foot traffic. I continued on to the picnic-table area before I turned. A minute later, the man who had something to tell me ambled out. Checking over his shoulder, he stepped behind the same tree I'd used to screen me Thursday night.

"I don't want Spooner knowing I've talked to you."

I nodded. "He's on the phone. Long distance, but I don't know for how long. Did you have something to tell me about Hashimoto?"

"What you were asking, about did anyone have an axe to grind with him? Someone might."

"And who would that be?"

A grin split his begrimed face. He did an exaggerated sideways dance step, cocked his head, and gave an expectant smile — aping Spooner to a T.

CHAPTER EIGHTEEN

"Spooner?" I wanted to make sure I was right in my interpretation.

He nodded, half turning so he could keep an eye peeled for anyone coming out of the building.

"That was the chatter from some of the women that work upstairs with him, anyways. At lunch break, if the weather's nice, there's a bunch squeezes in around these picnic tables. One day I heard some of them laughing how Spooner was always hanging around Mr. Kirby's secretary, Phyllis, talking to her and maybe flirting a little. Then when Hashimoto and the others started to work here, she began shooing Spooner away. She let Hashimoto talk to her, though. That made Spooner huffy. At least that was the story. The girls joked about it for a couple of days."

He shifted, preparing to bolt. Not because he feared Spooner, but because he had a good job and wanted to keep it, I suspected.

"Is there a bar where people from here go?" I asked before he could escape. "That way, if I need to ask him about this, I can say I heard something about it there."

"Inky's." He started to walk. "Owned by a man who used to work here." He looked back. "Not the Japanese fellows, though. I think they go someplace of their own."

"Hey," I called, making a quick decision to trust him. "That girl with the taped-up glasses — I think she knows something she's not saying. Tell her to give me a call if she wants to talk."

He nodded.

Not long after the Linotype man was safely back inside, Spooner came hurrying toward me. I could see where he might annoy a woman enough with his silly jokes that she would tell him to quit pestering, but I couldn't see him committing arson. One of the first things I'd learned as a gumshoe, though, was how deeply some people buried their true natures.

Zenzo didn't appear to fall into that category. Did Spooner?

"Well, you see what my schedule's like every day." His fists churned in a chipper suggestion of speed as he approached. "You said you needed something else?"

"Silly me." I sighed. "I forgot that I'll need to talk to the night shift."

"But they didn't work with the fellow. They wouldn't know him. I'm afraid I don't see the point."

"They're the ones who were there when the fire happened. They'd recall details."

"Oh. Of course."

It knocked him into at least four seconds of silence. His mustache drooped.

"I'm afraid it can't be tonight. A barbershop group I'm in is performing. Part of a larger program. It's been scheduled for months…"

"I can manage on my own."

"No, no. Against company policy."

I sighed again. And waited.

"I…uh…it is a much smaller crew working night shift. I suppose I could speak to the man who's night foreman down there and have him go around with you. He can pop up here too when you're ready to talk with the proofreaders."

"That would be fine. I'll try to be here early — five-thirty, maybe, so I don't interrupt when they're going full steam."

***

It was going to be a full day for me, what with talking to the night-shift workers and then hustling over to spend time with Maire. I caught up on work at the office and set aside checks to put in the bank when I went out for lunch.

At thought of my bank, temptation rose to sway in front of me like a hypnotist's watch. I resisted. Minutes passed. I succumbed. Picking up the phone, I called and made an appointment for later that afternoon to see someone about the possibility of a home loan.

On Saturday I hadn't had time for a newspaper, and on Sundays I read one of the ones delivered at Mrs. Z's. Today when I'd wanted one with my breakfast, Heebs hadn't been at his usual corner. Now, faintly uneasy as I recalled how preoccupied he'd seemed the last time I saw him, I detoured to get one. Half a block away, I realized another kid was standing there in his place.

As I drew closer, I realized I knew the kid. Heebs had taken him under his wing when the kid was eight or thereabouts, a skinny, shy little thing. He was probably twelve now, still skinny, still shy, but able to belt out a cheery sales pitch, thanks to Heebs' coaching.

"Heebs sick?" I asked as I gave him a nickel.

His name was Con, short for Connor, I guessed. He'd switched corners with Heebs a time or two when Heebs was helping me with something, so he recognized me. He sold a passerby a paper, then looked down and toed the sidewalk.

"Army took him, I guess. He was going down Saturday for his physical. Said if I didn't see him on Sunday, he'd be on his way to basic training."

He looked up, his young face miserable and a little scared at being the bearer of bad news.

"He said tell you he was real sorry not to say goodbye, but he was afraid you'd stop him....Paper, mister? Thanks....He said tell you he's going to be okay, and he'll write when he can."

I was biting my lip, trying to hold back the anguish erupting inside me.

"He's not old enough!"

The paperboy shrugged and paused to make change for a customer.

"He paid some woman to sign a paper saying he was."

He avoided my eyes. I turned mine heavenward, hiding the moisture in them.

"Thanks." I cleared my throat. "Thanks for telling me."

I crossed the street without seeing traffic and stopped at the first store window I came to, pretending to look at the items displayed there, so strangers walking past wouldn't see me bawl.

***

My eyes were only a little red by the time I arrived at Seth Rowe's house. His daughter, who let me in, was bustling about in a nurse's uniform as she prepared to leave for work. When I said I'd do my best not to upset her father, she chuckled.

"You won't upset him at all. Dad's always been one who loved to go over details. Growing up, it drove us kids crazy. Mom too. But I guess when something like a fire happens, it's useful."

What she said didn't jibe with the picture of

someone so shaken by an event that he'd quit working. My interest in talking to the recently retired watchman increased. I followed his daughter through the house and out the kitchen door to the back yard.

"Dad? The detective's here," she called to a lean man a few inches taller than me who sat in a slatted lawn chair with his legs stretched out and arms folded behind his head.

When we shook hands, I noticed arthritis knobs on his knuckles, but his eyes were clear and if he was jumpy, I saw no sign of it. I told him who I was, and that I'd been hired to have a closer look at what happened that night. I didn't say who had hired me.

"So, you're not police, and you say you're not anything to do with insurance," he mused. "Sure, I don't mind talking to you, then, long as it doesn't make more trouble for the business. It's bad enough for them with equipment damaged and work lost, and they've been real good to me."

I opened my mouth to reassure him, but he was still talking.

"Not that it didn't make me sore, getting put out to pasture like it was my fault the Hashimoto boy got away. Oh, they didn't come right out and say it, but I know that's what they were thinking: Somebody younger would have been faster; they could have caught him and tackled him. Well, let me tell you, I'd like to see them try, the head start he had, standing there where he was.

"I lunged off running. Of course I did. Anyone

would. But I hadn't gone half a dozen steps when I saw it was useless, and that maybe I ought to be trying to stop the fire instead."

His blast of information overwhelmed me so I wasn't sure what I wanted to ask first. He was saying something about a spigot now. I interrupted.

"Do you mean you didn't tell them after the fire that you wanted to retire and start drawing your pension?"

Rowe snorted.

"Why would I do that? Nothing wrong with me now that wasn't wrong before the fire. Sure, I was worn out for a couple of days, what with all that talking to police and answering questions. But no more than anyone else. Cleaning things up took twice as long and more work too because of keeping out of areas the fire and police had marked off. Things that didn't have fire damage had gotten soaked putting it out. Do you have any notion how heavy a carton of paper that's soaked up water is?

"No, it wasn't my idea retiring. Especially not then when the company needed us all pulling together. That jolly-jaws manager and Mr. Kirby called me in and said the fire had put me through more than a man my age should go through, and that I should start drawing my pension and taking it easy. If that wasn't telling me they thought I hadn't been up to the job that night, I don't know what would be."

Had he mistaken honest concern for him as a questioning of his abilities?

"I know how it is when someone's just too far away to catch them," I said. "It's happened to me more than a few times when I wanted to nab someone. Could you show me more or less where Mr. Hashimoto was standing when you spotted him? It would give me a better idea which direction he might have gone, and whether he drove or walked or somebody picked him up."

As I spoke, I'd unfolded a map I'd drawn of the back area. The reason I'd given for wanting him to point out where Tosh had been standing was hogwash. If he'd been too far away for the watchman to catch, I was wondering if that meant he'd been too far away for such positive identification.

Sitting forward in his chair, the old man pulled the map to his knees and pointed.

"About there, between the door and those picnic tables. I was coming back along this side here and heard a sort of WHOOF. And screams. I tore around the corner, already running. I must've been about there when I spotted him."

He was indicating a spot a short way from the corner of the building. It made too great a distance for anyone except a sprinter to overtake a man who was standing where he'd indicated Tosh was. More important, as far as I was concerned, was a different factor.

"How could you see anybody standing that far from

the building well enough to tell who they were? I had a look around back there Sunday night, hunting you because I didn't know they'd changed watchmen. The light from inside only comes out to about there."

I pointed.

"Huh." He nodded at the diagram spread before him. "You're right. I used to worry, walking my rounds, how I'd never be able to tell if somebody was behind that tree. How they could wait for me to start around to the front, and then slip inside before I got back. From the tables most of the way to the door, that's dark too.

"It must've been the fire, I guess. How it flared up right when it started that let me see. There was a lot of paper back there, and all of it went up. Anyway, I could see his face plain as day those first few seconds, before he spun around and ran. That — seeing his face — and the way he was standing was what made me think he'd been coming toward the building, not running out."

"What?"

He nodded, knowing perfectly well I'd heard what he said and pleased by my reaction.

"Nobody listened, though, just kind of shrugged it off like they thought I was soft in the head. But look here." He handed the diagram back, warming to the realization he had a receptive audience. "When you're running and you want to look at something behind you and, like when you played hide-and-seek, say, how do you do that? Get up and show me."

Maybe he *was* going a touch goofy, insistent as he had become over this. To humor him, I got up and trotted a few steps toward the house, then paused to look back over my shoulder.

His slow grin spread from ear to ear.

"See there? See how you're standing? Which direction your feet are pointing?" His hand sliced the air to aim at the house. "Them and the rest of you's headed that way. It's only your head that's turned."

I began to see what he was saying.

"But if I'm headed somewhere and hear a big noise, or see something…" I hunted for words… "an accident or disaster where I was going, I might run toward it to see what was happening, and stop when I saw."

"And maybe throw up your arm to shield your eyes like that Hashimoto boy did," said the watchman.

CHAPTER NINETEEN

I sat in my car for so long digesting what Seth Rowe told me that one of his neighbors came out on her porch to stand with her arms crossed watching me. Was it possible Tosh Hashimoto had been coming *toward* Kirby Printing the night of the fire? Perhaps to retrieve one of the notes his sister believed he'd left and received at the picnic tables? Was it possible he'd heard the ignition of the accelerant that started the fire, or seen the first flames and run toward it? Had he intended to grab a hose or otherwise try to help until it hit him that his lineage and presence there when he wasn't working would make him a suspect?

It made as much sense to me as the theory that he'd started the fire, given what I'd learned about him so far.

Unfolding a map, I kept in the car for window dressing, I raised it enough to be seen by the vigilant neighbor and made a nice show of refolding it. Then with feet that were starting to turn a little bit cold, I headed downtown to talk to my bank about buying a house.

***

"I've worked up information on my average monthly income for the past year and on my current monthly expenses, business and personal."

I wasn't sure what sort of information was expected in something like this, but the two typed sheets I slid across the desk to the man who had ushered me into his office seemed admirably complete to me. Since my checking and savings accounts were both here, checking my financial records would be as simple as pushing an intercom button and sending a clerk for my files.

"Very handy, yes," he murmured studying them.

He studied.

I tamped down the urge to fidget.

"I've reviewed your balance with us for the past eight years and can't help noting that your income is considerably higher the past two years than it was before that," he observed.

"I have some new ongoing contracts."

"War related?"

"Yes…"

"Meaning there's no guarantee they'll continue. But no matter. The size of the loan you're requesting is relatively small. Assuming your husband's income is predictable, your application should meet our requirements. Is his account here? We didn't find another Sullivan at your address."

"I'm not married."

"I...see," he said when the clock on his wall had ticktocked half a dozen times. He fitted the pen he'd been holding carefully back in its stand. "I assumed...In that case, I'm afraid we can't consider your request. It would be against bank policy."

Returning my carefully prepared sheets of expenses and income, he rose with the friendliest of smiles and opened the door.

"We do appreciate the fact you thought of us. If there's ever anything else we can do, let us know."

Like that, I found myself back on the street. I stood and blinked at a packed streetcar letting passengers on and off,

and tried to decide whether I was miffed at the turndown or the assumptions behind it.

Walking half a block through familiar afternoon crowds restored my sense of equilibrium. Being told I couldn't do something had always been the surest way to make me try to prove I could. I looked around and spotted a drugstore that had a phone booth.

With houses in short supply, I reasoned, banks might be starved enough for mortgage customers to see me on short notice. The voice I reached at the one I picked out of the phone book assured me they would. Half an hour? Why yes, a loan officer could see me then.

Five minutes into the meeting, as soon as we got

into brass tacks, the enthusiasm faded.

"I'm sorry." The woman, who had probably stepped into a male colleague's shoes when he was drafted, gave me a celluloid smile. "If you had a husband or other male relative with a reliable source of income, we would consider it. Arranging a mortgage for a single woman is simply outside the bank's lending guidelines."

I thanked her and left.

That should have been that. It already was half past four. But my chosen way back to the office took me past another bank. On impulse I went inside.

"Is there any chance I could talk to someone about a home loan without an appointment?" I asked a girl at an information desk tucked in the corner. "Just some preliminaries on how much I want to borrow, and what my finances are? I brought some paperwork."

She smiled, but I'd seen plenty of friendly smiles that afternoon. She said she'd check and spoke to somebody on the phone. A minute later a balding man in a very nice gray suit came out to pump my hand and introduce himself.

"I'm afraid it's too late in the day to discuss anything related to an application, but I brought our standard loan forms for you to fill out and return if you're interested. If you like, I can put you on my schedule for a time convenient to you tomorrow. If there's a chance you might want to actually submit an application then, your husband will need to come with you, of course. Or if he's in the service, we have a special form—"

"I'm not married."

"Oh, dear." He drew back some papers he'd been about to hand me. "I am sorry."

***

I didn't need a husband to do just fine as a gumshoe, so I got back to doing that. Freeze was usually in his office around this time of day unless he'd been called out on something. One more turndown wasn't likely to spoil my day, so I popped up to see him. To my surprise, Boike was there.

"Uh-oh. Looks like she's in a bad mood," Freeze said as they spotted me.

His mood, on the other hand, had improved considerably since the last time we talked. I wondered if that meant Boike had changed his mind and picked up his badge again. Freeze sat tipped back smoking placidly. Boike leaned against his former boss's desk with one foot crossed over the other. Their manner with each other felt more casual than it had in the past.

"It's a special expression I wear to confuse cops," I said. "Underneath I'm my usual sweetness and light. Hiya, Boike. Good to see you around."

"So, what do you want?" Freeze's question lacked its usual bite.

"Seth Rowe."

"The old gent who was night watchman?"

"Right. Did he tell you it looked to him like Tosh Hashimoto was initially coming toward the building, not running away?"

"He started rambling on some crazy theory like that. It didn't make sense."

"It made sense to me."

Freeze stood and began shrugging into his suit coat. Boike's interest had sharpened.

"See there, Boike? Bet she never even considers she might be wrong about something."

"Yeah, I have a couple of times. I always hated myself the next morning."

"You're grasping at straws, but I'll have another look at his statement. Boike and I were just heading out for a bite. Want to join us?"

I hesitated. Given the good lieutenant's current surplus of amiability, I might get another morsel or two of information if I tagged along, but I was due at Kirby Printing to talk to the night shift, and after that Maire was expecting me. Besides, I had a sense the two men might enjoy each other's company more as a duo.

CHAPTER TWENTY

I cheered myself with the idea Tuesday was bound to be better than the previous day with its news about Heebs leaving and the turn downs by banks. That optimism lasted until I opened my office door. File folders had been dumped on the floor, photographs pulled from the wall, and a message scratched into the side of my oak file cabinet in inch-wide letters as if with a chisel:

**JAP
LOVERS
DIE**

I drew a slow breath, fighting anger. Someone had broken into my office. It wasn't the first time; the lock was lousy. It was, however, the first to show such viciousness.

A few more slow breaths, and I began to make a circuit of the room, arms crossed in front of me. Even the dead plant, which some years back had become a permanent fixture, had been dumped from its attractive pot. The pot itself had been smashed deliberately.

Intruders hunting something might dump the dirt from a flower pot to see what it hid. The ceramic of the pot itself couldn't hide anything. Smashing it would reveal nothing. The shards littering the floor in front of me proved, more than anything, that the destruction surrounding me hadn't been a matter of someone hunting for something. It had been a warning. An attempt to scare me off trying to prove Tosh Hashimoto was innocent. They wanted him to be guilty. Or appear to be.

Because I couldn't decide what I wanted to do, and whether there was any point in calling the cops about the vandalism, I righted my desk chair and called two banks and made appointments to talk about home loans. Then I sat back and surveyed the damage again.

On occasions when someone had actually been hunting something in my office, with no concern about leaving traces, file cabinet drawers had been left partway open. The folders themselves had been jammed back, or dropped on the floor beside the drawers that had held them. This time the folders had been flung far and wide. Malice, not searching, had been the goal of this vandalism.

As in previous break-ins, the intruders hadn't gone to the effort of hefting the heavy old Remington typewriter under which I kept the most sensitive information from a case I was working on. Now I took the precaution of removing the sheet that was currently there. It held nothing more crucial than the

Hashimotos' phone number and the names of some of Tosh's friends, but as a precaution, I retrieved it. Folding it and slipping it into my purse, I sat off on an unannounced visit to Kirby Printing.

***

Spooner's secretary was trying to straighten out something with one of the file clerks and motioned me absently into his office. Spooner was on the phone. Both volume and tone suggested frustration.

"Yes, apartment 3A. The manager will let you in."

His tie today was a subdued maroon with yellow splotches that might have been commas. Or comets.

"That's right, 3A…I don't care what the problem was last time, I want it done today." He hung up and noticed me. "Well, well. I didn't expect to have the pleasure of your company again so soon. Not angling for a job here, are you?"

"You might be too hard a task master."

Pointing an approving finger at me, he gave his jolly laugh. This was the sort of banter he liked.

"How did things go with the night shift?"

"Fine, thanks. Nothing useful. If you wouldn't mind, I have another question or two. Maybe in private?"

I pointed to his open door.

"Oh, of course. Of course." Bouncing up, he closed the glass-paneled door to his glass-paneled office. He folded his hands on his desk and sat up with the exaggerated correctness of a comic in a vaudeville skit. "Fire away."

I sat down. I crossed my legs. I swung the top one back and forth. I smiled.

"I overheard talk at Inky's that you and your boss's secretary had been an item until Tosh Hashimoto came along."

His joviality slipped. The frown that appeared had a childish petulance.

"Phyllis and I were not 'an item.' It's true I enjoyed stopping in for a chat, and she liked it, too. Then once Hashimoto showed up..." Touching his index finger to the tip of his nose, he tilted it up. "All of a sudden she didn't have time. Treated me like - like I had leprosy. No loss. Showed her true colors." He gave a tight smile. "I trust that sets the record straight."

"It does, thanks." I got to my feet. "It sounds as though I'd better have a talk with...Phyllis, is it?"

"What? Uh, yes."

His attention had wandered to something behind me. Looking around, I saw the platinum blonde saunter past. Was she just nosey or did she have her eye on the boss? Ambitious girls had been known to marry their way up in the world.

"It looks like someone needs to ask you a question," I said.

"What? Oh. Yes, no doubt." His mustache twitched

with annoyance. He stood. "Yes, talk to Phyllis, by all means. I expect it will embarrass her no end, now that Hashimoto's looking, well, very different from what he appeared. But all of us need to do what we can to get to the bottom of this, don't we?"

He opened the door. He didn't treat me to the sweeping gesture he'd made yesterday, but his peppy manner was returning.

"By the way, did you manage a talk with Seth Rowe?"

"I did."

"Did you get anything out of him that was remotely sensible?"

I leaned in confidentially.

"Now, Mr. Spooner. How could I advertise services as a private investigator if I didn't keep some things private?"

"Oh, Mr. Spooner, the performance last night was absolutely wonderful!" Velma, the gray-haired proofreader, paused when she saw him. Judging by her direction, she had been on her way to the ladies' room. "I laughed till my ribs ached at that last number."

"Thank you, Velma. Roger said he thought it was the best performance our group's ever given."

"Is Roger all right? I didn't see him at refreshments."

"Oh, perfectly fine. He felt a little stuffy, so he stood over by the window. He said he waved at you."

"Did he? Such a sweet boy. I must have missed it."

"My son," he explained as she went on her way. Her glowing review had made him forget he was vexed with me. "He hasn't missed a single performance of our barbershop group since we started. Most people don't understand that his hearing's perfectly fine. He can't make words like you and me, so people assume he's a deaf as well. Velma, bless her heart, gets it."

"That must be hard," I said awkwardly. "You liking to sing and him unable to."

"Oh, it all works out. That's what I've always told him. Do what you're good at and don't worry about the other."

He was padding along in the general direction of the accounting section. I went with him, mainly to antagonize the blonde, who was back at her desk pretending to work and glaring.

Spooner had warmed to the opportunity to brag about his son.

"In school, he couldn't recite like his classmates, but he excelled at the things he could do — written assignments, numbers, sports. Roger went to a regular school, you see. I insisted he try a very fine school for the deaf for a year, but he got too homesick. He said he'd rather put up with the names and not being included and stay right here at home. He's very bright, but no one sees it except dear old Dad." His chuckle, for a change, was sad.

"He wanted like mad to work in one of the

vacancies we had downstairs before we brought in the Japanese. But it all worked out. He got a better job, a raise. He's making more than he'd have made here."

***

Phyllis Chapman, secretary to the firm's founder, had a reserved air about her that made it hard to imagine anyone making so bold as to flirt. She probably tiptoed toward forty, which made her almost twice Tosh's age, but as I'd noticed on my first visit there, her looks were still sensational. In a beauty contest between her and the blonde who liked to strut her stuff, I'd give the older woman the blue ribbon every time.

"How long have you worked here?" I asked after telling her I was asking some follow-up questions.

"Thirteen years now."

"That's a long time."

"It's a good place to work. They treat their employees well. And I count my lucky stars daily to have such a reasonable boss. He's rarely asked me to work past quitting time — except when we were gearing up for the war effort and everybody was putting shoulders to the wheel. I don't believe I've ever seen him lose his temper, no matter what happened."

A shadow of concern passed over her as she said the last. Her eyes flitted toward Kirby's door.

"I hate to ask personal questions, but in an investigation like this, I have to," I said. "I'm told Mr. Spooner used to spend a fair amount of time chatting to you, but that after Tosh Hashimoto started working here, you shifted your interest to him and shooed Mr. Spooner away."

Every vertebra in her spine stiffened.

"If you're implying I encouraged Mr. Spooner's visits, or that there was anything untoward about Tosh's, you've been misinformed. Yes, Tosh came in to talk occasionally, but mainly because he was sort of the contact person for the other Japanese-American workers. If any of them had a question or problem, he brought it to me. It simplified things, since I see Mr. Kirby every day, and my handling it meant one less thing demanding his personal attention.

"I'll admit I found Tosh a more agreeable conversationalist, though. Mr. Spooner's clownishness can grow a bit thin. As to shooing him away, as you put it, once the Nisei started here there was more paperwork, the same as if we'd hired twenty of them. Reports to the Office of War Relocation and such. There simply wasn't time to indulge Mr. Spooner."

She folded her arms, not in defiance but in certainty of her own ground.

"I can tell you who I think Tosh was interested in, however. Laura Gray."

The woman referred to was one of the proofreaders,

the ivory-skinned brunette. She and her fellow proofreaders were nowhere to be seen when I returned to the open area.

"*They* get a break to rest their eyes," a girl in the clerical section told me enviously. "They're probably outside."

Since their extra break lasted only ten minutes, the quartet of proofreaders merely walked down the lane behind the building, turned at the street, and walked back, exercising legs along with weary eyes. I met them as they were starting back.

"Laura, could I have a word?" I fell into step with her. "I won't delay you."

"Yes, of course." Wariness tinged her tone.

Her coworkers sent her looks and moved ahead. The two of us followed more slowly.

"I keep hearing from people that you and Tosh were friends."

"Yes. So, what if we were?"

"Dating?"

"That's none of your business. We went to the pictures once. Met for coffee a couple of times. Again, what of it?"

We were almost at the bay doors opening into the back of the printing plant. A round-about approach wasn't likely to rouse any more goodwill in her than bluntness, so I spoke quickly.

"Did you ever leave notes for each other at one of the picnic tables?"

She stopped in her tracks. She gave me a scalding look. Then she began to walk rapidly toward the building.

"Just what do you take me for? Some moony high school kid?"

CHAPTER TWENTY-ONE

I'd barely gotten back to my office and was taking my hat off when the telephone began to ring.

"You're back. Stay there," said Freeze's voice. "I'll be there in fifteen minutes. We need to talk."

His assumption that I had nothing on my schedule that couldn't wait was enough to make me close my eyes and count to ten. Then again, Freeze usually had a reason for doing things, even if I thought it was cockeyed. Patronizing as he could be, I'd never known him to do anything just to flaunt his authority. With curiosity mounting, I hung my hat on the coat stand and waited.

He came in with the most perfunctory of knocks. The sight of young Dotson trailing him put me on guard that this wasn't a social call.

"What in—?"

He broke off, taking in the disarray of my surroundings. The only inroads I'd made toward restoring order had been turning my wastebasket right-side up and reuniting two file folders with their proper contents. The detective's attention had come to rest on the words on the file cabinet.

"This just happen?"

"No, last night."

"You report it?"

"No, and that's not why you're here." I waved them toward chairs.

Dotson righted one by the wall, but Freeze paced, stooping to pick up the larger piece of a dime-store ashtray I kept for guests and rubbing out the stub of his cigarette.

"You're right. What else did that old watchman tell you yesterday besides that business about Hashimoto maybe coming toward the building? I need to know. No games."

"Seth Rowe?" His terse tone startled me. I blew a stream of breath out as I thought. "He went through what happened that night a couple of times, but nothing that stands out. Nothing he didn't tell you or your men. That, and he groused about being handed his pension and put out to pasture when he wanted to stay. Hurt pride, I think."

Freeze halted.

"He wasn't the one who wanted to leave? So he didn't have to keep remembering it all when he walked his rounds?"

"Not according to him. But it could be he just misinterpreted what was intended as kindness. He thought the bosses blamed him for not being alert enough to keep the fire from happening, or due to his age, not being fast enough to catch whoever started it. Why this sudden interest?"

"Because he's dead. Somebody bashed the back of his head in."

It took me a minute to take in all the various implications.

"When?"

"Last night."

Freeze picked up the chair in front of my desk and sat down.

"It's just a formality, but I gotta ask: Where were you last night?"

"Doing my best to cheer up a young widow who buried her husband last week. If you want, you can see the bruise her youngest gave me for my efforts."

I kicked up my leg long enough to show the nasty purple patch the size of an apple, but lowered it before he could get the idea the act was flirtatious. Maire and Willie's fairy-like daughter had a kick that would shame a mule. She'd walked up and let go without warning or provocation. Looking at Dotson, who was taking the notes, I spelled Maire's name and gave her address and phone number.

"When did you leave?"

"Nine-thirty or a little after. Maire was arguing bedtime with one of the boys. Her mother called, so I answered, which caused her to give Maire an earful. Ever since grade school the mother's viewed me as a bad influence."

"Imagine," said Freeze.

"Do I get to know when Rowe was killed?"

"Nine-fifteen, nine-thirty. According to the daughter and son-in-law he lived with, he liked to go out into the yard and stroll around for half an hour or so before turning in. Said it helped him sleep."

Because he'd worked nights for so long, I thought.

"It's connected," Freeze said. "Him, the fire, this." He hooked a thumb at the filing cabinet.

"Yeah. Care to guess how?"

"Since you're busting to tell me, I'll save my breath."

"Someone's out to frame Hashimoto. Rowe got in the way. So have I."

He grunted.

"You got another candidate?"

"There's a rumor Spooner was jealous of Hashimoto. Story is, a woman Spooner had been making goo-goo eyes with lost interest once Hashimoto came on the scene. But I haven't found out who she was."

"Pretty flimsy reason for setting a fire to the place where you work. I have to go to the printing plant anyway, though, because of Rowe. Maybe I'll ask a question or two on the other."

Given a large enough crowbar, prying the man's mind open now and again might be possible. He got up, and went for a closer look at the words on my file cabinet.

"You want me to have somebody from burglary or fingerprinting come out?"

I shook my head.

"Fingerprints would be a waste of time, so many people come in here. The building's cleaning crew, my clients, friends who stop by." My voice faded on the last. Jenkins wasn't around to stop in anymore. Neither was Heebs.

"Dotson," Freeze snapped.

Scrambling up, the young detective closed his notebook and answered the summons.

"What does the way these letters were made tell you?"

"Uh…They're gouged pretty deep. Lots deeper than needed to scratch through the finish. Whoever made them was mad."

Still studying them, Freeze lighted a cigarette and nodded approval.

"I know you've got your handy-dandy little .38 to keep you company," he said to me, "but Rowe's killer came up behind him and cracked his skull with a single blow."

***

I stood at the window and watched the detectives leave and thought about observant old Seth Rowe who at this time yesterday had still been alive. Had some detail he'd noticed, something he hadn't told me, gotten him killed? Or was it only his assertion that Tosh had been coming toward the building before something caused him to turn and run? Testimony like that wouldn't be welcome if someone wanted to pin the fire on Tosh.

Across the way from where I stood, a train rumbled past. Soldiers in uniforms outnumbered men reading papers and women in bright dresses these days, another reminder of a country at war.

Husbands and sons and sweethearts of people in Dayton and places around it were dying in that war on battlefields far away. Gold stars in the front windows of houses bore silent testimony of family losses. Newspaper columns listed their names.

Yet people were killed every day right here at home as well. They were killed brutally with knives or fists or guns or by hit-and-run. They hadn't signed up to risk their lives. They weren't on a battlefield. Yet still they died violently. Some were innocent old men like Seth Rowe, caught in something of which he'd most likely had no awareness.

I didn't like to think my visit might have contributed to his death. That was one of the unfortunate parts of my work, guilt at being a billiard ball that knocked into other people's lives, setting off chain reactions and shifting the courses of events.

While my brain sorted through everything Seth Rowe had said to me the day before to see if I'd overlooked some scrap that seemed inconsequential, the rest of me got down on my hands and knees to retrieve papers and folders. Two hours later, when I had my next visitor, I was still at it. I called to the unknown person knocking to come in.

"Maggie?"

It was Connelly, perplexed that he didn't see me.

I stuck my head up from behind my desk and got to my feet.

"Just retrieving some papers."

Most traces of the disorder that had greeted me that morning were gone now, although half the contents of the file cabinet were stacked, unsorted, in chairs.

In uniform now, Connelly shifted his hat from one hand to the other.

"I just stopped in to apologize about Friday. For me, and for Kathleen."

I dropped the final sheaf of papers I'd collected onto my desk.

"Nothing to apologize for."

"Yeah, there is. To you. To Finn and Rose. I…we'd had a misunderstanding. Kathleen and I. She's…we're going to have a baby, and she's not quite herself."

"Congratulations."

He nodded. All at once he stiffened, his steel-blue eyes as incisive as knife blades. He'd noticed the file cabinet.

"What the—?"

"It's nothing. Apparently someone takes exception

to a case I'm working on." I moved protectively toward my scarred furniture.

"Don't make light of it, Maggie. These things escalate."

He'd come of age amid what approached civil war in Ireland. The realization he probably knew what he was talking about left my mouth dry.

He came closer, stooping to examine the scratched-in words more closely.

"Whoever did this was a strong bugger, and I'd say left-handed. See how it's dug deeper in this side than the other? With someone right-handed, the pressure's the other way."

I leaned in to look and could maybe see what he was talking about. When I straightened, we stood so near that our elbows were touching. We both stopped breathing, and after several seconds stepped apart as one.

"Take care of yourself." His smile almost reached his eyes.

I crossed my arms, creating a barricade. "You too, Mick."

I didn't turn to watch him go. The door closed softly behind me. For a good many minutes I stood with my eyes fixed on the words scratched into the wood in front of me while memories of other things Connelly and I had said to each other flooded in. Finally rousing myself, I tried to recall if anyone I'd talked to about the fire or Tosh Hashimoto was left-handed.

CHAPTER TWENTY-TWO

Two more banks turned me down for a loan before what could count as mid-afternoon. At the second one, the woman with graying hair who reviewed my paperwork went so far as to check with someone above her to see if an exception to bank policy could be made. When she came back she seemed genuinely regretful.

"If you have a male relative who might be willing to sign as a guarantor in case you proved unable to pay…"

"I don't have any relatives. Thanks anyway."

I stood up and we shook hands and that was that.

Funny how getting turned down makes you want something that much more, even when you know it might not be in your best interest. Banks weren't stupid. They probably knew the struggle I'd have making house payments better than I did. But I knew how to struggle. Since setting eyes on the pretty little house again, I'd grown increasingly attached to the thought of coming home to a place of my own.

By the time I'd walked several blocks, an idea had

formed. I called the lawyer who'd started this all by dangling the apple in front of me, and asked if I could borrow the key so I could have a look inside. He said I could. Next, I did something I rarely did, call Seamus at work.

"Any chance I can meet you at Finn's when you get off?" I asked.

"Well, sure. I was thinking of going there anyways."

"I might not let you linger long over your glass. We might go for a ride."

"All right."

I heard his puzzlement, but Seamus wasn't one to stick his nose in things he perceived weren't his business. It was one of the many things I loved about him.

With house key in hand, and the lawyer's reminder that I had to make a decision by the following day buzzing in my ear, I went to check one detail about the house on which that decision might hinge. A heavy smell of dust met my nostrils as I opened the door. Electric service had been turned off when Lettie Gannon left, but the now un-curtained windows let in sufficient light to see.

It felt odd walking through a deserted place without listening for sounds that might warn of an ambush, or looking around me for signs of a panicked departure or violence. All I saw now was empty space waiting to be filled. The only furnishings left were a large and nearly threadbare oriental rug in the center of the front room and the small gas cookstove in the kitchen. The bedroom didn't hold so much as a bedframe. But it was the narrow staircase leading up to the attic that interested me.

As I neared the top, light filtered down from dormer windows at each end. I stepped into a finished room that ran from the front of the house to the back. The center was tall enough to stand upright, but the eaves slanted sharply down. There was room enough under them for a chest of drawers, though, and a chair and a lamp. An iron bedstead for a single bed had been left behind. Its once-brown enamel was worn off in places. Where my shoes disturbed a thick coat of dust, the planks of the floor still gleamed with polish.

It was a bedroom. A lovely bedroom. It confirmed a vague recollection that had flitted into my mind of Lettie Gannon telling me sadly that she still kept her son's bedroom nice in case he showed up one day.

It also made me think of Daisy Hashimoto creeping up to find privacy in the attic where she lived, in a house shared by a dozen people. Scolding myself over too much daydreaming, I locked the house and headed back to see what inroads I could make in finding out what had happened to Tosh. It was one thing — maybe the only thing — which could make the current life of his family a bit more bearable.

***

Seamus finished his last half-inch of stout and turned from the bar when he saw me enter. I hooked my arm through his and caught Rose's eye to let her know I wasn't staying.

"We're going for that ride," I said when we were outside. "I want your opinion on something."

"My opinion. Well, now."

This time Seamus didn't try to hide his curiosity. When I made no move to ease it, he chuckled. A soft breeze warm with the sunshine of early April ruffled the waves at the crest of his silver-white hair. Even at sixty-six, with the start of a stoop, he was a tall man. His limp from an old knee wound was more pronounced now, I realized as we walked. He should be enjoying life, not putting in eight-hour shifts with a day off every three weeks.

At first we talked about this and that, how he'd spent most of Saturday replacing a porch rail for Kate, the widow of his oldest friend, who had died a year ago. Riding in a car these days was a treat to Seamus, who kept his eyes on the passing scene as he spoke again.

"That fire at the printing place, the one you asked me about, I heard today that the fire investigator has finally decided to call it arson." He hesitated. "Also heard you're asking questions about it for people

173

connected to the fellow the police think set it."

What Seamus thought of my actions mattered to me.

"You heard right. His family." I concentrated on driving more than was necessary. "So, how do you feel about that?"

He pursed his mouth and worked his gaunt cheeks in and out.

"You think the boy might not have done it, then?"

"I do, and the more I find out, the more I think that."

"Well, then. When it comes to helping other people, your judgment's generally good."

The way he phrased it made me wonder if he was hinting decisions I made in my own life might fall short of that mark. It wasn't a pleasant thought since I was just turning into the street with the little white house.

"Was that what you were wanting my opinion on?" he asked. "Trying to help the Japanese boy?"

"Nope," I said as I pulled to the curb. "I want to know what you think about this place."

We got out and went up the walk. When I took out a key instead of ringing the doorbell, Seamus gave me a sharp look.

"You thinking of selling real estate, are you?"

"Not exactly." I unlocked the door. "I know the woman who owns this. She's moved to California and wanted me to take a look at it."

Pausing in the center of the worn Persian rug that

remained in the front room, I turned to face the gentle old man who had been a part of my life since my earliest memories.

"The truth is, Seamus, she owed me money for work I'd done. Quite a bit of money that I'd never expected to collect. Monday her lawyer called me out of the blue to say she's living with the son I located for her, so she's settling things here, and in lieu of paying me, she's offering to sell me this place for nine hundred dollars. The lawyer's hoping I'll say no. The house would bring a good deal more than fourteen hundred, which is what she owed me plus the extra I'd have to pay.

"At first I thought it was crazy, but then I got to thinking. I wouldn't be paying rent, there's an extra bedroom I could rent out — to you if you were interested — and I'd have a place of my own. The thing is, I'd need to borrow six hundred dollars. I've talked to five banks now, and none of them's willing to lend it unless I have a cosigner, someone who'll agree to pay if I don't. I was wondering — don't say anything until you've seen the whole place and think it over — I was wondering if you'd consider that. The signing."

Seamus pulled at his ear.

"Well, now. Isn't that something." His expression was grave. Seamus was cautious to the extreme when it came to money. He pursed his mouth again. "I expect I ought to have a look. That's a big step, what you're talking about."

There wasn't much to show, but to my surprise Seamus made a slow, almost painstaking, tour of the front room, pushing at walls, squinting up at the ceiling, frowning at times and nodding at others. We went on to the small downstairs bedroom.

"I was thinking if this worked out and you did want to move, you could have this downstairs room so you wouldn't have to climb stairs like you do now."

He made a noncommittal sound.

He only poked once at the bedroom walls, and not at all in the kitchen, though he frowned at some holes in the linoleum where the refrigerator had set. "Nice big tub," he said of the bathroom. When I pointed out the stairs to the attic and told him it was finished and would make a nice room for me, he said he wouldn't mind taking a look anyway. He was able to stand upright in the center of the upstairs room, though the ceiling looked to be no more than half a dozen inches from his head.

"That shed in back's just about ready to fall down," he said stooping to peer out the window.

"I don't need a shed."

"You would, for a hoe and rake and that."

Heaviness started to fill my stomach as I came face to face with aspects of home ownership I hadn't considered. Neither of us spoke as we went back downstairs. We stepped out the back door. The porch was wider than the one in front, and had one more step, but otherwise it was the same unadorned wooden shelf.

"Well, will you look at that." Seamus was looking down with the same delight a kid shows when given an unexpected ice cream cone. "Sparrow grass, and a nice patch. Hasn't been tended for a few years though."

Here and there a tip of what most people called asparagus was nosing through the soil. I hadn't known Seamus was fond of it. He made the same careful circuit he'd made of the rooms inside. In some spots he nodded. In others he crossed his arms as though in thought. When the survey had brought us back to the porch, he faced me and crossed them again.

"Well, now. When you began explaining all this, and the banks and such, you asked me not to say anything till you'd laid it all out, and I gave it some thought. That's what I want from you now — to just listen.

"Living in a proper house with a yard to putter in would suit me fine. Having you around on top of it, well, that would be angel cake. The part about taking a loan out, though, I don't like that. I've got a better idea. I've got enough saved to pay the part you'd have to borrow. I'll give you that, you put it with yours and buy the house outright, and I get my room rent free."

"Seamus, I can't—"

"I'm not done yet. You'd get the money anyways, in my will. You might as well have it now and enjoy it. I'll still have my pay coming in, or my pension once the war ends, and I can retire. I'll be okay for money. What do you say?"

Too choked by emotion to answer, I wrapped my arms around him while my eyes leaked gratitude.

CHAPTER TWENTY-THREE

Girl. Glasses. Getaway.

I wrote the three words across the top sheet of the tablet before me and twiddled my pencil between my fingers.

Girl. Glasses. Getaway.

Somewhere in those three clumps of unanswered questions lay the truth about what had happened the night of the fire. Who was the girl Tosh had been seeing — if he was? Why had a pair of glasses he owned but didn't wear shown up? Where were they found, and by whom? And maybe most puzzling of all, how had he managed to vanish so completely?

I stole a look at the clock. A quarter of ten. Maybe Seamus wouldn't be able to get an hour off work. Maybe he'd overestimated what he had in savings. Maybe he would have second thoughts.

On my way to the office, I'd ducked into a second-hand store and purchased a cracked but intact replacement pot for my dead plant. I'd grown accustomed to the brown plant's company. Besides, I thought the delay might help time pass more quickly this morning. It hadn't.

I yanked my attention back to the sheet of paper that sat daring me to fill the space beneath the three topics with clever ideas.

Did the girl Daisy thought her brother had been seeing, and trading notes with, even exist? Phyllis Chapman indignantly denied involvement with Tosh apart from work. Laura Gray, although acknowledging she'd gone out with him a time or two, appeared to attach no great importance to the fact, and had been scathing in her views on exchanging notes.

Either of them could be lying.

Longworth, the typesetter who had told me that Spooner bore hard feelings toward Tosh over a woman, had also mentioned that the Nisei workers frequented a particular bar. The fellow with the injured hand at the house where Tosh and Zenzo and some of the others lived might know its name. He had indicated a group of them often went out for a "good time." Those were the sort of gatherings where, with beer flowing and camaraderie in full flower, men proved themselves worse gossips than women. They were the sort of gatherings where the name of the woman Tosh was supposedly seeing might have been dropped.

I might be able to catch the fellow with the cut-up hand at home again today or tomorrow. If he wasn't there, or proved unwilling to part with the information… Stuck for further ideas, I turned to the other two items on my list and made no better progress.

Working on something physical sometimes nudged my brain in productive directions. I got up and went to my file cabinet and stood staring at the words gouged into it. A good woodworker could possibly sand down the oak and apply a fresh coat of finish or two and hide all trace of the vandalism. I wasn't any kind of woodworker, nor did I know any, so I'd come up with another idea.

From behind the very piece of furniture I'd been studying, I pulled a framed painting. It had been a gift, the sort that makes you wonder why the giver had ever supposed it would suit your taste. Whoever had vandalized my office had been too intent on destruction to notice the painting in the two-inch deep space between cabinet and wall.

I'd remembered it yesterday, and hauled it out to check. It covered the words on the file cabinet with room to spare. Now, using a borrowed hammer, I drove a short nail into the side of the file cabinet. Given the hardness of the oak, I marveled that someone had managed to carve those three words into it so deeply. As Connelly had noted, that person had been strong.

When I was finished, the picture hung securely on the side of the cabinet first seen by visitors. They might wonder at my eccentric decorating, but I wouldn't get comments and unwanted advice because of the now-hidden warning.

I was putting the hammer away when someone tapped at my door and Boike came in.

"Hey, Boike. What brings you around so bright and early?"

"Had to turn my tube in so I could get toothpaste. I thought I'd stop up to see if you'd given that plant of yours a drink since the last time I saw it. Doesn't look like you have."

We both eyed the withered specimen in its replacement pot near the windows.

"I get the urge now and then, but it always strikes me that it would be a waste of good gin."

"Most people use water, I think."

"Water? Huh. Imagine that. Did they have toothpaste?"

Reaching inside his jacket he displayed a much-used paper sack wrapped around a shape the right size.

"They ran out three or four people after me."

I grimaced. My own tube of toothpaste was just about empty.

"Take a load off. Did Freeze talk you into coming back to work?"

"Nope." Boike settled himself in the chair by my desk and put his hat on his knees. "We had a good talk over supper, though. He's changed some. Not exactly easygoing, but carries on an actual conversation. It was kind of enjoyable, actually."

"Good. But since he's not making use of your brain, I'd sure like to, if you have time."

"I've got plenty of time. Shoot."

"One of the things that's bothering me about the business at the printing plant is what became of Tosh Hashimoto."

"Plenty of other people want to know that, too."

"Yeah, but the cops and whatever government office has gotten involved are looking at it in terms of him getting away. Unless I miss my guess, they had men watching trains and buses and even private landing strips from here to Timbuktu within the hour. They're probably still watching, all under the assumption he'd leave town. I want to look backwards, or sideways, or...I'm not sure exactly which way."

Boike was frowning. It pulled the scar tissue on the injured side of his face even tighter, which made its shine more pronounced.

"You think maybe he stayed in town?"

I lifted my shoulders and let them fall.

"I'm just wondering. How does someone like him disappear? You or I could dye our hair, dress differently, use a cane, maybe attach ourselves to somebody, so we appeared to be with a spouse or a parent."

"But he's a, uh...he looks different."

"Right."

"Can't do much to disguise that."

"Right."

"And a Japanese-American man, especially one traveling alone, and at night, is going to stand out."

"And most likely attract suspicion. On top of which, Tosh is taller than most other Nisei men, and has some kind of cowlick."

Boike's eyes narrowed in thought.

"But if he didn't leave, and his family or friends aren't hiding him…"

"…how did he disappear so thoroughly? Exactly."

"Foul play?"

"If a body had washed up somewhere or been dumped, does it seem likely to you that Freeze would keep that information under wraps?"

"No. But I guess it's possible he wouldn't know."

"You mean if Army intelligence or whatever we call them got notified and kept a lid on it?"

"Yeah. Something like that."

"Jeez, Boike. It's hard enough figuring things out within boundaries I know. I don't need a third party brought in. Let's set that one aside for the moment, which leaves two possibilities. One, Tosh is dead and we have to look for a whole new set of motivations. Two, he's alive and still in town, but where is he?"

"If somebody's setting him up, he could panic and run. In that case, I don't see how the person behind the setup benefits by Tosh being dead."

"That's what stumps me, too. And they'd have to catch him…find him…"

"When something starts to get that convoluted, I tend to think it's less likely, too. Better to set it aside until you've run out of simpler explanations."

"Okay, then. Let's say, guilty or setup victim, Tosh runs — or starts to. But he's smart. He recognizes his chances of slipping out of town are almost nil—"

"Because of how he'd stick out."

"Right. But he doesn't want to get his family or friends mixed up in his trouble. So where does he hide?"

Boike considered in silence.

"There aren't many vacant buildings these days, but I guess there are some. And backyard sheds or barns."

"He'd have to find food, which gets back to the visibility problem. A Japanese-American man, alone, creeping around in the night?"

"What about the church people?"

"What?"

"The outfit that brought him and the others up here."

"Ah." I considered. "I don't think so. It might be worth another talk with the man from the Church Federation, though." I made a note.

"When you said he wouldn't want to involve his friends, you meant the other Japanese-American workers, correct?"

I nodded. "A dozen or more of the unattached young men live in one house, four to a room, with residents constantly seeking out crannies where they can find twenty minutes of privacy. That's where Tosh was. There may be other, similar places, but I expect the problem of finding a hiding place would be the same. I'll check that, too."

"I was thinking of friends who weren't like him," said Boike. "Someone he'd met at work, maybe."

I recalled the young man he'd had lunch with, the one who was also a proofreader. Their acquaintance, though it seemed cordial, didn't strike me as close enough. There was also the fact the Nisei had gravitated to a bar of their own.

I sat up slowly.

"What about a girlfriend? His sister and a couple of others seem to think he had one, though no one knows who. Would a man in the sort of jam he was in ask a woman to hide him?"

Boike shrugged his broad shoulders.

"Would she do it? You're the woman. You tell me."

Before I could answer, the phone rang.

"Hang on."

"The money's all transferred to your account," said Seamus. "I guess you better call that lawyer and make an appointment."

"I guess I'd better."

Boike lifted his hand in a see-you-later gesture. I barely had presence of mind to acknowledge it.

"Are they going to let you have time off so you can

meet me there?" I asked Seamus.

"I dropped a word here and there that if I couldn't get a few hours off when I needed them, I'd put in retirement papers."

When I hung up a few moments later, I sat feeling mildly stunned. I wasn't sure which I found most difficult to absorb: that I'd soon be a homeowner, or that Seamus had put his foot down.

CHAPTER TWENTY-FOUR

I checked with the bank to make sure the amount I needed was in my account. It was, plus a small amount in my checking and savings besides. I called the lawyer and made an appointment for four o'clock.

"I'll want the legal documents to include a clause about who gets the house if I die. Right of Survivorship or whatever you call it," I said.

Once I'd been to the bank and gotten the check I needed, I put my nose to the grindstone. First on the list was an unscheduled visit to Willard King at the Church Federation. To my relief he was in, his shirt sleeves rolled up as he went through paperwork. He frowned when I told him the elderly watchman whose account of the fire varied slightly from other versions had been murdered.

"That seems to suggest Tosh might not be the one who started the fire."

"Yes, I think so, too."

When I asked who among the Church Federation members might hide the young Nisei, however, he began to shake his head before I'd even finished.

"No one. Everyone involved in the relocation project is too committed to its success. Hiding one bad apple — or even a good one — would jeopardize our integrity, as well as that of the very people we're trying to help. It might even risk the relative freedom that this program gives them."

"But surely there are one or two among your members whose zeal might lead them to act unwisely if they believed they were helping a man unjustly accused."

"Again, no. The participants, the ones housing Japanese-Americans and otherwise assisting are all mature individuals. Settled. They were carefully screened."

We went back and forth a couple of times, but his certainty didn't moderate. In the end, he wrote the particulars on two other places where small groups of single men lived. Of the volunteers housing family groups like the Hashimotos, only half a dozen had sons or daughters anywhere near the age of Tosh. Those adult children might be rash enough to take risks their parents wouldn't, I thought. Of those households, however, the pertinent sons in three were away in the service, the daughter of a fourth was attending college in Indiana, and daughters of girlfriend age in the remaining two were already engaged and planning their weddings.

Confronted with an undeniable dead end, I returned

to the office where I thought about what to do next, added notes to my file on the Hashimoto case, opened mail and prepared the latest batch of invoices for clients. I was licking the flap on the last envelope, and starting to eye the clock, when Daisy came in.

"You haven't been in the last two days." It wasn't a neutral observation.

"A charming young woman, but her initial greetings need a pinch of work," I said.

Her look would have withered my plant if it hadn't gotten there years ahead of her.

"I assume your complaint is that you've come by and I've been out?"

"A professional person keeps regular hours," she said primly. Dumping her book bag, she came to perch on the chair at my desk.

"A professional person makes appointments, and expects the same from their clients. Do you waltz into your dentist's office whenever the mood strikes you?"

She ignored me.

"I *assume* your absences indicate you've been out doing something to find my brother."

The kid was parroting my word and adding a bit of sarcasm to make sure I noticed. I fought to keep my amusement from showing.

"That's right. I have to see the fire investigator and people who know your brother whenever they can fit me into their schedule. I expect you're here for an update. There isn't much concrete yet, but everything

I've learned so far leads me to think your brother's alive and still in town."

"Why? I mean, why would he stick around? Do you think he's hurt?"

I glanced at the clock.

"No. As to why he'd stay, it's complicated, and I don't have much time. I have an appointment at four."

"Yeah, okay, I get it. I'll call next time. Tell me what you can."

"I'd rather ask you a couple of things that could speed things along." I heard her draw a breath of resignation. And maturity.

"Go ahead."

"You and your brother were close, right?"

"I guess. Closer than Haruto and me."

"I need to know about friends he'd made since you came here." I'd asked her before about friends, but she might trust me more now. "Anyone from the Church Federation? Did he talk about anyone at work? Anyone he might have gone to the movies with, say."

She got up and moved restlessly around the room.

"A woman, you mean?"

"A man or a woman."

Did her unwillingness to sit indicate anything or was it just Daisy, brimming with energy for which she had no channel?

"Nnnn…no. Not that I remember. He talked about

movies with one of the other proofreaders; said he was a nice guy. Honestly, though, with us split up and living different places…"

"What about groups? Books? Bird watching? Music?"

"I don't think so." She paused, surveying the framed print on the side of my file cabinet. She wrinkled her nose.

I was running out of ideas of where her brother might have gone to ground. My remaining question carried with it the risk she could muck things up even more than she helped.

"Daisy, I need to ask you one more thing." The seriousness of my tone got her attention. I crossed my arms on the desk and leaned across them to drive home what I was saying. "If I do ask, I'm sure you'll have at least a vague idea how I intend to use the information. So, before I do, I need your promise you'll let me be the one who acts on it. If you try to muscle in and do something on your own, it could spoil any chance of getting anything useful. Agree?"

"Agree to something without knowing what? I guess so."

"Agree as an adult, or agree as a kid?"

It startled her.

"As an adult," she said after several seconds. "No crossed fingers or any of that. See?" She held up her hands and made her way back toward the desk. "So, what do you want to ask?"

"There's a place the Nisei men go to sit around, have a few beers, talk. Tosh didn't go there, but some of the others do. Do you know the name?"

Her dejected look told me the answer before the shake of her head. Then her face brightened. Hoisting herself onto one corner of my desk, she turned my phone around to face her and dialed. Her eyes had narrowed with a purposefulness beyond her years.

"Hi, this is Daisy Hashimoto. Is Joe there? Thanks." She waited. "Hey, Joe. 'Bout normal. You? Good. Listen. That bar where you and the other guys go to drown your sorrows, what's the name of it? My parents have gotten it into their heads Tosh might have owed a bill there that they should pay off. Pug's? No, I don't think he would either, but thanks."

All that was missing in her smile of satisfaction as she hung up was cream around the whiskers.

"Pug's," she repeated.

"Thanks, Daisy."

She hopped down.

"You're going to go there and see if you can get them talking, is that it? I guess I can see how you'd be better at that than I would. You've had experience. Anyway, they'd all get in a tizzy over my virtue or something if I turned up there."

With a grin, she fluttered her fingers and held out a pinkie.

"May I please make an appointment for this time tomorrow to hear what you learned?"

"I'm not sure I'll go there tonight. I'll try, but I've got a couple of other things I have to do. Let's say Friday to be safe."

"Yeah. Okay." Her disappointment was unmistakable.

"And Daisy, if you start to get ideas about going back on your promise, there's something I think you should know," I said as she hefted her book bag. "A nice old man who was trying to make the case that Tosh wasn't even in the printing plant when the fire started got his head bashed in two nights ago. He's dead."

She swallowed.

"Is that your way of warning me not to go beyond my depth?"

"Something like that."

Her head bobbed once. She started to leave, then paused to look again at my file cabinet with her mouth twisting.

"That picture's not bad, but where you've hung it's dumb. Who's going to see it there but people coming in? People thinking of hiring you have other stuff on their minds. Not to mention it's way too low. You need to put it…"

She'd lifted it as she spoke. Her voice faded. For what seemed eternity she stood staring at the ugly words the picture had covered while my mind scrambled for the best thing to say.

"Daisy—"

"This is because of me, isn't it?"

"No."

"Because you're helping us."

"No. It's because some narrow-minded, ignorant bully thinks he can scare people into doing things his way. But I don't scare easily."

CHAPTER TWENTY-FIVE

Concern that Daisy might find the lure of the bar where her brother's friends gathered impossible to resist in spite of my warnings was the main thing that drove me there that night. I was still half dazed at finding myself a homeowner.

The scene in the lawyer's office, the shuffling of papers and signing, was all a blur. Almost six hours later, it seemed like something I'd seen on a movie screen, with people who looked like Seamus and me playing parts. When we'd stepped out onto the street, with two sets of keys and a deed, we'd walked for a block before one of us spoke.

"Well now," said Seamus. "I guess we'd better sit down somewhere and make up some lists of what's to be done. There'll be gas and electric to get turned on, and I guess we'd best have a phone. And a ration card. One of us will have to sign up for that."

In a vague way, I'd anticipated expenses, even factored them in somewhat in my calculations. Seamus' practical mind was making them concrete. I hadn't thought about a ration card — getting one, standing in line to use it. And furniture. Apart from the rug in the front room and the bedframe in the attic and my dad's easy chair, which I'd somehow have to move from my room at Mrs. Z's, we didn't have a stick of furniture. I was in shell shock.

Compared with the cold reality of all that setting up housekeeping would entail, worming information out of a group of Nisei fellows inclined to not-quite-trust me wasn't half as daunting. I pulled the DeSoto into a spot on the asphalt parking strip to one side of Pug's Tavern and sat for a minute assessing the place.

The tavern itself was brick, square, embellished only by its neat appearance. The asphalt area at the side gave way to gravel in back. The lone car I saw parked there when I took a small detour before heading inside nuzzled up to the back door as if waiting for someone who worked there. The neon sign on top was dark, probably because of the war, but a shaded light glowed above the front door. To my relief, there was no sign of Daisy.

Inside was the cleanest watering hole I'd ever set foot in, Finn's included. The wax on the linoleum floor held such a gloss I feared for my footing. The mirror of the back bar gleamed.

The place was half filled. Mostly men. Two middle-aged women with men too old for the draft at one table. And in one corner, a group of young Nisei men. My deliberately casual once-over was too brief to tell me whether I knew any of the Nisei, but when I'd taken a stool at the bar and ordered a beer, I looked again.

Yes, one of the young men was Zenzo, as I'd expected. I thought one of the others worked with him at Kirby Printing and had spoken with me, but I couldn't be sure. Another had a bandaged hand, surely Ken who had ridden with me from their boarding house to the library.

I sipped my beer and looked idly at the bar area. A pair of boxing gloves held pride of place in a glass case. Half a dozen framed eight-by-ten photos showed scenes from prize fights. I began to understand how the place got its name.

"That's you in those photographs, isn't it?" I asked the bar tender with a crooked, lumpy nose who had waited on me.

He looked pleased.

"Me a long time ago and twenty pounds lighter."

He patted his midsection.

"It must take guts to do that, go in night after night and let somebody take swings at you."

"Takes more guts to walk away from it when you're still making money, but my wife didn't want me ending up punch drunk, so that's what I did."

"How long you had this place?"

"Nine years, and made a profit every one of them," he said proudly.

He had reason to be proud. He'd gone into business in the middle of the Depression.

When I'd decided to come tonight, I'd given some thought on how to approach the men I wanted to talk to. Zenzo, in particular, wasn't likely to believe I'd turned up here accidentally. I wanted to generate as much goodwill, or at least as little ill will, as possible.

"That table of Japanese-American gentlemen, take them a pitcher of beer on me, if that's what they're drinking."

I put enough folding money out on the bar to pay for it. The ex-prizefighter looked surprised.

"You know them?"

"A couple. They come in a lot?"

"Few times a week."

"Anyone ever give them a hard time?"

Shoulder to me, setting a tray out and drawing the pitcher of beer, he shook his head.

"Felt kind of odd the first time or two they came in. After that, they just became another bunch of regulars. Nice fellows. Never a peep of trouble. Not that I have much of that." He grinned. "Want to tell me your name so I can say who's sending this?"

"You can just point me out."

I took a sip of my own beer, then turned on my stool to watch as the boxer-turned-tavern-keeper made his way across the room and set down his tray. I could see him talking. Polite man that he was, he nodded in my direction rather than pointing. The ones with their backs to me turned to look. I raised my glass in salute. Then I faced the bar again. Now to hope one of them approached me, so I didn't have to force myself on them.

Pug, which was what the owner said everyone called him, returned to polishing glasses and filling them. Five minutes or so elapsed before Zenzo appeared.

"I hope you don't think we're dumb enough to believe you turned up here accidentally."

"I'm here because I heard some of you came here sometimes, and I'm hoping you'll feel more inclined to talk about Tosh here than you are with Spooner sticking his nose in."

Zenzo made a sound of disgust. "Spooner."

"He make trouble for you? For Tosh?"

"No, he's just a jerk, trying so hard to be everybody's pal. Thanks for the beer, but you wasted your money. We already told you everything we knew when we talked at the plant."

"Believe it or not, I'm trying to help Tosh. Help his family, anyway. They deserve to know if he's alive or dead."

His hostile gaze wavered.

"I haven't met some of the men you're with. They may have a tiny detail or two to contribute. And I want to know about the woman Tosh had been seeing."

"Woman?"

It startled him.

"I keep hearing here and there that there might have been one, but nobody seems to know who."

"Ken said once, back before Tosh disappeared, that he thought so. We all laughed." He looked toward his companions as he spoke. "I guess you might as well come and sit down."

The faces of the men at the table were a mix of curiosity and wariness as we joined them. Zenzo made introductions.

"How's the hand doing?" I asked Kensuke.

"Good thing I wasn't planning on becoming a violinist. The doctor says one of the fingers may not move so hot."

I commiserated while the other men stole looks at each other. One, a fellow in a navy-blue jersey that came to his chin, narrowed his eyes at Zenzo.

"She says she's heard Tosh was seeing a lady," Zenzo announced. "Anybody know if he was seeing someone?"

"I told her I thought he might be," Ken said with a hint of guilt.

"As did several people at Kirby Printing and his sister," I said to deflect any animosity toward him raised by his admission.

Chatter followed. Speculation began. Tosh had spent a lot of time talking to So-and-So at the last social night they had with the people from the Church Federation? Yes, but they were negotiating some kind of trade of a book of optical illusions for one about solving crossword puzzles.

To my annoyance, sitting there with the young Nisei men left me vaguely unsettled. The nature of my work had, more often than I could remember, brought me into contact with groups of men I didn't know, and where I was the only woman. Still, this felt different. In the group at the table there were no blond heads, no redheads, no eyes any color but brown. Only height and weight and facial features varied.

"I saw him talking to that skinny girl that works a Linotype machine," the diminutive fellow who lugged cartons of printing to shelves with Zenzo was saying. "Just once, though. Something about her glasses."

"I tell you one who wouldn't have tossed him a rag if he was bleeding to death," the third of the men who worked at Kirby chimed in with a grin. "Mitzi Fitzgerald." All three from the printing plant hooted with laughter.

"A blonde who's a clerk of some kind," the one who'd brought up her name explained to the others. "Really trundles her stuff." He pantomimed thrusting his chest out. "Half the guys in the plant start to drool when she goes by."

"Not Tosh, though." Zenzo was loosening up. "The other women from upstairs were giggling about it. They don't like her much."

It explained the platinum blonde's sullen comment to me that Tosh was stuck up, I thought.

"Gossip was, she pulled out all the stops, too," said

the skinny one. "Sauntering past, asking him to help her with things, even perching on his desk a couple of times. But Tosh, he just acted polite, and that was that."

"And that was enough to make her sore?" I asked.

If she was accustomed to male attention, I could see her sulking if she didn't get it, or starting rumors. What I couldn't see was her getting angry enough to orchestrate something like the fire.

Zenzo shrugged.

"Having the women she worked with notice and whisper about it might have. She started to snub him every chance she got, anyway. We kidded Tosh when we first heard. I guess maybe that was the only time I ever heard him say anything snotty."

"Which was?"

"That she was so cheap she belonged on a shelf in the dime store." They all laughed again.

A man they called TK, a fellow of medium size distinguished by a pencil-thin mustache and little round specs, had spent the entire time since I joined them leaning back with his arms crossed. Now he yawned pointedly, glad to convey that he found the whole topic boring.

"I've gotta go."

When he was halfway across the room, Zenzo jumped up.

"I need to remind him of something." He glanced at me. "I'll be right back."

The others chatted some, still uncomfortable in my presence. I angled my chair enough to see Zenzo and TK talking just inside the entrance to the bar. TK wasn't happy. He waved his arms. Zenzo grabbed one and leaned in close to speak. TK shook free, made some reply, and stalked out. After a minute, Zenzo disappeared toward the gents. He came back lighting a cigarette.

"Looked like you and TK were just about ready to try out your own boxing skills and let Pug referee," I said.

"Ah, the jerk owes me five bucks. He's been making excuses for two weeks. It's not that I need the money, it's the principle of the thing."

We talked awhile longer. Two more men drifted away. I asked about the pair of eyeglasses found at the fire scene, but no one knew where they'd been found or by whom. I decided to take my leave.

If accurate, what I'd learned about Mitzi-the-blonde and her feelings toward Tosh eliminated one individual who might hide him. Unfortunately, it brought me no closer to some hint who might, I thought ruefully. As I walked toward my car, I consoled myself with the delicate scent of the April night and the prospect of soon falling asleep in my own house, lulled by the music of crickets and katydids when summer arrived.

I sensed a presence behind me before I heard it. I

ducked and whirled. The person behind me was faster, wrenching my arm up and forcing my jaw down with a spread hand so that I couldn't yell.

"Keep out of this. It doesn't concern you!" a voice hissed.

The hand on my jaw slipped down below the hinge and squeezed.

I tried to bring my elbow back to break my attacker's hold, but a black curtain dropped.

CHAPTER TWENTY-SIX

I awoke with my arm lashing out to ward off attackers, and no idea where I was. My back rested on brick. I was sitting. My left shoulder leaned against…garbage cans.

Clarity broke over me. I was propped up in the parking area to the side of Pug's Tavern. No one else was in sight. No cars were in sight except my DeSoto several spaces away.

As memory returned, I recalled the attack, and I became aware of oddities. For one thing, I'd been moved, but only a few yards. After leaving the tavern, I'd scarcely rounded the corner from the front of the building before I was grabbed. Probably there, where a fat little yew added flair to the entrance and was tall enough to hide a crouching assailant from departing customers or cars passing in the street. Now I sat at the opposite end of the building, near the back entrance.

The other odd thing was that my head didn't hurt, nor did my throat. Either the killer who bashed in Seth Rowe's head had decided to spare me that treatment, or I'd been attacked by someone else. But my throat…I'd been choked to the point where I nearly blacked out a couple of times. Afterward, my throat had been swollen, and so sore it hurt to draw breath. My temples had throbbed, too.

With a good deal of caution, I pushed myself to my knees and then to my feet. I felt slightly dizzy. When I considered the distance to the front entrance and that to the kitchen entrance, or whatever the right term was in place that probably didn't serve food, the one closest to me won.

Steadying myself with a hand on the top of the garbage cans, I made my way around them to a door that was cracked an inch to let out heat. I paused to let my eyes adjust to the light that escaped. Then I opened the door and stepped into what was largely a storage area.

A woman sat at a table counting cash and writing down figures. As she reached for the cup at her elbow, she saw me and stiffened. "Hey!"

Pug came through the door to the bar with a tray full of dirty glasses. He stopped in his tracks.

"Sorry to come in the back way," I said, discovering my tongue felt a bit thick. "I stepped wrong out there and twisted my ankle. Hit my head when I fell. I've been hearing birdies."

The ex-boxer set down his tray and pulled out a chair. I sank onto it.

"Thanks."

"You scraped your cheek, too," said the woman. "Want some water?"

"Please." Pug handed it to me and I drank gratefully. "Who's left from that bunch I was with?"

"Nobody," said Pug. "We closed fifteen minutes ago."

I pressed my fingers to my forehead, rubbing away a headache that didn't materialize. So much for narrowing the list of candidates for my attacker.

***

To my surprise, I awoke the next morning with nary an ill effect from the night before. My head didn't hurt. My throat didn't hurt. When I looked very closely, I thought my mirror image showed a faint, thumb-size bruise at the side of my neck, but I couldn't be certain.

I washed and brushed my teeth and dressed. Then, with a pang of sadness, I gathered myself for the hardest task I would face in leaving Mrs. Z's, giving her my notice.

"Oh, Margaret. I'm so sorry to lose you," she said when I told her. She reached for my hand and gave it a squeeze. "I'm happy for you, though, dear. There's been a sadness to you these last few years. You've always been more solitary than the other girls, and I think you must see some very unpleasant things in your work. I think having a place of your own will suit you. What do you need? In the way of furnishings?"

I chuckled.

"Everything. Except for the chair I brought here with me and my two pillows, I'll be camping out for awhile."

"Would a set of sheets help? There's a raggedy set I've been reluctant to use any more but kept for emergencies."

I thanked her and hugged her. There were tears in her eyes. Dabbing at a few of my own, I headed downtown to have some breakfast while I tried to fit what I'd learned from the table of Nisei men into what I'd learned so far.

Mitzi Fitzgerald now joined Spooner on the list of people who might have nursed a personal grudge against Tosh. I needed to talk to the blonde, get a better feel for what she was like, but I couldn't see her setting the fire. From the sounds of it, she attracted too much male attention. The fact she didn't work nights would have made her stand out even more.

She could have hired someone, but would being snubbed by a man make her that angry? I found it hard to believe. Nor did I think either she or Spooner could have sneaked up on Seth Rowe and dealt a fatal blow to his head. Both lacked the strength.

Who, then?

No answers sprang to mind as I drank my tea and

ate oatmeal with the meager splash of milk and teaspoon of brown sugar now allotted with it. What did seem logical, though, was that Seth Rowe had been killed to keep him from casting any doubt on Tosh as the arsonist. That meant hearing accounts by the other two witnesses of what they'd seen might be the smart thing to do.

When I finished my oatmeal, I headed across Main to Market House hoping Freeze was in. He was putting on his hat.

"I've got information to trade," I said.

"On what?"

"On Seth Rowe's murder for something related to my case."

"If you're withholding information—"

"I'm not. Was Rowe's killer left-handed?"

"How did—?"

"Because whoever carved up my file cabinet was. At least according to someone who seemed to know what he was talking about, how the letters went deeper on one side and that. Like you, he also noted that whoever carved up my woodwork was angry."

Freeze sat down at his desk.

"Yes, the coroner says the blow to Rowe's head came from someone left-handed. The fact that a single blow killed him could indicate anger. More likely it means the killer was a strong devil."

"Or both."

"I'm guessing you see some connection?"

"Don't you? For Pete's sake, Freeze. That threat decorating my file cabinet makes it pretty clear someone doesn't like me helping the man people want to pin that fire on. Rowe's account of things strengthened the possibility of his innocence, so somebody killed him to keep him from talking."

"That's farfetched."

"It's not, and you know it."

Young detective Dotson, who wasn't sure whether he should return to his desk, elected to stay where he stood. He shifted from foot to foot.

"Okay, it's one possible motive. I'll keep it in mind." Freeze stood again. "Now if you don't mind, we've got our own work to do."

"Not so fast. You haven't anted up your part yet."

"I told you the killer was left-handed."

"I'd already guessed that. I want to know who the other witnesses were who identified Tosh Hashimoto running away."

"The manager and one of the proofreaders."

"Spooner was there that night?"

"Wasn't unusual, according to people working there. He came in sometimes to catch up." Freeze beckoned to Dots and the two of them started around me.

"What's the proofreader's name?"

"Don't remember."

"You could look it up," I said to his back.

"I could. But *if* you're right about why Rowe was killed, telling you might place her in danger."

"Yeah, you're probably right."

Besides, he'd already told me all I needed to know. The night-shift staff was smaller. There were only two proofreaders. Just one of them was female.

CHAPTER TWENTY-SEVEN

"Again? When is this disruption of our schedules going to stop?" snapped Spooner when he saw me. Today there wasn't even a trace of Mr. Broadway cheer. I wondered what was eating him.

"I know. You're getting tired of seeing me, I'm getting tired of seeing you. We're starting to get on each other's nerves like an old married couple. That's what makes me run in the other direction when fellas start talking marriage."

Since he'd decided not to turn on the charm today, I decided I could skip it, too. I helped myself to a seat on the edge of his desk.

"The only ones I need to disrupt today are you, for a few minutes, Mr. Spooner, and Miss Fitzgerald. I don't anticipate much time with her either."

"Miss...Fitzgerald?" He looked sharply through the glass front of his office. "Why do you want to talk to her?" He mustered an ingratiating grin. And a chuckle. "If I may ask."

I waved blythe dismissal.

"Oh, a few things came up in the course of talking

to people. Nothing major, but I'm hoping she can shed some light."

"Well, er, I'm glad to help, of course. I'm sure she will be, too. I apologize for being cranky when you came in. I must have gotten up on the wrong side of the bed."

"I won't take up much of your time. I promise. If you could just show me where you were standing when you saw Tosh Hashimoto the night of the fire."

"Where I...?"

His cheeks twitched like he couldn't decide whether or not to be jolly.

"Lieutenant Freeze and I were chatting just now, and he reminded me that you were here that night. It had completely slipped my mind."

"Yes. Yes, I was. Catching up, you know. So many interruptions during the day that things pile up."

He paused to let it sink in. I waited.

"Er, I can't show you where I was, I'm afraid. Not up close anyway. I was on the back stairs, just above the part destroyed by the fire."

From where I sat, I couldn't see the wooden stairs that led directly down to the composing room, but I knew where they were. They were roped off with a DANGER KEEP OUT sign up here like they were at the bottom. The bottom stairs that supported them had been burned away.

"I'd just stepped out to go down and speak to the

night supervisor," Spooner was saying. "I heard something — a noise I didn't recognize — and then screams. Horrible screams. I ran down the stairs and I saw fire. Flames. Hashimoto was right outside the door, running away. It hardly registered then. All I thought about was the fire. I shouted to start the sprinklers, and turned and ran back up here for a fire extinguisher. I yelled — I don't know if it was to anyone in particular or just in general — to call the fire department.

"I ran back down and started spraying, but the bottom was already gone. My sleeve had caught fire, and…" His face had grown pale. "I didn't realize until later that people had died. It was…it was awful."

"And you're sure it was Mr. Hashimoto you saw."

"Oh, absolutely. Sadly."

"You saw his face?"

"Uh, well, no. He was running away. I saw the side of it, now that I think. His cheek. He must have glanced back, making sure he was getting away, I suppose. It was him, though. His hair had a place that always stood up." He gestured vaguely with his hand.

"And the other witness was standing where?"

"Other…oh. At the back window. It's next to the utility closet and the ladies' room."

I started to slide off his desk when something that hadn't been visible when I was facing the desk like a good visitor should caught my eye.

"Who's the handsome golfer?" I asked, indicating a

silver-framed photo of a young man in white sports attire. He was displaying a trophy and a radiant smile. I was almost certain he was the man I'd seen arguing with Mitzi Fitzgerald.

"My son." My switch to friendlier topics brought some of the color back to Spooner's face. He picked the photograph up, so I could have a closer look. "Roger's a wonderful golfer. All kinds of trophies."

"Is that how he and Miss Fitzgerald know each other? Both golfers?"

"I don't believe they know each other at all." Spooner looked and sounded completely startled.

"I saw them talking out front and assumed they were friends." I smiled and shrugged.

"Oh, no, no, they probably just met in passing some time when Roger came here to see me." All at once he frowned. "That's not why you want to talk to Miss Fitzgerald, is it? Surely you don't think Roger had anything to do with – with this."

The frustrated wave of his hand presumably meant the fire. A sheen of uneasiness appeared on his forehead.

"Farthest thing from my mind." Especially since I'd already asked her about Roger and she'd dismissed him as some creep who made a pass at her. "It's just some things that have come up in conversations that I hope she can add to. You know how it is, one thing leads to another. Thanks for your time.

I could almost feel his relief fill the room as I turned toward the door.

"Oh, I almost forgot. The glasses they found."

"The ones that belonged to Mr. Hashimoto, you mean?"

"The ones that turned up at the fire scene, anyway. Where were they found?"

"I...have no idea. You'll have to ask the fire investigator, I'm afraid. The fire department...well, to tell the truth, they took over as soon as the blaze was out. Quite bossy, actually. I suppose they have to be, but all the same. We were in absolute turmoil. Not really sure what had happened, or what to do next, and there they were scolding us not to walk here or there. It was almost a whole day before they'd even let us move around to assess damages."

He practically bounced with indignation. His fiefdom had been invaded.

CHAPTER TWENTY-EIGHT

Mitzi, in contrast, proved a tough nut to crack. Brazil-nut hard; maybe even black walnut.

"You're older than I thought the first time," she said as I closed the door to the small room once used by the director of personnel, whose duties now were shared by Spooner and the head of accounting.

"Meaner too," I said pleasantly.

She didn't know how to take it. Wariness began to erode her smug expression.

"Tell me again about how you got along with Tosh Hashimoto."

"I already did. He was stuck up."

"Because he wasn't interested when you flirted?"

She stood with one hip canted out and arms crossed, looking back at me with studied boredom. She smiled superiority.

"I don't have to flirt. I can have any man in this place I want with a snap of my fingers." She gave one in illustration. "Why would I waste my time on a Jap?"

"Let's see…He's good-looking; he's smart; he's polite. Oh, and because people here say you made passes at him, but he wasn't interested."

"Well, they're lying."

"Why would they do that?"

Red blotches that signaled anger seeped into her cheeks.

"You're not that dumb. All the other women are jealous of me because of my looks. They're always making dirty digs about me. But I'm not going to take this kind of-of insult to my good name lying down! The only time I even talked to Tosh Hashimoto was when it had something to do with work."

Since she was some kind of low-level clerk and he was a proofreader, I couldn't see where work would necessitate much contact between them. I waited. Her eyes narrowed.

"I guess some are desperate enough they'd go with a Jap. The one you ought to be talking to is Miss Secretary-to-the-Top-Man Chapman. I saw them parked in her car and they looked awfully cozy."

***

I didn't trust Mitzi any farther than I could spit. Before I antagonized — and embarrassed — Phyllis Chapman by asking her if she'd gone out with Tosh, I wanted to see if I could confirm the story I'd heard from the Nisei men about Mitzi making a play for Tosh and being rebuffed. I'd hoped I might get a chance to ask at least one of the proofreaders.

When the blonde and I parted ways, however,

Spooner was entertaining Velma, the one receptive to his jokes. It conveniently placed him where he could see where I went when I finished talking to Mitzi, and would hear any conversations I had with the proofreaders. The only other ploy I could try was going into the ladies' room and hoping one of the other women would happen in, but when I'd dawdled as much as I dared, I gave up and came out again. I thanked Spooner, who walked me almost to the front stairs and then waited to make sure I left.

As I reached the bottom, and started toward the end of the counter that separated the rest of the plant from the small front customer area, some unknown saint who was scattering acts of kindness dropped one on me. The fellow who proofed illustrations rather than lines of type was coming out of the composing area.

"Hey, can I ask you something, confidentially, before you head back upstairs?"

He paused.

"I guess."

The two of us moved to one side, so we wouldn't block anyone's way.

"Did Tosh ever mention Mitzi Fitzgerald flirting with him?"

For a second he hesitated. Then his eyes danced.

"*He* never said anything, but she did. I saw it. Usually I keep my nose down, but one day I looked up right when she was boosting that cute little caboose of hers onto his desk. Mitzi's a pretty hot gal. I'd have melted. But Tosh, he glanced up and went right back to what he was doing, no more interested than if some stranger on the street had asked him what time it was."

"Then what?"

He shrugged. "After maybe thirty seconds of sitting there swinging her legs and trying to strike up conversation, she jumped down and sauntered off."

"Could I ask a fast favor? Also confidential?"

This time he was wary.

"Maybe."

"You know which typesetter Longworth is?"

"Yes."

"Would you go back and tell him I'll be parked across the street from the lane in back at noon, and I'd like a word if he can spare me a minute?"

He nodded.

***

After giving Mrs. Z my notice that morning, I'd rooted through my room to find a few little dabs of cash I had squirreled away over the years but somehow never remembered when I ran short of cash. Three dollars stuffed in a pair of nearly worn out shoes so disreputable that I would wear them now only as a last resort. A crisp five-dollar bill hidden between a photograph and the cardboard backing that kept it straight in its frame. Another five here, two bucks here and there, and before I knew it, I'd found a total of thirty dollars.

My plan, when I got back from Kirby Printing, was to walk a few blocks past my office and deposit it in the bank, so I could rest a few breaths easier about my depleted balance. I got to the bank. I got into line, with cash in hand.

Then I heard my name called.

Looking around, I saw Jolene, one of the other longtime roomers at Mrs. Z's. Her wealth of buttery yellow curls had begun to escape the kerchief tied over them. She was still in the grease-monkey jumpsuit she wore for mechanic's work on the midnight shift at Patterson Field. She'd just come through the door from the street and was breathing harder than usual by the time she reached me.

"I was on my way to your office, but then I saw you across the street. I've been trying to catch up with you for a block." She noticed the money I held in my hand. "Oh, good. Maggie, I need to talk to you."

Hand hooked through my arm, she was already urging me from the line, which had added another half-dozen people behind me.

"Jolene…"

"It's – it's important, Maggie. And it can't wait!"

There was an edge of anxiety to her voice that I'd never heard before. She came from a farm in the next county over and was smart as a whip. Generally, she was levelheaded, too. I let her draw me aside.

"Maggie, I've got a business proposition for you. One that's guaranteed to make you money. Three times, four, what you put into it. Maybe more. I know that sounds like I'm peddling snake oil, but I'm not. You know me, Maggie. I've got a head for business."

"I know you do, Jolene, but—"

"Just let me tell you, okay? It's bees, Maggie. See, what with sugar rationed, honey's become real popular. You can use it in cooking, except you have to tinker with recipes some. Dad's kept beehives for years. He's always had jars of honey for sale right along with those vegetables he sells at the market."

Her family grew wheat and corn and raised some kind of animals, hogs, I thought. Twice a week her father also brought in a truckload of whatever was in season from their sizable garden and sold it at a sprawling outdoor produce market a block from my office.

"Well, ever since rationing started, Dad can't keep in honey," she went on before I could open my mouth. It sells out in the first hour or so. There's a farmer up the road from us who has hives too, but he's getting old, and his grandson that helped him got called up, so he wants to sell his hives. Since we've already got bees and know how to take care of them, he's offered Dad the first chance to buy them.

"Later in the year that wouldn't be a problem, but

right now's when farmers are short of money because they've just bought seeds for the rest of the year, and Dad's thirty-five dollars short of what old man Morris is asking. Well, that much short of what he thinks it's safe to take out of his account and still be able to cover bills and emergencies — and that's after I've kicked in from what I was saving to start a business after the war. So, I racked my brain, and I kind of recalled that you have more work than you used to, and I know you save, and there's not much else to spend it on, so like I said, I was on my way to your office to see if you'd kick in."

I was laughing in spite of myself. Jolene's ability to reel off words without pausing to breathe was phenomenal.

"Jolene, I wish I could. It sounds pretty smart. The problem is, I just bought a house, and I don't have a nickel extra to spend."

She looked pointedly at the cash in my hand.

"You've got however much that is."

"*And* I don't even have a bed to sleep in. The only stick of furniture I have for the place is an easy chair. Mrs. Z, bless her, is giving me leftovers of that black lining she used to make blackout curtains, so we won't get cited for a violation. My godfather, Seamus, is in the same fix. He's lived all his life in rented rooms. He doesn't own much of anything except for his clothes, and he used up most of his savings helping me buy the place."

"That nice old gent who doesn't say much?"

I nodded. "He'll be living there, too. And besides needing furniture, there'll be the little matter of keeping food in our mouths. Not to mention a skillet or something to fix it in."

Jolene's blue eyes were round. Appreciation of how thinly stretched my resources really were had rendered her silent. Then she broke into her sunny smile.

"None of that will be a problem. There's an old daybed on our screen porch that nobody ever uses. Dad could bring it in on the truck on Monday, deliver it right to your door. If you slip the measurements for your windows under my door, and maybe the colors you'd like, I'll call Mom and she can whiz curtains up this weekend and send those too—"

"Jolene—"

"And since you'd be part owner of the bees, you'd kind of be part owner of the farm, too, so Dad could drop you off a basket of stuff every time he came to town — or maybe you'd have to go over and pick those up at the market. Vegetables and eggs and stuff Mom's canned. You know how much you loved Mom's jam that she sent when we used to be able to use the kitchen at Mrs. Z's on Saturday mornings…"

CHAPTER TWENTY-NINE

I sat in my car across the street from the lane leading into the rear of the printing plant wondering whether I was competent to do detective work. So far this week I had become not only the owner of a house, but an owner of honeybees and, according to Jolene's logic, owner of about a square inch of a farm in Greene County. So far this week I had not learned the whereabouts of Tosh Hashimoto, or his fate, or who had started the fire of which he was accused.

With relief, I watched employees start filtering out through the bay door for their lunch break. Most of the women from upstairs crowded around the picnic tables. The men, including the one who worked with the proofreaders, sat on the ground or stood stretching. One of the men detached himself from the others and continued on in my direction.

Longworth had an easy, swinging gait. As I watched him approach, I noticed the two women Linotype operators, the young one with taped-up specs and the older one, both stuck with their male coworkers rather than joining the women from upstairs.

"Is there some kind of class system, upstairs versus

down?" I asked as Longworth came around to slide into the passenger seat. "The Linotype gals aren't sitting with the other women."

He gave a wide grin.

"Something like that. Mostly I think Betsy and Ro think the ones from upstairs are kind of silly, the way they twitter on about men and who's doing what. Which reminds me."

He handed me a scrap of paper from his pocket.

"Ro says she forgot to tell you something. She said tell you she'd be having supper at this place at five if you want to talk."

As he spoke he wiped his hands on a freshly ironed bandana. "Mind if I eat my lunch while we have our cloak-and-dagger meeting?"

I chuckled.

"Go ahead, but I'm not sure it qualifies as cloak and dagger. It just rubs me the wrong way having Spooner stick his nose in every time I'm talking to someone. I thought it might spare you a little grief if he found out, too."

"Spooner doesn't scare me." Flipping open his lunch pail he pulled out a sandwich wrapped in wax paper. "You want a piece? The missus always makes me two sandwiches."

"No thanks. I had one at my desk. What can you tell me about Mitzi Fitzgerald?"

He'd just taken a big bite of sandwich. He paused

with it clutched in his teeth like a dog with a bone, grinning.

"She's like catnip to men," he said when he'd chewed enough to get words out. "And she knows it. She likes the power. Likes dangling herself and watching them fall all over themselves trying to get a nod or a hello."

"She comes downstairs then?"

"Oh yeah, probably once a day, more to cause a ripple than because she's got any real need to, if you want my opinion."

"Flirt with anyone?"

"Downstairs? Nah. She likes men's attention, but the only ones she wastes her time on are ones who could advance her lot in life. She set her cap on a young fellow in accounting not long after she started here. Then she dropped him for the head accountant — caused that fellow to break his engagement if rumors are to be believed. Then he up and enlisted. Guess that left her with pretty slim pickings."

"What about Tosh Hashimoto?"

He folded the waxed paper from his first sandwich and unwrapped the second one as he considered.

"That would make sense. I didn't hear anything about it, but he was smart. It was plain to see that he was going to make something of himself. I wondered what your interest in Mitzi had to do with the fire."

"Probably nothing. It's just that I've heard she made,

ah, overtures to Mr. Hashimoto and he ignored her. If that's true, would it have made her sore?"

"Sore enough to be spiteful, or tattle on him or stir up trouble. But set a fire, if that's what you're thinking? I doubt it. Besides, she's always worked days, so plenty would have noticed if she'd been in the building that night."

***

Bernadette Howell, one of the two proofreaders I'd spoken to when I interviewed night-shift employees at the printing plant, had seemed completely open in her answers. She had not, however, mentioned seeing Tosh there when the fire started. Then again, I hadn't specifically asked her.

She and her husband lived in the top half of a frame house that sat opposite some sort of church. Thanks to Freeze's disclosure that morning of two other witnesses who'd reported seeing Tosh at the fire, I'd called from my office to ask if she'd let me stop in for a few minutes. As I climbed the unsheltered outside staircase on the side of the house, I hoped the short drive from downtown wouldn't be wasted. I was raising my hand to knock when the door opened under it.

"Oh, yes. I recognize you now," the proofreader said. She stepped aside so I could enter. "This is my husband."

We exchanged nods.

The couple were both somewhere around fifty. Bernadette's hair was coal black, heavily threaded with white, and she had it wound into a Victory Roll under a snood, already getting ready for work by the looks of the ironed white shirt she wore.

"You said on the phone that it would be safer if I didn't tell anyone you were coming here," she said. "I don't get it."

"You will when I've asked you some questions. It may be unnecessary precaution, but Longworth, who told me how to reach you, seemed to think it was a smart idea, too."

Husband and wife exchanged looks, their foreheads wrinkling.

"You were one of the people who identified Tosh Hashimoto as being at Kirby Printing the night of the fire. I'd like you to tell me everything you remember, every detail."

"I've already told the police several times, and the man from the fire department," Bernadette objected.

"Do you think she made something up? That she'll change something?"

The husband didn't sound pleased. I held up a placating hand.

"It's not that at all. Sometimes the right questions aren't asked. Little things can come out when they are. Things that don't seem important." I paused. "A detail like that came out when I talked to Seth Rowe, and it calls into question assumptions about what happened that night. Only no one else had mentioned it, and the night after I went to see Mr. Rowe, somebody killed him."

"And that's why you think my wife might be in danger? Because you think she might have noticed it, too, and you came and talked to her?"

"Yes."

Bernadette's husband sat down on a sofa that was starting to sag although its green upholstery was still in pretty good shape. Bernadette joined him. She patted his knee.

"It's okay, hon. Now that I know what's going on, I'm not going to turn tail if I might dredge up something that helps."

He nodded. I sat down facing them.

"I want you to take me through where you were and what you saw that night. I'll hold up a finger to stop you if I want to know more about something you just said. Okay?"

"Yes."

"First, tell me how you knew it was Hashimoto rather than one of the other Japanese-American workers. They worked days, you work nights."

Bernadette cocked her head.

"You're not suggesting all Japanese look alike, are you? They don't, not any more than we do. There were several get-togethers, so we could all meet them when they first started working there. And I trained

Tosh for a week so the other proofreaders didn't have to keep stopping to answer questions. He'd already proofed part-time on a magazine where he lived, but every place has its peculiarities. I made sure he knew ours, and I took him around and made sure he knew who was who downstairs. Longworth kind of wanted to poach him because the kid also knew how to use a Linotype."

She thawed enough to show amusement.

"Even someone who didn't know him could probably pick him out. He had wild hair. A cowlick, I guess you'd say, although it was more like two or three of them right together. Or maybe he rumpled it while he worked—"

I put a hand up. "You convinced me. And thanks. Now. Where were you when you saw him? How did you happen to see him?"

"There's a window in back. Down by the restroom."

"I know where you mean."

"I'd used the restroom and gone to the window to stretch. I do that a couple of times in the course of a shift. There aren't half a dozen working upstairs at night, so it's pretty informal. Anyway, that's where I was when I heard a big commotion downstairs and noticed him standing there."

Standing there?

But I wanted to follow another thread first.

"That window isn't blacked out?"

Some factories had elected to paint their windows black to keep lights from showing if they ran night shifts. Bernadette shook her head.

"It's dim down there, just a little dinky light bulb."

"Still, there'd be some light, and the lane leading up to the loading door is dark except for that puddle right at the door that goes, what, maybe two feet out? Was he that close?"

She'd have been looking straight down. And the closeness would be damning to Tosh.

"No, he was farther away. Fifteen feet, maybe more." Her eyebrows raised in dawning comprehension. "You're wondering about contrast. How I could see him at all with him in the dark."

"Yes."

"But he wasn't. Those houses beyond the fence on the left of the lane, the first one down has an upstairs bathroom that looks out on the lane. They don't have a curtain there, just a roller shade to pull down. Only they don't." Her mouth gave a twist of amusement.

"You can't *see* anything but the wash basin — I expect the bathtub's under the window and the toilet at the other end — but there's at least one of them who comes in at night and flips the light on without lowering the shade. I expect if there was a drill on, they'd pull the shade and get it blacked out. But there wasn't a drill the night of the fire, and light from up there was pouring out like a stage spotlight. So yes, I'm sure it was Tosh. He was standing there right in it until he turned and ran.Right then's when I realized something was wrong downstairs. I raced back and crashed right into Mr. Spooner as he came stumbling up shouting to get the fire extinguisher. His face was as gray as his tie—"

I held up a finger.

"Tosh was standing still at first?"

"When I first noticed him? Yes."

"Standing how?"

Her brows drew together. The question puzzled her.

"Was he bending down? Holding anything?"

"Oh. He was standing straight. He had one arm up shielding his eyes, and…No, come to think of it, he wasn't standing straight. He was leaning forward like he was looking for someone or thinking about running in."

Her eyes, which had been focused elsewhere as she thought, raised to mine. "Only why would anyone go back into a fire they'd started? Why would you even waste time looking? All you'd think about would be getting away."

CHAPTER THIRTY

Freeze and Dotson were walking toward the car they used when I rounded the corner, headed for Market House, and saw them. I broke into a run.

"Hey, Freeze! Wait!"

"We're in a hurry," he said as I caught up with them.

"The proofreader who said she saw Hashimoto there the night of the fire, there's something she left out of what she told you."

"She kept something back?" He started to bristle.

"Not deliberately. I've just come from talking to her. It didn't come out until I pressed her for details — how he was standing, did he have anything in his hands."

I paused to catch my breath.

"The thing is, Freeze, she told me the very same thing that Seth Rowe did. She says Hashimoto was standing stock still, facing toward the building. She says he had his arm up shielding his eyes, like he was trying to see what was happening inside, and maybe whether he could get in to help.

"A few hours after Seth Rowe told me pretty much

that same thing, somebody killed him. I'm worried someone could go after her. She's at work now, or on her way. She swore she'd come to see you tomorrow to add that part to her statement, but tomorrow's a long time away."

Freeze wiped thoughtfully at his upper lip.

"Spooner didn't say anything about Hashimoto looking into the building. He put him right outside the door and already running."

"Well, Bernadette claims your suspect was fifteen feet or more away, and the way she pinpoints it is pretty convincing. If he'd been as close as Spooner says, why didn't Seth Rowe catch him? Rowe was spry for his age and took some pride in it. In fact, Rowe was upset thinking that might have been why the company shoved him into retirement, because they blamed him for not being fast enough to catch Hashimoto. It could have been pride talking, but he claimed Hashimoto had too big a lead."

Freeze had started out fidgeting. Now he leaned against the car. He got out an Old Gold.

"Are you suggesting Spooner could be lying? Why would he?"

"He blamed Hashimoto for spoiling a flirtation he had going on with Kirby's secretary. It wasn't reciprocated, by the way, and the secretary says she just got too busy with extra forms every week because of the Nisei workers and other things to keep humoring Spooner."

"You think that would be reason enough for Spooner, who's got to be drawing a decent paycheck, to set fire to the place he works?" His skepticism was clear. "If I buy that, or even just that he lied, then I have to also think he's involved in Rowe's murder."

"A second reason I thought you should know."

"Spooner has a rock-solid alibi for the time Rowe was killed."

"Yeah, I know. He was part of a singing group performing in front of a few hundred people. He could have hired someone."

Freeze flapped his lips in dismissal.

"Please note I haven't asked for anything in return," I said instead.

He motioned to Dotson to get in the car.

"I'll send Dots home in time to grab a few hours' shuteye. He knows what the proofreader looks like. He can keep an eye out for her when she gets off work and tag along to make sure she gets home safely."

As precautions went, it didn't make me jump for joy. In any sort of crunch, young Dotson would be as much help as a Raggedy Andy doll.

***

My curiosity itched worse than poison ivy over what Ro, the skinny girl who operated a Linotype, might have to tell me. It was still too early to meet her, but too late to do much else productive. I now faced an additional problem as well. Given the direction my last conversation with Spooner had taken, showing up to ask more questions at Kirby Printing might alert him to my suspicions.

At the moment, I wasn't completely sure what those suspicions were. His account of where Tosh had been and what he was doing the night of the fire was at odds with those of the other two witnesses. He blamed Tosh, rightly or wrongly, for causing Phyllis Chapman to lose interest in him. Both suggested he'd had something to do with the fire, in my opinion.

On the other hand, there was his alibi. As loath as I was to admit it, Freeze also had raised a good point about whether a man with as much to lose as Spooner would risk it for spite.

Without time to pursue other options before I met Ro, I sat at my desk thinking of ways I might butter up Spooner well enough to navigate around him without setting off alarm bells. After fifteen minutes of rotating side-to-side in my chair, and staring at my defaced file cabinet, inspiration struck.

Baked goods.

Cookies, fruit bread, a pie. Anything on that order.

Peace offering…something I thought a couple of single fellows like him and his son might enjoy…etcetera, etcetera.

The trouble was, with sugar rationed, such treats were in short supply. It would also be an expense that I didn't need right now. Something purchased wouldn't be as persuasive as something homemade, either.

Finally, a solution came to me. I was reaching for the phone to make the call that, if I was lucky, would make it possible, when it rang under my hand.

"Thought you might want to take down our new telephone number," Seamus said proudly.

Aware that I was as tickled as he was, I did.

"What about the others? Do we have electricity?"

"That and the gas on, too."

He wasn't due for a day off for another week, but he'd managed to trade with someone. When he'd called the three utilities and they'd learned he was a policeman, they'd been accommodating enough to fit him into their schedules.

"A beer truck that makes deliveries to Finn's was nice enough to drop off the table and chairs he's loaning us from his back room," he said. "So, I guess our kitchen's all ready to go, except for a skillet and stewpan and something to eat on."

"I'll give Kate a call. I'm sure she'll let us borrow something."

"You haven't talked to her, then?"

I thought I heard something odd in his voice.

"No, why?"

"She's giving me some tools that Billy used. I was kind of hoping if it fit into your schedule okay, you'd pick them up and bring them over when you finish up for the day. She said she'd be there. I thought I might as well sleep here tonight. I brought my sheets and a towel and some things on the trolley this morning."

I was smiling.

"I'll pick us up some sandwiches, too. I've just got a thing or two to finish up here, and then I'll head for Kate's."

As soon as I hung up, I dialed Maire. I didn't hear kids whooping and yelling in the background. Either they were still grieving the death of their dad or she'd shoved them outside.

"Oh, Maggie, you don't know how good it is to hear from somebody my own age," she sighed.

"Well, I'm kind of embarrassed at why I'm calling, but you know that mountain of food you were showing me Monday that people have brought you?"

"Are you going to come over and help us eat some? Say you will. None of us have much appetite, and they keep bringing it."

"I can't tonight, honey. I'll be busy with things until bedtime. But I was wondering…Could you spare a dozen cookies? Something the kids aren't partial to. It wouldn't have to be cookies—"

She gave a faltering laugh.

"If you promise not to tell, so many have brought us molasses cookies the kids have started to turn up their noses at those. I guess, well…"

"They wanted to do something nice for you and the

kids, but it's hard enough to stretch their sugar ration as it is."

"Yes."

Molasses was another sweetener people were using instead of sugar. It had a strong taste, though. Things made with it either just tasted like molasses, with maybe some raisins or nuts thrown in, or people hid the taste under spices. I suddenly wondered what kind of rival it was to honey.

I told Maire I'd swing by for the cookies after she'd packed the kids off to school the next morning. She said she'd have the kettle on. I wasn't sure yet if I'd tell her how I meant to use the cookies.

CHAPTER THIRTY-ONE

Ro, the Linotype operator with the taped-up glasses, was already digging into the blue-plate special in a little joint where you ordered your food, then carried it to the table yourself.

"I thought you might like some pie," I said setting one of the slices I carried next to her plate. "All they had was rhubarb."

"That's real nice of you. You didn't have to."

I nibbled the point of my pie to put her at ease. It could have been sweeter, but the crust was first rate.

"You come here every day?"

She shook her head, either shy or wary of talking now that she'd initiated it.

"There's three places feed you good for not very much money. I kind of rotate. Can't get in my room till six. That's when the ones who sleep days have to have their bedrolls stowed and be out, so we can put ours on the bunks."

She said it casually, but it made me see how Mrs. Z's, even now, would be heaven to someone like her.

"Longworth said you'd thought of something you forgot to tell me."

She poked at a pea with a single tine of her fork.

"Not forgot so much as didn't. I didn't tell the police because where I come from, it's mostly sheriff deputies, and they're mean cusses. Hurt people. Throw their weight around. 'Specially with women." Her eyes flicked up to mine for a moment blue and somber behind her thick lenses. "When you came 'round talking to people, I didn't want to say anything because Mr. Spooner was there."

I nodded as if I understood. I thought I did. Spooner held the girl's job in his hands.

Ro mopped up a last bit of gravy from her potatoes.

"But Mr. Hashimoto, like I said, he was real nice. It kind of seemed to me like it was the right thing to do, telling you." She popped the bit of bread and gravy into her mouth. "See, he didn't just ask how I busted my glasses, he brought in an old pair of his."

I paused with my fork in midair. "The ones they found at the fire."

It was her turn to be startled.

"I didn't know they found any. These were kind of old people's glasses. Wire frames. He said he knew the lenses would be wrong, but maybe there was a way an eye doctor place could fit my lenses into the frames, or maybe trade me for frames that would fit. He said he knew frames were probably hard to come by, what with the war."

The girl pulled her slice of pie toward her, but ran

her fork along the edge without cutting into it. Shyness claimed her again.

"I thanked him and said I appreciated it, but I'd just wait. Truth is, I like these I have, tape and all, better than I liked those frames. And I don't need charity. I've got money enough for a new pair, but I'm saving."

She ate some pie now, a hefty chunk.

"Mr. Hashimoto looked kind of disappointed. He said he'd leave the glasses in his box till the end of the day in case I changed my mind, but I didn't."

"By box, do you mean a tray on his desk?"

"No, his coatroom box. There's a little room in that hall to the restroom. It's got coat pegs for the people who work up there, with things like great big pigeon holes over each one."

A room where anyone working upstairs could slip in and pick up a pair of glasses unnoticed, I thought.

***

I'd been coming to Kate and Billy Leary's house since I was a child. Billy, a rosy-cheeked cop who'd been a constantly grumbling fount of advice, had been my dad's partner, then Seamus', then Mick Connelly's. He'd died last year. I was still smiling at memories of his well-meant efforts to mother-hen me when Kate answered the door.

"Maggie, love, it's so good to see you." She hugged

me. "Mind you, don't trip over the toolbox there. I put it by the door so we wouldn't forget it. Come on into the kitchen."

"Thanks, Kate. I guess Seamus must have told you we bought a house?"

"He did, and that's grand news. You work hard, both of you."

"I don't know what he's found to fix so soon, but he's as tickled to have things that belonged to Billy as he is over the tools themselves."

"Truth be told, I think Seamus may have used those tools as much as Billy did. Every time he came over, there was Billy standing supervising while Seamus did something that Billy had been putting off."

"With Billy saying twenty words to every one from Seamus," I added.

"Ah, don't you know it."

Memories made her eyes mist, but she was smiling. We'd reached the kitchen. A box whose circumference would fill my arms sat on the counter. Another, of equal size, occupied one end of the oak kitchen table. The other end held two pretty cups and saucers and a creamer and sugar.

"Will you have some tea, love? Or can you stay for supper? It's in the oven."

"Tea sounds lovely, Kate. After that I'd better scoot off to see what Seamus is up to. He's been at the house by himself all day." I poked through the box on

M. Ruth Myers

the table. "A skillet, two sizes of stewpans…big spoons and a pancake turner. This is wonderful, Kate."

Back toward me, she was pouring hot water into a teapot that matched the cups on the table. She nodded.

"There's a butcher knife rolled in an apron down at the bottom, so watch you don't cut yourself. There's some tea towels in there, too. This box here on the counter has enough dishes to get you started."

"Thanks, Kate. You're a lifesaver. I'll get it all back to you as soon as we get our feet on the ground."

Kate's shoulders froze.

"Seamus didn't tell you then?" She turned to face me. "I'm selling this place. I won't be needing them."

My dismay must have shown.

"There, now, it's for the best. I've been thinking it over these last six months. I decided last week."

We sat down and Kate folded her hands. Her gaze shifted back and forth between them and me.

"This makes me feel like I've decided right, you getting a place now and needing things when I won't. I'm going to live with my sister and her husband up in Piqua. She's been after me to do it ever since Billy died, but I didn't want to take that big a step right when – right when I couldn't even make sense yet of what had happened."

The calm practicality that had been a part of her for

as long as I'd known her began to appear as she spoke.

"I thought being here in this house where I'd see reminders of Billy in every corner would be a comfort. I thought being in the place we'd been together in most of our lives would ease the pain. Now I wonder if all those reminders just kept it fresher.

"Anyway, I started trying to be broader-minded about moving in with my sis and brother-in-law. The three of us all get along. The last of their kids has moved out, so they've got more room than they need. We'd make good company for each other. And Sis and I would end up with only half as much work each."

She gave me an impish look with the last part. I squeezed her hand.

"You'd all look out for each other." And Kate wouldn't be alone. "It's a good idea. I'll miss you, though."

We sipped our tea.

"I'll take our bedroom set and some other things," Kate said abruptly. "I'm going to sell a lot of things too, but some...If you can use it, if you have room and want it, I'd give you John William's bed. It was practically brand new, it and the mattress, and I can't stand the thought of it going to strangers."

John William was their son. He'd died when he was ten or twelve. I barely remembered him.

"Oh, Kate!"

***

Seamus was watching for me when I pulled up in front of the house. He came down the front walk to meet me and we each carried one of the big boxes into the house while I talked almost as fast as Jolene about seeing Kate. Then we made a couple more trips to and fro for the toolbox and other things.

"She even sent us some dinner. It's in that basket," I said pointing. "She took it out of the oven — scalloped potatoes with onions and some bits of ham — and dished up our part into that pie plate. If we eat it now, it still ought to be warm."

Seamus chuckled. "Or, we could put the oven low and set it in there while we have a beer on the porch. One of the young fellows dropped off an ice chest with ice in it on his way to second shift. I guess his wife used to put food in it for when he and his brother went fishing, but he'd heard we didn't have an icebox, and doesn't figure he'll go fishing again till after the war, so he said we might as well use it."

I marveled at our telephone, and the overhead lights coming on when I flipped the switch, and at having a stove. Then we went out and sat on the back step and clinked our bottles of beer in a wordless toast. For a long time, we sat there side by side, each of us lost in contentment so profound we needn't express it.

"Reminds me a lot of us sitting out on the back steps at your folks' house," Seamus said finally.

"That's what I was just thinking." I hugged my arms around my knees, lost in wonder between past and present. "You reading to me before I could do it myself."

"Shelling peas together and you snitching every third one until you got a bellyache."

I hadn't realized until then how much I'd loved the simple wonders of that little backyard world, or how much I'd missed it. It made me think of Daisy and her family. They might not have shelled peas, but they'd had a home, a private place where things were ordered the way they wanted them. They'd been torn away from that. Now all they had was each other. And one of them was missing.

CHAPTER THIRTY-TWO

Unlike Seamus, I elected not to spend the night in our electrified, phone-equipped house that night. I went back to Mrs. Z's keeping my fingers crossed I'd get a half-decent night of sleep. I had a list of things a mile long to do the next day.

I started with the fire investigator, hoping to catch him before he got busy with something else. It turned out to be a less-than-wise choice.

"I'm not sure I should have told you as much as I did last time, let alone anything more," he growled.

Maybe he hadn't had coffee yet. Maybe the household ration of it had run out. Running short on coffee was one of the things I heard the most grumbling about. Whatever the reason, the man glaring at me from behind his crossed arms wasn't the amiable fellow I'd met on my first visit.

"Did anyone take you to task for talking to me?" I asked.

"Not in so many words," he said darkly.

"Well, I am sorry. I suppose you know Lieutenant Freeze and his men have another homicide to investigate at the moment. Since they have their hands full with that, and you probably know the answer to this better than they do, a pair of glasses was found at the scene. Where, exactly, were they found? And when?"

He grunted.

I held my breath.

By hitting him with the question outright, I hoped he wouldn't have time for overlong consideration of whether to answer or not. Still looking out of sorts, he rose and went to one of the file cabinets. He returned with a folder that he smacked on the desk with enough force to convey his displeasure.

With his eyes locked on mine, he sat down, opened the folder, shuffled through it, and stubbed his finger down on a diagram, all without speaking.

"There," he said, sliding the drawing toward me with the finger he'd affixed to it.

"Outside?"

"That's right. Uhhh…" He glanced back to read something else from the file. "Twenty-seven inches from the side of the building."

"Had they snagged on something?"

He shrugged. "I just know they were found there. You wanted to know when?"

"Yes, please."

"The next morning. During the first daylight search."

"There'd been searches during the night?"

"As soon as we got the fire out. Even before, making the last few rounds to be sure it was out. The men know to keep their eyes out for things that are dropped or might be important. But using artificial lights, at night, you miss things." He warmed to his subject. "There'd been confusion, too, with people from the printing plant running around trying to put out the blaze before we got there. Somewhere in there, the glasses got stepped on."

He was getting interested now.

"You think time is important?"

"Probably not. You've explained pretty well how they could have lain there all night without being noticed. I wouldn't mind knowing, though, if you have it handy, who found them."

He shuffled some papers.

"One of our men. I don't want to give you his name unless you bring me some kind of authorization saying I should."

"I don't need his name, thanks. Just curious." I stood to reassure him I was on my way out.

The fire investigator cocked his head. His earlier ill humor had largely dissipated.

"Were you thinking that if one of the employees at the printing plant had found them, it might suggest something there needed looking at more closely?"

"I expect we both like to look at everything closely. We're trying to answer the same question: Who started that fire?"

***

Maire fretted that the molasses spice bars she had done up for me might be getting a little bit stale.

"Don't worry about it," I said with a grin. "I'll just be using them to bait a mousetrap."

Her face fell.

"You're going to waste them on mice?"

"The two-legged kind. They're for buttering somebody up, so I can dig around for information I need."

"You're going to use them in your detective work?" Her eyes grew wide. The shadows under them weren't quite as dark as they'd been the last time I'd seen her. "Cookies. Who'd ever think of something like that?"

"Hopefully not the man I'm trying to snooker. Now I've got something to tell you you're not going to believe."

Over the tea she had ready, I entertained her with my venture into home ownership and how unprepared I was. While I talked and she gasped and asked questions and even giggled once or twice, a good part of my mind was on what I'd learned from the fire investigator.

What he'd told me about the glasses confirmed my belief they were part of a plan to make Tosh look guilty. Where they'd been found up so close to the building, they couldn't have fallen off in his haste to get away. They hadn't been noticed until the morning after the fire. Anyone who'd been at the printing plant that night, or the next morning, could have left them when no one was looking. Frames of wire-rimmed glasses were too thin to yield anything, but I wondered whether the cracked lenses held any fingerprints.

***

After all my careful plotting, Spooner was out when I arrived at Kirby Printing. I asked his secretary if I could leave the cookies on his desk along with a note. The secretary gushed and said of course. When I was done, I moseyed toward Kirby's office for a chat with his secretary. I was almost there when Kirby himself came out.

"Miss Sullivan," he said, and smiled. He looked more settled than he had the first time I'd met him. "Are you making progress?"

"Yes, I think so, if only by inches."

He nodded. The jitters that had plagued him were nowhere in evidence. He looked tired, but no longer numb from exhaustion and the magnitude of his loss.

"Phyllis told me you'd been here several times and had talked to lots of people."

"It's actually your secretary I was coming to see."

"I won't keep you, then. I'm sure Phyllis will take good care of you." He started on, then pivoted. "Somehow, knowing someone not connected to insurance or the war department is sifting through all this makes everything seem more manageable. I'm not entirely sure that's a good thing, since it meant my wife was able to drag me out to our bridge group last night. It did lift my spirits some, though, thinking of other things for awhile."

We exchanged a few comments more, then continued our respective ways. Phyllis Chapman raised her head from whatever she was typing away at when I entered.

"I'm afraid you've missed Mr. Kirby."

"Actually, I ran into him on the way in. It's you I've come to see."

"About?" Her coolness hadn't diminished since last time.

"Something that's come up since the first time we talked."

She folded her hands and sat perfectly straight.

"Go on."

"You told me you had no dealings with Tosh Hashimoto outside of work. I've been told you pulled up beside him one day and he jumped into your car."

A smile devoid of amusement flitted across her attractive features.

"The Fitzgerald girl. The platinum blonde. I wondered when she'd get around to telling you."

"You don't deny it, then?"

"I do not. Yes, I pulled up and asked if he wanted a

ride. Yes, he jumped into my car. It was pouring rain at the time. It seemed like the decent thing to do. And yes, we stopped at a little café and had coffee together and talked for a very long time. Did she tell you that part? Perhaps she didn't know.

"I was…hungry for conversation." Her voice broke. "Male conversation. Not flirting. Simply talking to a man. Can you understand that? I haven't had that since my fiancé died, and I miss it." Her lips pressed together as she struggled to control her emotions. "I was lonely. So there you have it." She raised her chin.

I gave her a minute, hating that I'd made her expose herself.

"I figured it would be something like that."

"You believe me?" She looked surprised.

"A lot more than I believed Mitzi Fitzgerald. I had to check. Now that I have, there's reason to think Miss Fitzgerald may have nursed some resentment against Tosh. What can you tell me about that?"

A faint line formed on her forehead.

"Resentment? I can't imagine why. I don't hear much in the way of office scuttlebutt, though. Being the boss' secretary is…isolating. When I first got promoted, I found a wall had gone up between me and the other women. Even the ones who'd been friends. They'd clam up if they were chatting and I came up. It's why I don't go to lunch with the rest of them.

"There's a lovely retiree named Ethyl who comes in three times a week to help with filing in personnel and accounting. It's usually afternoons, but it happens she's here now. She might have picked up something. I expect whatever you heard was just irritation on the part of whichever girl told you, though. Miss Fitzgerald does like to rub her attractiveness in. Now I really must get back to work."

I nodded and moved toward the door.

"It was from men, actually. Several of them," I said over my shoulder. "Miss Fitzgerald might be disappointed to know how many men are immune to her charms."

Wrists already poised, she didn't look up from her work.

"Not all men are immune. I wouldn't say anything about her to Mr. Spooner if I were you."

CHAPTER THIRTY-THREE

Luck was with me, meaning Spooner still wasn't around when I left Phyllis. Knowing he could pop up at any moment, I lost no time beating a path to the cramped little personnel office. There I introduced myself to the bustling retiree who was Ethyl.

"Oh, yes. Mrs. Kirby called me last week and said she and Mr. Kirby had every confidence in you, and that I should help in any way I could."

When I asked if she'd heard any rumors concerning Mitzi Fitzgerald and Tosh Hashimoto, her eyes twinkled.

"I don't know any particulars, but I did hear a whisper or two about him not liking the way she kept trying to get his attention. 'Having to fend off her advances' as one of them put it." She smiled in silent conspiracy. "It put a funny picture in my head, like those old silent movies where the girl tries to pull away from the oily villain, only with the roles reversed."

Using the desk chair on rollers as an improvised dolly, she wheeled a carton of file folders over to one of the cabinets.

"I hope you don't mind if I work while we talk, dear. I only come in three half-days a week."

She already was opening a drawer. The sight of her working away at a single cabinet in a row of eight or more made me realize the room where we stood wasn't as small as I had initially thought. It was the number of file cabinets that ate up space. Through the open door I saw the oldest of the proofreaders, the one who always laughed at Spooner's jokes, looking our way with interest.

"Is Velma a tattler?" I asked as I took a few steps, so I could pretend to study a wall of framed photographs that faced the file cabinets.

"Oh, not particularly. Why?" Ethyl's nimble fingers danced across the contents of the drawer in front of her.

"She's looking this way. And she always laughs her head off when Mr. Spooner cracks one of his little jokes."

Ethyl smiled as she plopped a folder into the space she'd found for it. "I think Velma just likes the attention."

"If she or anyone asks, including Mr. Spooner, I came in here to look at the record of who missed work the week leading up to the fire. You do keep something like that?"

"Of course. It's right over here."

"I don't really want to see it. What I would like is the

addresses for these three employees."

Taking the paper with the names on it from my pocket, I unfolded it and handed it to her.

Mitzi Fitzgerald

Laura Gray

Phyllis Chapman

When she came to the last one, Ethyl looked up, startled.

"That one's just for elimination purposes," I said. "Dotting my *i*'s."

The volunteer file clerk wasn't quite as trusting now.

"Is this so you can question them? Away from work?"

"That's not my intention. I just want to see where each one lives. It will give me a sense of them."

That wasn't exactly true, but it was enough to reassure her. She moved to another cabinet, opened one drawer, then opened another. In both drawers, she removed files and jotted down information. When she handed it to me, the curious proofreader no longer was watching.

"I don't like what the war's done to us," Ethyl said as I thanked her. "The war and this fire both. I don't like keeping secrets."

The only reply I could think of was to nod agreement and take my leave and hope she would stick to the story I'd asked her to.

***

A short detour on my way back to the office took me past the pleasant white bungalow where Phyllis Chapman lived with her mother and aunt. A handful of gussied-up women were just going in. The way they were chattering and laughing indicated they knew each other, and one carried a covered dish. It had the looks of some sort of club or a bridge group whose festivities were going to incorporate lunch. It didn't seem likely Phyllis could hide a man with such activity occurring, even with cooperation from her aunt and mother.

I'd take a look at the other two addresses that afternoon, after I'd picked up a sandwich and made a phone call. Mary Minerva sounded reasonably friendly when I gave my name and asked to speak to Boike.

"What's up?" he asked a minute later.

"I need the help of someone with a truck and a strong back tomorrow. I know it's asking a lot for you to use up gas on a trip into town—"

"Mary Minerva delivers plucked chickens and milk from a neighbor to a couple of little restaurants on Saturday morning. I'll make the run for her. What do you need with a truck?"

"I have an easy chair from where I'm staying and a bedstead and some other things from Billy Leary's place that I need moved to a house. They won't fit in my car."

"You elope or something?"

"No, I bought a house."

"Funny. What are you really up to?"

His reaction brought me up short.

"I'm serious, Boike. I bought a house. Granted it's small, and I came by it partly in settlement of a client's bill, but is that so hard to believe?"

"Let's say I'm having a little trouble picturing you pulling weeds. Sure, I'll help you get things from one place to another. Is nine-thirty, quarter till ten okay?"

"It's fine. Thanks, Boike."

I called Rachel Minsky to ask if she'd have one of the men from her building firm take a quick look at the house in case there were any immediate problems that needed addressing.

"Have you any idea what you're getting into?" she inquired.

"Probably not."

We'd been friends a long time, so her bluntness didn't rankle the way Boike's amusement had.

"Ah. I thought as much. How fortunate you have a construction genius like me to bail you out, then. Give me the address and we'll meet you there after work if you like."

I thanked her and shifted my attention to the sandwich on my desk. By the time I finished that, and a couple of background checks, there was just enough time to take a look at the lodgings of Mitzi Fitzgerald and Laura Gray, the proofreader who had acknowledged having coffee with Tosh a few times. They would have to be fast looks. I didn't want to incur Daisy's wrath for arriving late at the appointment she'd reluctantly made.

***

Laura's address was in a quiet neighborhood near Miami Valley Hospital. The eight-unit, brick apartment house had a linden tree in the front yard and a hedge in need of trimming between it and the neighbor on one side. From what I could see from the street, it had a back yard, probably not very deep but more generous than the strictly utilitarian strip found at many apartment places.

All in all, not a bad place for hiding someone, I thought as I made a second loop past it. People would be coming and going in the building itself — tenants, dry-cleaning deliveries, a handyman and someone cleaning the halls. The street outside had foot traffic at all hours too, since the neighborhood was prime living space for people who worked at the hospital. Still, it made a more likely spot than Phyllis Chapman's had with its arriving covey of chattering women. I ducked inside, where mailboxes were labeled with apartment numbers and last names of tenants.

Mitzi Fitzgerald, unlike the other two women, lived close to downtown. She, too, enjoyed the luxury of an apartment, but in a building larger and older than the one I'd just seen. A quick trip into the lobby with its wall of mailboxes told me units were smaller here, and nearly twice as numerous. Most were shared by two or three people. Two of the boxes had the name Fitzgerald under them, and both were shared.

Given all that I'd heard about her anger at Tosh for rebuffing her overtures, Mitzi had been an unlikely candidate for helping him evade capture. Still, I was dogged by the idea she was connected to his disappearance in ways I hadn't yet discovered.

The brief encounter between her and Spooner's son that I'd witnessed puzzled me most. She claimed he'd made a pass. Spooner had dismissed the idea Roger and Mitzi even knew each other. If the girl had managed to charm Spooner, as Phyllis Chapman suggested, would Mitzi keep quiet about his son's unwanted attentions? Possibly, if it furthered her own interests.

Or had the disagreement I'd witnessed been about something else entirely?

I was still weighing those and other possibilities when Daisy strolled into my office at four o'clock.

"Good afternoon, Miss Sullivan. How have you been?"

Her sarcastic politeness made it hard not to laugh.

"Quite well, thank you, apart from someone attacking me outside that bar where I talked to your brother's friends."

The grin she'd been hiding faded.

"Yeah, I heard about that. It wasn't me."

I chuckled. "It hadn't occurred to me that it was." I straightened up from my comfortable lounging position. "Any chance you've heard who it might have been?"

She shook her head. "I'm sorry, though. Honest. I never imagined that looking for Tosh would get…you know…" She made a vague gesture that included my defaced file cabinet. "Ugly."

"That's the nature of my work, Daisy. And talking to those men who knew Tosh actually helped me quite a bit. So, thanks."

"You learned things then?"

"A few."

"Like what?"

I gave a breath of resignation. "Let's just say I now know the names of two women he might have gone out with and one who didn't like him much."

"Who? I might recognize names, somebody he mentioned."

"You've told me repeatedly that you couldn't remember him mentioning any women by name."

"I don't!" She shifted her nose to the side and looked over my shoulder. "Hearing you say them might jog my memory."

"Nice try."

"You don't trust me."

"You're too much like me."

"That's…" She sputtered.

"That's what? An insult?" I grinned. Patting the edge of my desk with my fingertips, I stood. "I've got to go, Daisy. I know you're sore at me, but I think I'm finally starting to make progress."

In imperial silence she rose, slung her book satchel over her shoulder, and went to the door. Just before she opened it, she spun around.

"Anything you found out, I can find out, too."

CHAPTER THIRTY-FOUR

Rachel Minsky gave me some good-natured razzing.

"You may have carried the spare modern look a hair too far," she said as she took her first look at my front room with only the faded oriental rug to relieve its emptiness.

I told her grandly that furniture would arrive the following day, we had martinis with the fixings she had thoughtfully provided, right down to a small jar of olives, and the foreman from one of her construction projects inspected the roof and everything else on the place and pronounced it sound as a dollar. As a housewarming present, they left behind the ladder he'd used.

The phone rang as I was waving goodbye from the porch. It was Seamus, saying he was working late, filling in for somebody sick on the next shift. I sat on the back steps a few minutes thinking how odd and yet natural it felt to be answering the phone at my own place. Then, since I had packing to do at Mrs. Z's, I headed for Finn's to think about Spooner's son Roger while, with luck, enjoying a bowl of the Irish stew Rose made only on Fridays.

"Good thing you weren't later," she said as she set a steaming bowl of it before me at the table I favored in a back corner. "Two or three more servings and it's gone for this week."

Rose never advertised the stew, but longtime pub regulars knew to ask for it. Even without meat, it was rich and thick. I dipped a chunk of soda bread in it and tried to get my taste buds under control as I thought.

Roger's connection to his father was obvious, and possibly closer than the average father-son link. Spooner had raised him, mostly single-handed. He was the only one who could understand the boy. He'd even tried to get his son a job where he worked. Roger, in turn, went to his father's concerts. They appeared to be pals.

The link between Roger and Mitzi, on the other hand, was a puzzle. His father seemed surprised that he even knew her, yet he also acknowledged that Roger sometimes came to the printing plant. Had Roger met Mitzi in passing and misinterpreted her politeness for interest in him?

The problem with that theory was, I couldn't see Mitzi being polite.

I ate another bite of soda bread, savoring the texture of the whole grain on my tongue.

Maybe I was looking at this from the wrong angle. Maybe I should be exploring how Mitzi connected the two men. Was she manipulating one of them, or both, to win some sort of advantage with the other? Or maybe just to further her own purposes?

At work, she could be cozying up to Spooner in hopes of becoming his girlfriend, or even his wife. She'd have to be a glutton for punishment to endure his jokes at the breakfast table, but maybe she hadn't thought that far, or expected to just turn over and snooze more while he got off to work.

Let's say that was her agenda and she'd already been seeing Spooner after hours. Roger might resent it. He was a grown man, but because of his dependency on his father, he could resent sharing him as much as a kid would. Maybe more. The episode I'd witnessed on the street might have been him trying to warn her he didn't want her around his old man. It would explain why they appeared to know each other more than casually even though Spooner had been startled to hear I'd seen them together.

If Mitzi had made some attempt prior to that to win Roger over, she'd bungled it. It was the only reason I could think of that she'd want to butter him up, though. Granted, he was a good-looking fellow, but he wasn't one who could help her get ahead in the world except through his father. Unless…

I'd been slouching. I sat up.

Mitzi had, by various accounts, seethed with indignation when Tosh rebuffed her. I'd put money that she'd be happy to see him blamed for trying to burn down the place where he worked. She couldn't have started the blaze herself without being noticed, but Spooner might manage to. So, possibly, might his son.

I took quick, shallow sips of Guinness to keep pace with my thoughts.

I liked to believe Mitzi wasn't so cold-blooded as to let two innocent men die horrible deaths to achieve her ends. No one but Walt Kirby had known they would be there that night. What she could be self-centered enough to do, though, was persuade either Spooner or Roger to start the fire and make sure Tosh showed up to be blamed. But Tosh had escaped, and Seth Rowe stuck stubbornly to his account that cast doubt on the frame, so Rowe had to be silenced. And while Mitzi might not be heartless enough to sanction murder in her initial scheme, she wouldn't blink at one that became necessary to save her attractive backside.

***

When I parked at Mrs. Z's, I sat for a minute absorbing the fact that this was the last time I'd be coming home to the white house that had welcomed me for the last seven years. For some of the girls who lived there, Friday meant the work week was over. They were heading out giggling in twos or threes for picture shows or a beer or two or a USO dance.

The pleasant memories swirling around me evaporated when I opened the front door and nearly collided with the mouthy girl I'd tangled with over her loud music.

"Word is, you got kicked out as of tomorrow," she smirked.

I smiled.

"Maybe you ought to have your hearing checked. I'm moving out because I bought a house."

I sailed past her while she stood gaping. My foot was on the first step of the gleaming staircase when I heard her yell.

"Hey." She came trotting over, leaving her two companions to wait at the door. Her voice dropped. "You want a roommate? Give you a buck a week more than what we pay here."

When I was capable of uttering sound, I burst out laughing.

"I don't think the man I'll be living with would like it much." My belly was still quivering with laughter when I reached the top of the stairs.

My ruminations about the triangle presented by Spooner, his son and Mitzi had exhausted themselves for the evening. I'd recognized as much back at Finn's. There came a point, after a time of feverish ideas and connections and possibilities when my brain began to dull and refuse to go any farther along the path it was following. The packing and cleaning-up task ahead of me was just what I needed. It required organizing, but not much thinking. Things that needed doing were obvious.

Lingerie and personal items went in my suitcase, along with my blouses. For lifting furniture and carrying boxes tomorrow, I'd wear my gum soles. My other three pair of shoes went into an old pillowcase. I took the pillowcase out to the trunk of my car, and made another trip to add the clothes on hangers from my wardrobe. The suitcase and a couple of boxes could go in tomorrow before Boike came. Apart from my father's chair that would go in the truck, and two hat boxes that I could put on the passenger seat, all my worldly belongings would fit in the cavernous trunk of my smallest-of-the-line DeSoto.

CHAPTER THIRTY-FIVE

"I guess you weren't pulling my leg about getting a house." Boike slammed the tailgate of Mary Minerva's pickup closed and secured it. Using the back of his sleeve he wiped sweat from his forehead and upper lip.

"Have any concrete proof?"

He chuckled at my Freeze imitation.

"That bedstead that weighs as much as a sack of concrete."

I passed him a quart jar of water and he drank down half. We leaned against the truck, taking a breather. We'd spent much of the morning at Kate's house, part of the time over coffee and homemade cinnamon rolls she'd had waiting. Now we had to do it all in reverse at my place, minus the cinnamon rolls.

"Boike, I never imagined there'd be this much work involved," I apologized.

"Change of pace. Don't worry about it. Besides, it's the first time I've been upstairs at a girls' rooming house."

"You're kidding. With all the suspects you must have talked to over the years?"

273

He started to scratch at the healing scar on his face and caught himself.

"At regular boarding houses that have men and women both, a cat house or three, but never like your place. Those doodads on the doors, and the smell of furniture polish instead of Lysol."

"Mrs. Z was a terrific landlady."

Other than Jolene, only two other women from my early years still lived there, so last night's goodbyes hadn't taken much time. After a morning of loading a hodgepodge of furniture and other items into the pickup and thinking about where they'd go, my time at Mrs. Z's was already starting to feel like a dream.

I'd driven to Kate's in my own car, so I wouldn't have to go back for it. Waving away Boike's offer of the water jar, I slid into the DeSoto and led the way to my place. The perspiration gumming my shirt to my back had just about dissipated by the time we got there.

"Are you still looking into that fire and the Hashimoto boy disappearing?" Boike panted as we eased the iron bedstead from Kate's through my front door.

"Yeah. Is Freeze?"

"Don't know. Haven't talked in a couple of days."

"If you're still willing to toss ideas around, I'd like your opinion on a couple of things when we take a break."

He gave an indecipherable grunt. "I'm expecting a beer or two after this."

"They're on ice."

More precisely, they were on half of what remained of last night's chunk of ice and half in the very cold water left by the melted part.

Even though the bedstead was the main part of the furniture, it took most of an hour to carry in the rest. My front room still looked woefully empty with a single floor lamp and assorted boxes clustered around my dad's easy chair. In the kitchen, with two chairs and the small table borrowed from Finn's taking up floor space, we had to step over boxes.

"Nice of Mrs. Leary to send sandwiches with us, too," said Boike as we finally sat on the back steps devouring them and drinking cold beer.

"Kate's as good as they come." I squinted in sun that was still too high overhead to allow for much shade. "I didn't go see her as much as I should have, and now that she's leaving I wish I had."

Boike lounged back on his elbows.

"So, what about this business at the printing plant? What did you want my opinions on?"

"Since people seem to think he had a girlfriend, or at least was involved with a woman, I decided to follow up some on the idea we kicked around of a woman hiding him."

"I take it you've found a likely candidate for the girlfriend?"

"Not exactly. What I've managed to do is narrow it down to three possibilities, two of whom might have been cozy with him and one who, by various accounts…well, she may not have hated his guts, but she'd have been plenty happy to see him in trouble."

"Huh." Boike started on a second sandwich. "You think that one would what? Tie him up for some reason? Stash him somewhere?"

"I don't know. She's up to something, but it might not have to do with him at all." I gave a loud breath of frustration. "The thing is, I've only got a couple of things besides that left to follow. I have the addresses of all three women. I've been by them to look. One seems like it might be okay for hiding someone; one seems unlikely but maybe possible; number three, I can't see any way at all to manage at that one."

"And you want me to take a look at that one and see what I think?"

"Actually, I was hoping you'd have a look at all of them if you're willing."

"Sure. Let me have the addresses."

I went inside, stepping over boxes, and retrieved my tablet from the corner of the closet where I'd put it to ensure I had paper to write on no matter how chaotic the move became. With three addresses copied, I went outside and handed a scrap torn from the tablet to Boike. He gave it a glance and stuffed it into his pocket.

"What else did you want my bargain-basement opinion on?"

I laughed.

"You've worked on plenty more cases than I have, Boike. You're several floors above the basement on what your opinion's worth." I gathered my thoughts. "In a way, this has to do with your idea about bicycles. There's a rack of them at the place a dozen or so of the Nisei men live, by the way. They take them and bring them back as they please. That may not be important except that it started me thinking about styles of attack."

His forehead had wrinkled. I wasn't surprised. So far I wasn't explaining my reasoning very clearly.

"The man who grabbed me through the car window and tried to choke me — the one where I heard the sound that made you think of a bicycle — that was kind of basic, everyday alley fighting, right?"

"I guess. So?"

"So, for one thing, they might not necessarily have meant to kill me. On the other hand, the old night watchman who might have squelched the idea Hashimoto started the fire was killed with one hard blow to the head. Violently. Then I got jumped outside a bar where I'd been talking to some of the Nisei—"

"What?"

I waved off his look of concern.

"By someone who could just as easily have finished me off the same way, but didn't. Instead they whispered a warning and gave me a whack on the side of the neck that knocked me out.

"Add to that the vandalism at my office, and a warning there that was more like a threat. What does all that suggest?"

"That if you were smart, you might consider another line of work."

Boike drained a second beer bottle, set it aside, considered. Finally, his blond head shook.

"Beyond the fact someone doesn't like you digging at this, I don't see a pattern. The old man got killed because the killer believed he presented more of a threat than you do, that's all."

"Or how about this." I shifted to face him. "What if it was two different people? One killed Seth Rowe and ripped my office apart. Someone entirely different attacked me."

Again he considered, eyes crimped in thought.

"Maybe. So, what did the message in your office say again?"

"*Jap lovers die.*"

"And the one outside the bar?"

"'Keep your nose out.' Something like that."

"It's milder, I'll give you that."

"And after Rowe's murder. Why not 'You could be next'?"

"You have a theory?"

"I'm wondering if my attacker's purpose — both times — was protecting one of their own."

"One of the Nisei, you mean."

"Yes."

"While the warning in your office showed…"

"Hate."

Boike nodded. "Of course, the words could be a deliberate attempt to throw you off, make you suspect anyone but a Nisei."

"Hel-loo-ooo," a call from the side of the house interrupted.

The woman who came into view was skinny with rounded shoulders and exuberant white curls. Each lapel of her gray dress sported a Victory pin. Cradled against her chest was a robust, excessively green philodendron the size of a basketball.

"I'm Nora Sanford from next door. I thought I'd stop over and introduce myself and bring you a little welcoming gift. Nothing makes a house feel quite as homey as a plant does, don't you think?"

Boike made a gurgling sound. He followed the transfer of the plant from her hands to mine as if mesmerized.

"Ah, thank you. How very thoughtful." I set the plant on the steps and dusted my hand. "I'm Maggie Sullivan."

"I noticed you coming and going the last few days. I take it Mrs. Gannon decided to sell?"

She was angling to find out if I was just renting. And

now that I had recovered my balance, I admired the skill of her questioning.

"Yes, Lottie finally decided to make a permanent home with her son in California."

Despite her age, there was a lovely arch in the bones from her nose to her eyebrows. The eyes beneath it glowed with satisfaction.

"And this must be Mr. Sullivan," she said turning to Boike, who had risen politely. To her credit, though she flicked a curious look at his injuries, she didn't react.

"No, he's a friend who's been kind enough to help me move what furniture I have at this point."

"Oh." Nora waited a moment to see if more information might be forthcoming. "And the white-haired gentleman — such lovely waves he has on top — he's your father?"

"Godfather. He'll be living here, too."

"How nice. Well, I look forward to getting better acquainted with both of you. If there's anything you need while you're settling in…"

"That's very kind of you, Mrs. Sanford."

I began to walk toward the side of the house and she hadn't much choice but to toddle along toward her own house. When I saw her go up the steps there, I returned to find Boike still standing. Hands in pockets, he was staring mournfully down at my new plant.

"I feel like I've just been a witness to premeditated murder," he said.

CHAPTER THIRTY-SIX

Boike helped me move a couple of things, then said he needed to get back and do some chores for Mary Minerva. On his way out of town he would drive past the three addresses I'd given him. He promised to call that evening with his assessment.

The reality of having nowhere to put the contents of my dresser at Mrs. Z's had begun to stare me in the face when the phone rang. I heard the strain in Seamus' voice the minute he spoke.

"Seamus, what is it? What's wrong?"

"That wife of Mick's — she's killed herself. Stepped in front of a train."

I sat down hard beside the upturned crate that served as our telephone stand.

"I'm heading over there now to be with him and help with the kids," Seamus said. "Don't know when I'll be home. I'll let myself in." He hesitated. "You going to be okay, staying there by yourself the first night?"

"Sure. Fine. I...Seamus, I don't know if it's right, but if there's anything I can do..."

"I'll call if there is."

A full minute passed before I became aware of the droning dial tone and set the receiver back in the cradle. Kathleen was dead. I hadn't liked the woman. Had despised her, in fact. Yet now an unaccountable bleakness seeped into me.

Her poor, poor kids. And Mick. Based on the little I'd seen, and heard, theirs hadn't been the best of marriages, but surely it hadn't been the worst either. He must be crushed by her loss.

I leaned my head against the kitchen wall and closed my eyes. All Mick had wanted from life was a home and a family. He'd thought he'd found them, readymade. Now this. An accident would have been bad enough, but for her to take her life deliberately… Did I bear part of the blame for what he was going through now? I'd urged him to find happiness with someone else because I was too big a coward to try and give it myself.

After an interval of sitting and staring at the linoleum around me, I got up and went back to work.

***

Boike called around four o'clock that afternoon.

"I think all three of those places could be possibilities."

"All *three*?" I wasn't sure I'd heard correctly.

"Yes. I agree the small apartment house where the

Gray woman lives looks like the best bet — on the surface. But with only eight units, tenants are likely to have a sense of each other's habits, schedules, whether a neighbor's apartment is quiet during the day or has somebody at home and moving around. Things like that.

"The house where the secretary lives with her mother and aunt has an attic. Stash somebody there, and as long as they don't move around to make noise, they could go undiscovered for months as long as they had someone to slip them food. And if Mama and Auntie were persuaded to help, having groups of ladies in and out would make a fine smokescreen."

I digested it.

"Maybe. But the third one, the big apartment house, you can't seriously think someone could hide out there, someone who looked so different they'd stand out like a goat painted purple."

"Put a Western Union cap on the goat and give him a messenger bag and you might get away with it."

"What are you talking about?"

"A building with that many unit's bound to have their own maintenance man. Maybe more than one. The Nisei they brought here are filling all kinds of jobs."

I jumped onto his train of thought.

"Get a toolbox, or even a rag and a wrench, and Hashimoto could stroll right in. If anyone noticed, all he'd need to do is smile and nod and say he was going to take a look at somebody's leaky pipe."

"Something like that. Alternatively, the Fitzgerald woman you mentioned could have a roommate who's away, although I think that one's more of a stretch."

The flaw I saw in either of those was Mitzi. If she'd been as miffed by Tosh's lack of interest as people let on, why would she help him? The alternative, that she'd taken him captive and was keeping him stuffed in a closet, was even more farfetched.

"I guess it's worth talking to a few people there," I said. I nudged the potted plant from Nora Sanford with my toe.

Boike cleared his throat.

"There's not much to be learned watching from the outside there, but if you wanted, I could keep an eye on one of the other places on Monday. There'll be too much coming and going tomorrow, people heading to church and Sunday dinner and that. Too much chance of my car being noticed."

"Boy, would I ever appreciate that."

It would free me up to do something else I wanted to do — talk to occupants of the houses that looked out on the lane leading from the street to the loading door at the back of Kirby Printing, the route along which Tosh had fled the night of the fire.

***

By the time I'd found the sheets and gotten my bedroom set up, unpacked a few boxes and gone for a new chunk of ice for the ice chest, I was tired and sweaty. I took a long, long bath in my very own tub. No one knocked on the door wanting their turn. It was heaven.

Sunday, I awoke with muscles as stiff as if I'd traded punches with a couple of thugs. It was raining. After a day of dusting and cleaning with a bucket of rags and other necessities Kate had anticipated I wouldn't think of, the stiffness was gone and the contents of boxes stacked tidily in the areas where they belonged, or as tidily as they could be without furniture to hold them.

The activity mostly kept me from thinking of Connelly and his bright little stepdaughter with ears that stuck out and her younger brother, who had been just a toddler this time last year. It also gave me time to formulate a plan for getting into Mitzi's apartment building and asking some questions on Monday.

"Well. This looks a different place," Seamus said when he came in the back door Sunday evening undoing his uniform collar. Every inch of him showed weariness. The lines of his gaunt face were deeper, and sad.

Then a weak chuckle escaped him. His eyes had come to rest on the philodendron.

"A potted plant and everything."

"The woman next door brought it over." With my

head I indicated which neighbor. "Her name's Nora Sanford."

"Sharp-nosed woman?" He lowered himself into one of the kitchen chairs with a sigh he couldn't suppress. "Been sweeping her porch a lot. Front and back both."

"Want a beer?"

"No beer, but tea would go down good."

Water was already heating in the small saucepan. The larger one held potatoes boiling in their jackets, which were the only thing I could make besides scrambled eggs and toast.

"No milk," I said. "We need a ration book. I'll sign up for one Tuesday. Tomorrow Jolene's dad is supposed to drop off some things when he's done at the market, so I need to be here, and the rest of the time I've got legwork to do on my case."

"That's fine. Don't you think that plant ought to be where it gets some sun?"

"It'll get some tomorrow in my car. It's going to earn its keep."

CHAPTER THIRTY-SEVEN

Monday morning, I watched from a coffee shop across the street as Mitzi Fitzgerald's apartment building emptied of workers. Mitzi's hair was light enough to stand out when she appeared in a cluster of other girls. As soon as she was past where she could see me, I hurried out. Keeping far enough back she wasn't likely to notice me if she looked around, I followed until she joined the line at a bus stop and boarded a bus. Then I went back to my car and retrieved the philodendron.

"Trust me," I told it. "The odds you'll survive are better this way."

I tried the manager's bell at the building on Wilkinson. When he buzzed me in and came out to meet me, I waltzed through the door with my arms wrapped around the potted plant like a dancing partner.

"What do you need?" The manager wore a tan cardigan accessorized by carpet slippers with a bunion pushing through the left one.

"I promised Mitzi Fitzgerald I'd bring her a plant,

but I don't know which number she is."

"Mitzi. Real light hair? That shade of blonde people call whatchamacallit? Platinum."

"That's her."

"She's not here. Saw her head out for work a few minutes ago. I'll take it up and put it by her door."

He reached for the plant. I drew it protectively toward me.

"I wouldn't *dream* of letting a poor plant sit in a hallway all day! Besides, Mitzi was very insistent about wanting me to place it where it would be happiest."

The manager stared. Men are quicker to think a woman's flighty than to think she's smart. If they think she's flighty, it doesn't cross their mind that she could be up to something. I smiled.

"Maybe you could go in with me and wait while I found the right spot. It wouldn't take two minutes, I promise."

"Look, lady, her roommate just came in from her work. She saw Fitzgerald and tossed her a package of gum, which is why I noticed them. The poor gal probably just put her head on a pillow. I'm not going to bother her. Sorry."

I pressed my lips together in thought, then leaned in.

"Couldn't one of those nice Japanese-American men you have working here go up and let me in? I understand they're very quiet and *very* polite. I'd tiptoe, too."

His expression now questioned my sanity.

"We don't have any Japs working here, or living here either. If I saw one I'd run, and then call the police. Or maybe the FBI. Now, do you want to leave the plant or not?"

I sniffed and nuzzled the plant.

"I most certainly do not! I'm having second thoughts about letting Mitzi have a plant if she lives in a place this unfriendly."

***

Five minutes later the plant was in my passenger seat and I was starting the DeSoto.

"Maybe it's for the best," I told the unresponsive clump of green. "Our neighbor's bound to come over and we'll end up letting her in one time or another. She'll ask where you are if she doesn't see you."

Seamus might remember to water the plant. Seamus was patient.

Meanwhile, it probably wouldn't do its innocent leaves any good to go up to my office while I did forty-five minutes or so of work. The dried-up brown specimen in the corner wasn't exactly reassuring, and for all I knew had succumbed to some sort of disease instead of neglect.

I had just about finished the tasks on my desk when the telephone rang.

"Meet me at your house at noon," said Rachel. "It's urgent."

"Rachel—"

"Urgent."

Rachel and her entire family seemed to think they owed me a lifetime of favors because I'd gotten her out of a very tight spot. I didn't see it that way, but for her to use a demanding tone surprised me. It must be important.

"Okay, I'll be there."

"I'll bring sandwiches."

She hung up.

That would cut into my time for talking to people living in houses along the lane Tosh had run through the night of the fire. Nevertheless, I managed to cover four of the six houses on the north side. At one a woman told me her brother and three nieces were all out working. Her brother and one of the girls had been the only ones awake. I'd have to come back. A bleary-eyed man at another house said he had worked until midnight and the rest of the household had all been asleep. Residents of the other two places had still been awake or had been awakened by the commotion, but no matter how I probed they didn't remember anything useful. When I asked outright if they'd noticed anyone standing in the lane and looking at the blaze, the answer was a definite No.

I was running out of possibilities, however slim.

***

"You look glum." Rachel sauntered to meet me as I got out of my car.

A van with the words Used Furniture on it was parked behind her Buick.

"Rachel, what—?"

"Unlock, please." She made an impatient gesture. "They haven't got all day."

Two men had hopped out of the van and were lifting down a small Frigidaire.

"Rachel, I can't—"

"Mama and the girls wanted to give you service for four in sterling. Be glad I talked them into something practical."

The "girls" were her sisters-in-law.

"It's a used one," she continued before I could speak. "Used a great deal more than I would have liked, but as you may have heard, appliances are hard to come by. So, don't be an ingrate."

"Rache, I don't know what to say."

"'Thank you, Rache. I love the color,' will suffice."

I laughed. Like every other Frigidaire I'd ever seen, it was white.

"Consider it said."

The delivery men maneuvered it deftly through my front door. We followed it into the kitchen.

"And thank you a hundred times over."

"My motives were selfish. You'd be utterly useless to

me if you came down with ptomaine, which you were sure to with that." She snatched the ice chest away from the patch of worn linoleum which marked the spot of a previous fridge. "Then who would I laugh with over a drink?"

With a speed which left me lightheaded, the men positioned the Frigidaire, plugged it in, listened for the hum that indicated it was working, and left accompanied by a wave from Rachel. Like that, Seamus and I had a working kitchen.

I brought in the plant and she got the sandwiches, sliced tongue on rye with horseradish mustard and a big dill pickle.

"I don't suppose you'd care to trade jobs for the afternoon," Rachel said as we settled in at my borrowed kitchen table.

"Come to think of it, you might be better than I am at shaking loose information from people who may not have any."

"Yes, but I doubt you'd do the Outraged Boss Firing Someone Who Begs For Another Chance nearly as well as I do."

"You're going back to fire someone?"

"Yes, and a foreman, too, damn his eyes. I could strangle him."

"Doesn't sound as if there'll be much acting involved. What did he do?"

"Siphoned gas from two of the trucks, the idiot, so he could ride around with his new girlfriend. It's been going on for over a month. Didn't it occur to him I might keep tabs of how much each vehicle uses each week and notice a jump with no explanation? What possesses a hitherto trustworthy middle-aged man to do something so stupid?"

"Suddenly finding himself a prized commodity with so many younger men gone off to war?"

Something fluttered at the back of my mind. Spooner Senior and Mitzi? No...not that, but...Whatever it was had to do with what Rachel had said.

"I take it you're not going to give him that second chance?"

"He had one, some years back. I shouldn't have been soft then."

CHAPTER THIRTY-EIGHT

That afternoon I got proof of what I'd long suspected: the work I did didn't lend itself to having a home life. I talked to people in the other houses north of the lane behind Kirby Printing. Then I went through the same routine and questions at houses on the opposite side. My failure to come across even a crumb of anything new was identical to that morning.

The cops, it was no surprise to learn, had done a thorough job.

They also had questioned occupants of the three houses facing the mouth of the lane, the place where anyone running out that way would turn onto the street. Since not much time remained before I had to return to my own house to meet Jolene's dad, I decided to put the dwellings facing the lane off until later. Instead, I could make fast visits where the police hadn't been — the two that flanked the lane but faced away from it toward the street.

Most likely the cops hadn't tried them because a big sycamore in the back yard of one blocked the view of the alley, while a high board fence and a utility pole interfered on the other. Even if a resident of one or the other had been coming in from a night shift or was getting a drink of water at exactly the right time, they would have a clear view of only a small wedge of the lane.

When I reached the porch of the one with the fence, I found it had been converted from a dwelling into a series of small offices. Tenants included three doctors, a real estate agent, an insurance office, a lawyer and a stenography service. It seemed unlikely any of those would be working at the time of night I was interested in, so I moved on to the one with the big tree.

A rumpled old fellow with wild white eyebrows and navy suspenders stepped out onto the wide front porch when I rang the doorbell. He held a *National Geographic* as if he might swat me with it if I got annoying.

"Hi, I'm Maggie Sullivan." I gave him a smile. "I know the police have probably already talked to you, but I'd like to ask some follow-up questions about that fire they had at the printing plant a few weeks ago. Can you spare a few minutes?"

"Is this to do with insurance or something?"

"Not insurance. Some of the people involved hired me to get a better picture of exactly what happened." I extended a business card.

"Private detective. Huh." He stuck the card in his magazine and gave me a good look. "Can't say I like the idea of getting mixed up in other people's business, but I guess there's civic duty and that. No, the police never talked to us, and I don't know what I can tell you, but you might as well come in."

He started to open the door behind him. "Unless you'd rather sit out here. It's quieter. The wife and I watch our two grandkids while our daughter works. Little wild Indians those two are."

Through the partly open door I heard shrieks.

"Out here's fine."

With his rolled-up magazine, the man of the house indicated a pair of wicker chairs. The porch was covered, with a railing around it. Even without screaming kids to avoid, it made for a pleasant spot.

"Were you up when the fire happened?" I asked curiously. His comment about civic duty and other things in his manner suggested he had been, and that he might have seen something.

"I was." He grunted slightly as we sat in the chairs. "I like a cigar in the evening, before I head up to bed, usually. The wife doesn't like me smoking them inside with us keeping the boys every day now. One has asthma and she claims smoke makes it worse."

"You were out here?"

My interest quickened. The chairs where we sat had their backs toward the printing plant, and from this vantage point only the entrance to the lane was visible. He could have seen whoever ran out though, and possibly what became of them.

"Sitting right where I am now," he affirmed. "Even without a cigar, I like to come out for awhile once the weather gets warm. Sit in the dark, watch the cars go by. People too, now and then. It's relaxing, the dark and the silence. Lets my brain empty out. And sometimes there's entertainment too — a woman begging her dog to do his business so they can go in, a lovers' spat — nothing very big."

I nodded encouragement.

"And that night?"

He squinted at the street. I knew he was picturing it again in his mind.

"This young fellow came along whistling, not a care in the world. I couldn't see his features or anything, just that he had a cowlick, the kind you can't help but see."

At his mention of whistling, my breathing had slowed. When he got to the cowlick, I had to remind my lungs to function.

"Go on."

"Well, he turned in that little service road." He indicated the lane to Kirby Printing. "I couldn't see him after that, but I could still hear him whistling. It wasn't ordinary whistling, it had flourishes and sometimes it seemed like two notes at once — really worth hearing. Anyway, that went on for a little. Then all at once it stopped. A minute later — and I mean it wasn't much longer than that — he came tearing back out like the devil himself was at his heels."

The man gave a nod of conclusion. His story was over.

"That's all I know about it. Like I told you, it doesn't amount to much. The only reason I noticed that young fellow was his whistling, that and how happy-go-lucky he seemed going in and how scared he was when he came out.

"Then I started to hear people yelling. I went out in the yard to see what the commotion was, and I saw the flames. Then a fire engine came, and I watched for a while, but it looked like they got it under control pretty fast, so I went to bed."

I glanced at my watch. I had to get going.

"I do wish the wife had been awake to hear that whistling, though. It was one of those show tunes she's so fond of."

On the edge of the wicker chair, haunches tensed to rise, I froze.

"You recognized the tune?"

"Well, yes, but not exactly. It was from some picture show she dragged me to. Not that long ago, either. But danged if I can remember the name of the picture, or the song either. Real nice though."

***

Miraculously, I didn't get stopped for speeding on my way to the little house that was now my home. It wasn't worry that Jolene's dad might have to wait that drove me. It was a hunch, one that I needed to talk to Daisy about in order to confirm. With luck I might squeeze in a phone call to her before Cecil Fields arrived on his way home from the produce market.

"Daisy's not home yet," said the woman whose family had opened their home to the Hashimotos. "My bunch just came in, and she's usually at least half an hour later."

I hoped the frustrating young woman hadn't taken it into her head to pay one of her unannounced visits to my office in spite of my talk about making appointments. Rapid knocking rattled my front door.

"Could you please have her call me as soon as she gets in?" I reeled off the number.

The knocking sounded again.

"It's open," I yelled as I hung up the phone.

Jolene came in beaming with a stack of fabric overflowing her arms.

"You're going to love the curtains Mom made, Maggie. Oh, look! They're going to match your rug too. This is a cute place. I guess I'd better put these in that chair, huh? Since it's either that or the floor."

Her father came in after her, grinning. Cecil, whom I'd met a few times at the market, was slim with a face roughened by working outside and twinkling blue eyes that seemed to acknowledge his daughter's eternal fountain of words. He handed me a peck basket filled with jars of tomatoes, green beans and jams. He introduced a brawny man beside him as his neighbor.

"I needed to bring my bigger truck because of the furniture. It left plenty of room for what he brings to market, along with mine, so he saved some gas and I get help carrying."

The first item they brought in was a big old wooden kitchen cupboard, the kind where you stored plates and cups in the top of it, with a work or storage surface under that and more storage at the bottom. It took up the entire free wall in the kitchen. While it made that small space snugger still, it would hold most of the dishes and kitchen equipment now in boxes.

"It was out on the screen porch with the daybed, and just had card games and stuff tossed into it," Jolene narrated. "Mom said if you didn't have furniture it would come in handy. She scrubbed it up good, but it probably got all dusty coming into town."

After two trips with light things — two table lamps from her family's attic; a wooden chair with no back, which Jolene said could fill in as a handy little table; and what looked like a brand-new quilt — the men brought in the daybed Jolene had promised.

"I didn't realize so much of the paint was worn off," she lamented as her father and his neighbor sat at the kitchen table drinking cool water from the pitcher I'd put in my new refrigerator before I left. "And those flowery cushions don't go that well with the curtains and rug…"

I assured her they were fine. Half my mind was still

back on my conversation with the old gent who had heard Tosh whistling. *"From some picture show,"* he'd said. Did that tell me the name of the woman Tosh had been seeing? Was Daisy home yet? Would she even know the answer?

"Maggie? Are you okay?"

"Yeah. Fine. I'm just…overwhelmed by all the stuff you've brought me."

I was, too. My modest investment in her family's honey business had gotten me started on furnishings faster than I could have found things, and they were already in place. A bushel basket with fresh produce and a dozen eggs, plus a loaf of freshly baked bread, had joined the jars that came in earlier.

"If you want a ride partway to your place, we'd better get going," Cecil said to his daughter as he and his neighbor came into the front room.

"Cows to milk when he gets back," Jolene explained.

Thanking them several times, I waved them off from the door. Then I made a beeline back to the kitchen and called Daisy's number.

"I was just getting ready to call you," she said when she answered. "What's going on?"

"I need to ask you a question. You said something about Tosh whistling a tune so much it drove you crazy. I think you said it was new."

"Yeah. From a movie he'd liked."

"Do you happen to know the name of the tune?"

"Sure. *'Laura.'* Why?" She sucked in her breath.

"Wait a minute. Was he whistling it because it was *her* name? The woman he'd been trading notes with? It is, isn't it? What's—?"

"Thanks, Daisy." I hung up softly.

CHAPTER THIRTY-NINE

Boike and I had flipped a coin, metaphorically speaking, and it had landed on the wrong side. He'd spent all day watching the wrong house. With a hasty look around the kitchen to see if there was anything that needed to go into the refrigerator, I grabbed my keys and headed out.

When I got to the street where the head secretary at Kirby Printing lived with her mother and aunt, Mary Minerva's truck was nowhere in sight. I was on the verge of leaving, and hoping my volunteer helper had for some reason decided to watch Laura's place instead, when I noticed a blunt head sitting behind the wheel of a car across the street. I pulled close enough to talk. Boike rolled his window down.

"It's the wrong house, Boike. I've wasted your time. I'm sorry."

He shrugged.

"We knew going in that it was a tossup. You must have turned up something on your house-to-house, huh?"

"Yeah, and then got confirmation from the little

sister. Let me buy you a beer somewhere to make up for wasting your day."

We agreed on a spot that was on his way back to Mary Minerva's. Boike wanted to hear how I'd come to conclude that Laura was the woman to be hiding Tosh, if that was, in fact, the way he had managed to disappear so quickly and thoroughly. Boike shook his head when I explained how the old man's mention of movie themes had made my mind scurry through shows that had been popular lately and click on one that made sense.

"I wouldn't have made that jump," he said.

"You've been away. And I don't imagine you got to see a lot of movies when you were working with Freeze. Where'd you borrow the car?"

"It's mine. I left it with my folks while I was away. Technically I still live there, and since they're a fair piece out and I have medical appointments to keep, the rationing board said I could have it."

His windshield had an A gas sticker, I'd noticed, the same lowly category I was in.

"What time does the other woman — Laura Gray, is it — leave for work?" Boike asked.

"A quarter of eight or thereabouts, I'd guess. But since we've zeroed in on the one to watch, I can keep an eye on her myself now."

"Not on her and her place at the same time. Don't you have other leads you want to check?"

"Well, yes, but…"

"You get here in time to follow her leaving for work. I'll be here by a quarter past. Once she's at the printing plant, you can follow up on other things until it's time for her to clock out. Tail her home and you can take over sitting outside her apartment house for however long you want. This is different from watching a place to see who goes in and out. If I don't see activity in the lady's apartment while she's at work, and nothing catches your eye after a couple of hours, chances are Hashimoto's not in there."

"Boike, are you sure you want to spend another day on this? A bottle of beer isn't much of a salary."

"It's another day I can put off deciding what kind of real job I want to apply for, though."

He was missing police work. I thought about it all the way home. Why couldn't he and Freeze work out some kind of agreement?

It was too late to follow Laura home from work today to see if she made any odd stops along the way. I could sit and watch her place tonight to see if anything happened. What could I expect to see, though? Silhouettes on the shade? Two people where there should be only one? With curtains lined in black these days, there wouldn't be any silhouettes. Besides, both Laura and Tosh were smart enough to stay well away from windows.

I opened the front door and called out that it was

me. When Seamus yelled that he was in the kitchen, I realized how relieved I was to catch him at home, even if he went out again. I wanted to hear how Mick Connelly was doing, and to see how much of a toll helping out there on top of work was taking on Seamus.

His expression when I entered the kitchen wasn't one of weariness, however. It was one of utter bewilderment. Standing in the middle of the floor he looked from me to the newly arrived refrigerator to the big wooden cupboard to the fresh potatoes and spinach, eggs, jars of jam, and homemade bread.

"Maggie, what on earth happened to this kitchen?"

***

I missed having a morning paper to read over breakfast. I missed having Heebs around to sell it to me. When was some Army mook going to wise up to the fact the kid wasn't as old as he claimed and send him home, I wondered as I finished an egg and toast at my own kitchen table. Even without the paper, my new situation beat breakfast at McCrory's lunch counter.

Seamus had already left for work. He'd gone over to Connelly's for a few hours the previous night, and his report on Mick and the kids was pretty much what I'd expected. The little boy was taking his mother's death especially hard, Seamus said. I cleared the table and washed the skillet. Thanks to Boike, I now had most of a day for detecting.

Once I'd followed Laura to the printing plant and watched her go in, I headed to the neighborhood around the school where Spooner and the barbershop group had performed the night of Seth Rowe's murder. The school's tidy system of tracking whether any cars left and then returned had done away with my theory that Roger Spooner might have slipped out to kill Rowe. He couldn't have used his father's car. You didn't catch a trolley to a murder scene. The distance he'd need to cover was too great to get back in time to be seen at refreshments.

Rachel Minsky's frustration yesterday over siphoned gas had given me another idea. I trudged to houses on one side of the school, then on the other. Waving the clipboard I kept in my car, I blathered about a study of vehicle security.

"Car theft! Mercy me, no!" gasped a woman in pin curls who answered the door six houses away from the school. "Word about that would certainly get around, too. We're a very close neighborhood."

She started to close the door. I leaned against the jamb with a pasted-on smile so she couldn't. Given my years of experience talking with strangers while I stood on their doorsteps, I should take up peddling encyclopedias.

"Well, not theft precisely, just joyriding. Has

anyone's car been taken and brought back? Or gas siphoned off?"

"Goodness no. This isn't some railroad neighborhood. Mrs. Murphy with the blue roof went around saying her car was moved while it sat in the garage, if you can believe it, but the way she rattles on, nothing she says is worth two cents."

I thanked her and made my way three doors up to a house with a blueish-green roof. A fiftyish woman in trousers and clip-on earrings like clumps of grapes opened the door. At her heels, a fat little dog with a caved-in face started barking the minute it saw me and kept it up throughout our ensuing conversation.

"I understand you believe your car was used recently without your permission. Would you mind telling me more about it?"

She broke into a smile.

"You're the first to show any interest at *all*. Won't you come in, Miss—?"

"Sullivan. Maggie Sullivan." I offered my hand.

"Are you with the police? They sent a young fellow out, but he just scratched his head and asked a few questions and left. I don't think he believed me."

"Actually, I'm a private detective." I gave her a card. "I'd like to keep that between the two of us, though, if you've no objection. I told your neighbors I'm collecting information related to vehicle safety across the city."

"Goodness!" She stared at my card with delight. "Well, mum's the word, then. Hush, Chipper. Be a good dog."

The mutt had possibly barked himself deaf since he only barked louder. At his owner's invitation, I perched on a chair.

"I'd gone to a concert down at the school — walked, of course. That's one of the lovely things about this neighborhood, the programs they have down there. The next morning, when I realized someone had taken the car, I worked out that might have been when they took it. Of course, it could have been any time that night they took it. I just know that next morning when I went out to use it, it was obvious someone else had as well."

I phrased my next question carefully so she wouldn't misconstrue it as doubting her.

"What made it obvious?"

She looked at me as though I were dim.

"Why, my logbook, of course."

"What?" I raised my voice to make sure she heard me. My left ear was starting to ache.

"My logbook. I keep a little notebook and pencil stub in my purse. If I drive somewhere, I jot down the date when I set out. When I come back, if I'm not going to use the car again that day, I jot down the mileage on that thingamabob on the dashboard. It helps me keep an eye on how much I'm driving, and whether I might use up my gas ration. When I opened my notebook that morning, the miles I'd written down the day before were lower than the ones on the dashboard."

CHAPTER FORTY

My fingers got a workout typing up pertinent information from the past twenty-four hours. Yesterday there'd been the hitherto unknown observer who'd noticed the whistling man. This morning brought Mrs. Murphy with her wonderful notations on dates and mileage. The latter didn't prove it was Roger Spooner who took her car. It did, however, strengthen my theory on leaving the concert and coming back. Freeze might need more convincing.

Signing up for my first ration book used a chunk of the afternoon. By the time I managed to use it on coffee and a few other items, it was time for Laura Gray to get off work.

It had started to rain, which made it tricky to spot her amid the umbrellas being unfurled by workers leaving the printing plant. She opened hers, and Velma, the gray-haired proofreader who giggled at the drop of a hat, trotted up to hold it over both of them while Laura put on a headscarf. The scarf had splotches of red on the back which made it easier to keep track of the two women as they hurried through the rain and boarded the trolley together.

Half a dozen blocks later, Laura got off alone. She dashed into a door marked Dry Cleaners and Laundry, emerging with a bundle of clean laundry clutched to her chest. After two more trolleys and stops at a butcher shop and a magazine stand, she got off near her house and started to walk. I let out a breath of relief.

The rain that at times had made it hard to spot the bright pattern on her scarf was slowing now. It became a steady drizzle. I turned into an alley and made a quick circuit that brought me out on the opposite side of the street, a short distance away from the front of Laura's apartment house. Up ahead, she was bobbing toward me, her various purchases stowed in a canvas shopping bag.

I scanned both sides of the street for Boike's car, then realized as I passed it that Mary Minerva's truck sat at the curb. A car was parked in front of it, but the space in front of that was free. I pulled in. My rearview mirror, above the roof of the car between us, showed Boike's distinctive shape in the cab of the pickup. As soon as Laura nudged her way through the apartment house door, I left the DeSoto and hurried over to join him. He opened the door.

"You're drenched," I said as I slid in, shaking off rain myself.

With a nod, he tossed me a towel so wet that

wringing it out seemed more practical than using it.

"I didn't want to give up my spot where I could watch front and back both." He tipped his head in the general direction of Laura's apartment. "There's somebody in there, all right. A man. He's smart enough to stay away from the windows, but he has to use the can now and then. That room has a window shade that stays down all the time. There's nothing covering the window over the kitchen sink, though. You can see through it into a hallway or room they have to pass through to answer a call of nature. I've caught glimpses of him there, going back and forth."

"It probably never occurred to him — them — that they could be seen there."

"Or that anyone would be watching."

I twisted and looked back, attempting to see what he was describing.

"You'd have to be closer than you are here in the truck. How'd you manage that?"

"Hedge trimming."

"Hedge trimming?"

I looked back again. The first time I came here the hedge between the apartment house and its neighbor had been shaggy and overgrown. Now it was neat, and two feet lower.

"Sitting here all day, even in a car, risked attracting attention. When I got here this morning the truck was all loaded up with tools and a wheelbarrow. I went right to the manager's apartment, gave him a spiel about being a newly returned vet trying to start a lawn care business. When I got to the part about doing the hedge for free in return for a letter of recommendation, he just about danced."

"And you think the man you saw in there was Tosh?"

"All I could make out was dark hair. But having it turn out to be someone else would be mighty coincidental. "So. Shall we go in?"

"Just me. If it is Tosh, he'll be less likely to clam up. Two people would make him feel threatened the minute he saw us."

"No."

"He's not dangerous."

"He's cornered. You don't know what he'll do."

"I'm armed. I doubt he is."

"You're not thinking of trying to keep this from Freeze if it is Hashimoto, are you? I couldn't do that."

"If it is Tosh, I'll call Freeze myself. Just give me ten minutes. Then you can come up and see for yourself one way or another. Meanwhile, having you down here is insurance he won't get away if he decides to make a run for it."

After a long minute of hesitation, Boike nodded.

***

I added my partially closed umbrella to others in a rubber tray in the lobby of the apartment house. Shaking at least some of the raindrops from my coat and hair, I climbed the stairs to Laura's apartment. There was no response to my knock.

"Laura?"

I tried again. Just as I was wondering if I'd need to knock a third time, the poised brunette proofreader opened the door enough for us to see each other.

"Yes? Oh…What do you want?"

I gave a smile I hoped would reassure her.

"It takes a bit of explaining. May I come in?"

"I suppose."

It wasn't the warmest welcome I'd ever received. On the other hand, she wasn't quaking with nervousness. She'd removed her wet shoes. The seams she'd painted on her legs to look like stockings were smudged from the rain. That and her bare feet made her look vulnerable. With the same reserve she'd displayed in the workplace, she crossed her arms.

"Well? Why are you here?"

"To talk to Tosh Hashimoto."

She gave a breathless laugh. "You're mad. You expect to find him here just because we had coffee together a couple of times and went to a movie?"

"No, because you were more than that. Enough more that he drove his kid sister crazy whistling the same tune over and over, one with a title the same as your name, *Laura*."

"That's—"

"Look, I happen to think Tosh is innocent. I have the evidence to prove it, except for some bits about what happened that night that only he can provide. Otherwise, he's a handy scapegoat, for whoever set the fire and for the police. A witness who thought Tosh might have been running in to help that night, not running away, has already been killed. I'm his best hope for getting a fair shake."

Eyes clamped closed, and paler of face, she was shaking her head.

"He's not here."

"Yes, I am."

From the back part of the hallway separating the living room from the rest of the apartment, a man I'd seen only in photographs stepped into view. Tall and good-looking, with black-rimmed glasses, it was Tosh Hashimoto. He caught Laura's hand as she turned to him with her poise collapsing. He gave her knuckles a kiss.

"It's no use, Laura. I've put you through enough."

His other hand brushed her cheek, where tears were starting to slide. He drew a breath of resolve, then turned to me.

"What is it you want me to do?"

"I want you to tell me about that night."

Tosh sank down on the couch, with Laura beside him. Removing my wet coat, I folded it inside out and sat down across from them. His voice was calm.

"Not long after I got home from work, Gene Spooner called. He said they'd hired a new night-shift proofreader who had experience but needed someone to spend a couple of hours going through how our particular system went — where to find things, where to put things, a few stylistic peculiarities of military usage. He wanted to know if I'd come in at ten that night and run through it so one of the regulars on the night shift didn't have to stop work to do it. I said of course."

"And you're sure it was Spooner who called? You recognized his voice?"

"Ah. Sorry. I should have been more precise. It was actually Spooner's secretary who called. Miss...uh..."

"That's okay. I don't know her name either."

"And no, I couldn't say if it was really her, just that it was a woman. I realized afterward that I'd been snookered. At least I believe that's what happened."

"Could the voice on the phone have been Mitzi Fitzgerald?"

"Mitzi?" The question startled him. "The predatory little blonde?"

I nodded.

"But why—?"

"I'm not sure."

He rumpled his hair with both hands. The result was a patch that stood straight up.

"So, you were going in the back way," I prompted.

"That's right. The woman who called said I should, that the front would be locked. I didn't mind. It was a nice night, and I was in a good mood. The day before I'd asked Laura to marry me, after the war when things aren't as…complicated, and she'd said she would. I was still on Cloud Nine."

He sent her a fleeting smile.

"When I was almost there, maybe thirty feet from the door, I heard a sound. A *whump* like when you put a match to a stove burner. And then…I don't know how to describe it. Flames as tall as my shoulders all across the back there. I heard someone yell…shriek.

"I remembered I'd seen a hose somewhere back there, and I started to run, thinking maybe I could do something. I didn't get very far before I realized I couldn't see in anymore…."

When he'd stopped with his arm up.

"Right then, in what seemed like a single second — I don't think I was actually conscious of any one of them — all these things hit me at once. That someone was yelling at me. Saying 'Stop!' Running toward me. That I was there, right outside where a bad fire had started." He swallowed. "That looking Japanese, never mind where I was born, was enough to make me guilty in the eyes of lots of people."

Rain spattered into the silence that followed his words.

"So, you turned and ran."

"Like a fool. Like a coward," he said bitterly.

"You were scared."

"And made myself look even worse. I see that now. By the time I'd run a few blocks I started to realize it, but I didn't know what to do. If I went to the police, were they going to believe me? What if they locked me away somewhere and didn't let my family know? Because of the war, I thought they probably could.

"I didn't want to go to my parents, or any of the fellows I lived with, or the Church Federation. It might make them look involved. I-I thought of the one person who might take me in, the one the police, if they started hunting for me, would have no reason to contact."

"Laura."

He nodded. "I called her from a pay phone. I told her I'd understand if she said No. I only meant it to be for a couple of days—"

"I wanted him safe!" she cut in. "This was the only way. And they did hunt for him, and then you started, too."

"His family's frantic. They don't even know if he's dead or alive." I gave Tosh a wry look. "And your sister doesn't take No for an answer."

He chuckled despite the worry lines etched on his face.

"No, she doesn't. So, what now?"

A glance at my watch told me it was almost time for Boike to make an appearance.

"Now I call the police — a man I know, a

detective." I'd already spotted the phone on a stand next to the short hall that gave access to kitchen and bath. "I'll stay with you when they arrive. There won't be any rough stuff. I'll follow you to the station and make sure your parents and the Church Federation know where you are."

I picked up the phone.

"There's a policeman — ex-policeman — in the back yard," I told the pair on the couch. "He said I could have ten minutes with you before he came up. Don't panic when he gets here. He's a good guy."

Tosh swallowed and nodded. I dialed. To my relief, Freeze was still there. I didn't have a plan for if he wasn't.

"It's Maggie," I said. "I'm with Tosh Hashimoto."

"Where are you?"

"First, I need your guarantee no weapons will be drawn. He's unarmed. He won't resist."

"Tell me NOW before I charge you with impeding a police investigation!"

"Do I have your word?"

"Okay, fine. No weapons unless he presents a threat."

It was the best I'd get. I gave him the address.

"One other thing," I said as I turned. "You took a pair of glasses to work with you one day. Why?"

The question clearly puzzled him.

"To see if one of the Linotype operators could use the frames. She'd broken hers."

"Did she take them?"

"I don't know." He was frowning now. "She said she didn't want them, so I put them in these cubbyholes we had for stowing our lunches and that. They disappeared."

I nodded.

"I'll let you have a minute alone to say your goodbyes." It would be their last time together before life tore them apart, maybe for good.

Bypassing the kitchen that had afforded Boike his view, I went into the bathroom that had a small window facing the back yard as well as one on the side. Rain had brought darkness early. When I raised the shade to get a look at the back yard, objects were only shapes against a lighter gray. Boike's blocky form already was moving toward the back door.

As I watched, another figure burst from a clump of bushes beyond the hedge at the side of the house. He grabbed Boike from behind. Boike swung and spun. The attacker's arm shot up, descending with lightning speed. Boike fell, motionless.

CHAPTER FORTY-ONE

"Back door?" I shouted as I burst into the living room.

"Right and straight." Laura pointed.

The apartment door banged as I flung it open, heedless of someone else going the opposite way behind me. I slid down the stairs. By the time I jerked the building's rear door open, my Smith & Wesson was in my hand. I ran.

"Boike!" I dropped to my knees. He still had a pulse.

"Go!" he said thickly. He gestured.

Between the hedge and the side of the building a figure was fleeing. He glanced back. His arms and legs pumped. I tried to close the gap between us and slipped on the wet grass. Rain was soaking me. Boike's attacker disappeared around the corner of the apartment building.

Even as I regained my feet, I heard an ear-splitting squeal, one which would have been a scream if it hadn't been so distressed. Disregarding safety, I plunged around the corner without checking to see what lay in wait. The man I was after leaped over a female form that lay sobbing. He ran down the street.

I pursued him half a dozen steps, then slowed. I'd never catch him, and I didn't dare let off a shot in near darkness, in an area given to foot traffic. Behind me, steps that were none too steady approached as Boike caught up.

"No use," he puffed. He bent over to catch his breath. "Too much of a lead."

"You okay?"

"Yeah."

I dropped to my knees by the sobbing woman.

"Daisy?" I said in disbelief.

She lay curled in a fetal position, and drew her knees tighter at the sound of my voice. I tried to help her sit. She resisted.

"He punched me," she sobbed. "Tosh punched me." She cradled her jaw in her hand.

"It wasn't Tosh who punched you, sweetheart. I don't know who it was, but it wasn't Tosh."

She let me ease her upright.

"But I heard him! I followed you, and I heard him up there! Then you yelled something about the back door, and I knew you were coming out, and I didn't want you to see me, so I ran out the front. He came out right behind me, and when I heard him and turned, he hit me in the chin — hard! Then he knocked me..." Her last word was lost in a hiccuping sob.

"It wasn't Tosh," I repeated. "It was somebody else who was in the back yard."

"Who is she?" Boike had joined us.

"His kid sister."

"Hashimoto's?"

"Yes."

A car screeched to the curb and the doors flew open. Daisy shook off my hand and got to her feet.

"What the hell's going on?" Freeze demanded. Dotson and another detective were at his heels. "Where's Hashimoto? Why aren't you with him?"

"Upstairs. Boike was in back watching that door. Somebody ran out of the bushes and jumped him. I came down."

Freeze gave Boike a murderous look.

Another police car, this one a black-and-white cruiser, had pulled to the curb.

"Pierce. See to things down here and have two uniforms check the back yard. Dotson, come with me."

Freeze yanked the front door open hard enough to rip it from the frame. I caught up with the startled Dots and joined the party. Freeze glanced back.

"Where do you think you're going?"

"With you. I promised them I'd stay with them when you came. I gave my word."

He swore.

At Laura's door, despite the agreement I'd extracted

from him on the phone, his hand moved into easy reach of his sidearm. He pounded on the unlatched door.

"Police."

There was no response.

Behind us, I was aware of one of the uniformed officers. Moving to one side, and indicating we should do the same, Freeze nudged the door open. The sound of sobbing filled the room. Laura lay on the couch, collapsed on her side, as we flooded in.

"He's gone!" She pushed upright, and it was me she spoke to, grief saturating her voice. "I tried to stop him, but he's gone!" The hand she pressed to her mouth couldn't hold back her heartbreak. One side of her Victory Roll had come undone.

At a nod from Freeze, Dots and the uniformed cop began to check rooms. The woman on the couch scarcely noticed. She looked at Freeze with dazed comprehension that she should be talking to him.

"When she — Miss Sullivan — ran out asking about a back door, we went to the window and looked. We saw a man on the ground and someone getting away. She tried to catch him. And then the man on the ground got up and staggered off after them. Tosh said something was wrong, something bad had happened. And - and then he said he was going to get out while the coast was clear."

Her eyes, which had briefly been dry, overflowed

again. "I tried to argue, but he wouldn't listen. He panicked!"

Daisy and the others had come up in time to hear.

"Where's he going? Where could he be going?" Freeze demanded.

"I don't know."

"If you lie, you will be charged with—"

"I don't care what you charge me with. I DON'T KNOW!"

The intelligent, self-possessed proofreader began to emerge again. She slowed her sobs almost by will.

"Some people had been working out a plan to move him somewhere else. I don't know who or how. He wouldn't tell me. I don't think it was very far along though. Or it may not have existed. He only mentioned it a few days ago, to stop me from worrying."

She was wrung out. Drained. Freeze turned on me now, jabbing a finger toward Daisy, whose slacks and blouse were streaked with mud, as I realized my own were.

"Who's she and what's she doing here?"

"She's Hashimoto's kid sister."

Other times, Daisy would have objected. Now she merely swallowed a sniffle. Laura blinked and looked at her with real attention. Daisy returned the favor.

"As to what she's doing here, I have no idea."

Freeze gestured irritably at two of the uniforms.

"Take all four of them downtown. Yeah, you too, Boike."

I owed Boike an apology, here and now. At the moment, however, my main concern was for Daisy. Even though I wanted to strangle her, I stepped to her side.

"Come on, Freeze. She's a kid. She's still in high school, for Pete's sake. She hasn't done anything wrong. Let me take her home to her parents. They'll be terrified if they hear she's at the police station, especially after what you put them through over her brother. And now this? You'll be all over them again. Please. I'll come down on my own after I've seen to it."

He wavered.

"You've got one hour."

***

We were halfway to where Daisy lived before either of us spoke.

"I jimmied the lock on your trunk," she said in a small voice. "I knew you knew where to find her. Laura. Once you had that name. But you wouldn't tell me.

"I wanted to see her…what she was like. It was too late to do anything yesterday after I talked to you. I had to find the right kind of wrench and plan some. So, I watched when you came to your office today, and I knew where you parked your car, and when no one was looking, I undid the trunk and got in. It wasn't that hard."

I didn't trust myself to speak.

"I didn't damage the lock any," she added hopefully.

"Do you mean to tell me you've been in the trunk of my car all day?"

"Just since noon. I had tests this morning. I knew I might have missed it, but there was an equal chance I hadn't."

We rode in silence again.

"If it makes you feel any better, it's miserable back there with that metal floor and all those bumps."

I shifted my jaw to the Locked position.

"What's going to happen to her? For helping Tosh?"

It was something I'd been considering.

"I don't know. They'll question her till she's ready to drop, to learn what she knows and to get her to cough up anything she's holding back. Then they may decide to hold her in a cell overnight." I glanced across at her. "That could have been you, too, Daisy. For God's sake, don't do anything else so they regret letting you go. And if Tosh contacts you or your family, call them."

***

"Five minutes more and units would have been notified to bring you in," Freeze greeted from the top of the stairs at Market House. Flinging his cigarette into an ash can, he stalked into the detective squad room, leaving me to follow. He stepped behind his desk and stabbed a finger at a vacant chair in front of it. "Sit."

To my surprise, Boike occupied a second chair. Did Freeze intend to question the pair of us together, out here at his desk, rather than grilling us separately? Or had Boike become an official detective again? The smell of coffee from the thick tan mug in front of him made my stomach growl. It was twenty past nine and I hadn't eaten since lunch.

Freeze didn't offer me any coffee. He glowered.

"Talk. Or you get the same treatment we're giving the girlfriend." A jerk of his head indicated an interrogation room.

Boike nudged the handle of the still-warm mug toward me. I shook my head. In the twenty minutes or so I'd spent with the Hashimotos, they'd brought me a towel to dry myself and a thimble-sized glass of some rice wine that unleashed more heat going down than any whiskey I'd ever swallowed. My clothes felt clammy against my skin, but I'd been in worse shape a few times at this time of night.

I talked.

"And this old man you talked to that gave you the idea where to find Hashimoto, doesn't even live on the alley?" Freeze didn't hide his skepticism as he made notes. He had another Old Gold going in a flimsy metal ashtray the size of a pancake.

"No, but the house is situated where someone there can see movement into and out of the back lane," I said patiently. "Which is why I checked that group of houses."

"But didn't see fit to let anyone in this office know what you'd learned."

"That I had a theory because of a song title? You would have laughed me out of this office."

He didn't have an answer to that.

"And Boike here was helping you because…?"

"I offered to," said Boike before I could say I'd recruited him.

"You didn't mention that when you told your part."

Apparently, the former detective had given his account before I arrived. He'd settled back into the silent facade he'd worn when he was Freeze's assistant.

"You didn't ask me. You don't like hearing details unless you ask."

Freeze didn't have an answer for that either. Instead, he put us both through our accounts two more times, with occasional interruptions while he checked on the interrogation of Laura Gray. When I heard Boike's story of what had happened to him for the first time, and he told about getting a blow on the side of the neck that knocked him out momentarily, I felt obligated to tell Freeze about visiting the bar frequented by the young Nisei men. It led to another patch where Freeze wasn't happy with me.

Finally Freeze said I could go. My lower eyelids felt as though they had wads of putty weighting them down. I sneezed a couple of times as I got up.

"Mary Minerva claims putting a bay leaf in a mug of hot water and adding a splash of whiskey chases a cold off," Boike volunteered.

Not being the sort of gal who kept a jar of bay leaves in the kitchen to use in stews, or maybe it was slaw, I went home and slathered myself with Vick's Vaporub. I even put a little dab on the roof of my mouth.

CHAPTER FORTY-TWO

My trusty elixir of camphor and eucalyptus worked its magic. I woke up the next morning without a trace of sniffles, only to spend most of the day spinning my wheels.

Topping my list of concerns was what had befallen Daisy and her family after I left them. I'd known the police would be calling on them, and a flurry of activity shortly after I settled in for my cozy evening with Freeze made me suspect it was afoot. A call to the woman of the house where they were staying eased my worries at least temporarily.

"Daisy's here. She stayed home from school," she reported. "Her parents didn't go to work either. They were all up very late, I think. Would you like to speak to one of them?"

"No, I just wanted to make sure they were okay."

I finished my tea and brushed my teeth and put on slacks and a Windsor jacket. The woman I'd spoken to hadn't indicated whether Tosh had been captured or not. Only when I got downtown and bought a paper did I find out. A small item on page three got to the essentials:

A man wanted for questioning related to an incident two weeks ago eluded police last night. Tosh Hashimoto is a Japanese-American, five-foot-ten, with dark hair and glasses. Anyone with information on his whereabouts is urged to contact the police at once.

It wasn't the best of situations, but it wasn't the worst, either. Had I opened Freeze's mind to the possibility Tosh might be innocent? Had Tosh's decision to flee for a second time cast him as more of a public safety risk than he'd been before?

I phoned Laura, but she didn't answer. It could mean she was still downtown being grilled by the cops, or it could mean she didn't want to talk to anyone. I called Boike to apologize for the mess I'd landed him in, but there was no answer there either. Maybe he and Mary Minerva were out worming some kind of livestock, or maybe they didn't want to talk to me, or both.

Going to the window, I stared down at Patterson while contemplating my failure. If I felt like splitting hairs, I had done what the Hashimotos asked of me. I had found out what became of their son. I had brought them the good news he was alive. Yet a nasty little voice inside kept jeering that in finding him, I had made his situation worse.

The only way I saw to better it was to prove him innocent, which meant proving who had set that fire. Proving it indisputably, beyond the shadow of a doubt.

Spooner Senior.

Roger Spooner.

Mitzi.

One of those three was responsible. But which? And how? And where would I find that indisputable proof?

If I'd made any headway with Freeze — and maybe if I hadn't — he or some of the other detectives would be paying a visit to Kirby Printing today. I didn't think he'd get anything useful, but I hoped he would. He could throw his weight around. I had to be diplomatic. Mitzi would lie if he asked her whether she'd made the phone call to Tosh, and she'd do so without batting a darkened eyelash. Spooner's secretary and Phyllis Chapman were, in my opinion, far less likely to have made the call, but considerably more likely to break down and admit it if they had.

Unable to stand the inactivity, I turned to the hatrack and snagged the tan fedora with a bright blue ribbon that was my favorite with slacks. Laura didn't answer the door when I knocked. Calling out who it was didn't improve the results. I hadn't learned anything, but it felt better than brooding.

At Kirby Printing, I found cop cars aplenty, two used by detectives and one black-and-white. Cheered that Freeze was stirring things up again, which in itself was enough to make the guilty parties squirm and not be as careful, I went inside. I didn't expect Spooner to be receptive to a visit from me, and I knew the cops wouldn't, but I might be able to pick up some scuttlebutt from the front office staff. Given the article in the paper, not to mention the police presence, speculation must be flowing like a draining bathtub.

"No one who doesn't work here allowed in today," said the girl at the counter before I could open my mouth.

"Gee, aren't customers miffed when you tell them that?"

She pursed her lips in irritation.

"We don't say that to customers. Just others. You in particular."

"I'll bet Mr. Spooner told you that. He's such a kidder. Just tell me how long the police have been here, then."

A tinge of embarrassment rose on her cheeks. Her eyes avoided mine.

"I'm not allowed to tell you anything either."

"Maybe he didn't like the cookies I brought him," I said with a sigh. "Men are hard to figure out, aren't they?"

***

The tan-brick building where Spooner lived with his son had an established look to it, and the units were spacious, judging by the small row of mailboxes in the lobby. When nobody came along during the ten minutes I lingered there checking my watch as if waiting for someone, I decided to have a look around.

From the snatch of conversation I'd overheard in Spooner's office, I knew he lived in 3A. There were four floors, three units each. I got a gander at the first three floors as I climbed the carpeted stairs. Black metal numbers marked the polished wood doors. The one identifying 3A was on the left.

My plan, having seen the layout and the quiet that prevailed here, was to go back to the lobby and loiter again until a resident who seemed inclined to gossip happened along. I didn't get a chance to try it. A woman emerged from the unit down the hall from Spooner and drew a bead on me with her eyes as she strode toward me. With the instinct that forms a significant part of a gumshoe's arsenal, I knew she could mean trouble.

"May I help you?"

Her tone could inflict frostbite. She'd hit fifty and kept on going, with bobbed rust-colored hair that didn't give a fig for fashion. Her mint-condition handbag looped obediently over her arm.

"Just dropping something off for a friend, thanks."

I smiled agreeably. She looked me up and down. I ground my teeth. I didn't want Spooner to know I'd been sniffing around, and this place was small enough that residents probably talked to each other.

"This is such a lovely building." I fell into step with her.

She sniffed and didn't reply.

All I could do was hope I'd allayed her suspicions.

***

My remaining option for discovering anything worthwhile related to the Spooners was to try the businesses near where they lived. There weren't many in what was now a mostly residential neighborhood. The beauty shop up the street didn't seem like a very good prospect. The line of people waiting at a mom-and-pop grocery store was so long I decided to save it for last. That left an easy-to-miss lunch counter across the way and an old three-story building whose use I couldn't determine to the immediate east of Spooner's abode.

I decided to start with the lunch counter. In spite of the fact it was almost noon, there wasn't a crowd. Two women sat at a counter with eight stools, and a lone male at a table by the café's single window. A tired-looking waitress shuffled over to take my order.

"One of those corn muffins, please. To go." Like the rest of the place, they looked past their prime. "And I wonder if you could tell me whether any of the people who live in that building across the street need extra help because they're blind, or can't talk, or use crutches…"

Her shaking head stopped me.

"None of the Ritz crowd come here. Not fancy

enough for 'em, I guess. I get mostly girls who work at the beauty shop, and from that school place over there."

I turned to look at the rambling old building next to Spooner's.

"That's a school?"

She shrugged, lifting the glass cover over the muffins and taking one out with a square of parchment.

"Something like that. Piano lessons and such, near as I can make out from what they say."

I paid her and thanked her and left. I walked to the corner to cross, not from any qualms about jaywalking, but so I could ditch the muffin in a trash can without her seeing. Wasting food that was probably perfectly good gave me a twinge of guilt. Not ten years ago, in the grip of the Depression, hungry people had picked through trash cans hunting any scrap they could eat, spoiled or otherwise. Putting that guilt behind me, I took a good look at the place where I was headed.

The building housing "piano lessons and such" was nicely kept and robin-egg blue. People who knew about such things probably would call it Victorian. Its parking lot abutted the one where Spooner lived, but separate driveways led into each. Between the two, a parched strip just managed to sustain a pair of struggling spirea bushes. Even by my standards, it was cruel to the plants.

In front of the building, a painted sign the size of a bath mat identified the place as Letterman Concert Hall. As I turned to go in, a side door that led into the parking lot opened. A man in shirt sleeves and vest shooed a skinny boy of about fifteen out in front of him.

"Payday's tomorrow, kid. No advances. Now run on, beat it."

The side door slammed.

Sensing an unplanned route that might save me some time, I changed course. The kid was too busy adding scuffs to his shoes and glaring at the door that had closed behind him to notice me as I approached.

"Tough boss?" I commiserated.

He shifted his animosity to me and didn't answer. I tried again.

"I take it you work here?"

"What's it to you?"

He had lank hair and shoulders with the defiant thrust necessary to keep a chip on his shoulder. Pimples made a line down one side of his nose.

I held up a dollar bill.

"What it is to you, is a chance to earn something to tide you over till payday."

CHAPTER FORTY-THREE

The kid's eyes had fixed on the dollar the instant he saw it. He took a fist from his pocket and reached for the money, then drew back.

"What do I have to do?"

"Just tell me who works here at night and anything you might know about two men who live there." I indicated Spooner's building.

A smirk had formed on his face. He crossed his arms.

"That's worth more than a buck."

"You got a better offer?"

He wavered, then held out his hand. "Okay, but I get it now."

"Half now, half if you deliver." I made as if to rip the dollar bill in half.

"Stop! You can't do that!"

"Watch me."

"Okay, okay! Keep it till I finish. Me." He hooked a thumb toward his chest. "I work nights. Six-thirty to eleven, out here keeping an eye on the cars so nobody siphons gas or swipes a windshield wiper. And the first time, *the first time* I ask can I get part of my pay two days early, that skinflint of a manager turns me down! He knows I won't quit 'cause I'm not old enough to get anything better, so he takes advantage. It's as bad as my old man charging me a buck a week for food and sleeping in the same bed I always have—"

"Yeah, life's tough." Why more wise-aleck kids weren't strangled before they got old enough to blight public sanity escaped me. "Are you telling me this place has music recitals of some kind every night?"

For the first time, he gave the hint of a smile.

"Naw, recitals are usually once a week, and sometimes it's dance, not music. Some theater group uses it once a week to rehearse. All the other nights it's a Bingo parlor. You wouldn't believe how those old biddies pile in here. Men too, but not as many. Daytime's different, people give lessons, I guess. Music on second floor, tap and ballet and stuff on three, I think is how it is." The scowl returned. "They're making money hand over fist, and I get peanuts."

I digested it. What he was describing meant plenty of people were here at night, but only he was consistently outside in a position to notice comings and goings of the residents next door.

"There's a man in his early twenties who lives over there." I nodded. "Dark hair, lives with his father, who wears gaudy bow ties."

"You mean old…?" Twisting his face up and contorting his body, he tottered around making ugly animal sounds and having a fine time.

"He's not deformed and he doesn't have trouble walking," I said coldly. "He hears perfectly well and reads and writes, probably better than you. He just can't talk. But yes, that's the one."

He straightened up, but he clearly didn't see anything wrong with his performance.

"Well, what about him?"

"I want to know anything you can tell me about him or his father. Do they go out at night? When do they come back? Have you seen either one with a girl?"

He was curious now. "Why do you want to know? Are you thinking of asking one of them out?"

"I'm interested." I smacked a business card into his hand. "And if you tell me anything substantial, I'll give you four bits on top of the dollar. I've told plenty of lies and heard plenty of lies, so don't make it up."

His eyes had begun to narrow. Now they shifted sheepishly. He stuffed his hands back in his pockets and scuffed at the gravel where we were standing.

"Okay, there's not much, but I'll give it straight. It gets boring standing out here by myself. When something happens on that side, I usually notice. Yeah, they go out sometimes, usually together. Every now and then when they come out the old man's wearing a striped jacket, red and white, and has on one of those stiff Katys, so I think maybe he's in one of those barbershop groups."

"They go off together and come back together?"

"Yeah, sure. The older one's always yak-yak-yakking. I figure that's because the mor— the other one can't. He tries, though. That's how I know the kind of sounds he makes. Awhile back they were having a real set-to when they got out of the car. The son was yowling away like a cat in heat."

"When?"

"Uh, three or four weeks ago. It was still cold at night."

"Any idea what the argument was about?"

"Uh…not really. The kid was upset about something. The old man was trying to calm him down." He closed his eyes and bared his front teeth in thought. "He said, 'Hasn't your old dad always looked out for you?' Something like that. The son kind of shoved him and went agw-agw-agw. The old man told him nothing was going to change, but hadn't he earned the right to enjoy some things on his own? Then the son shoved him harder and gargled and waved his arms and stormed away."

"What did the father do?"

"Stood there a minute, then went off after him."

"Is that the only time you've heard them quarreling?"

"Yeah."

He held out his hand. I put the dollar in it. He waited. So did I.

"Oh, yeah," he said after a minute. "Girls. I never saw the son with one, but then he's kind of a freak, you know? Pop, now, I've seen him coming in with a girl now and then these last few months, and does she know how to strut her stuff. Blonde, real curvy, but way too young for him if you ask me."

***

Freeze was coming out of my building when I got back. He dropped his cigarette on the sidewalk and ground it out as he watched me approach.

"What steams me," he said with deceptive mildness, "is Boike working for you instead of me."

"He isn't working for me. He said he got bored now and then, and if he could help with something that didn't involve talking to people, he would. I'd narrowed down possibilities on places where Hashimoto might have gone to ground. I wanted to keep an eye on Laura's place to see if anyone moved around inside during the day—"

"Yeah, yeah. You told me that last night."

"Well? What would you have done if you also wanted to follow up other leads? What was wrong with getting help from someone experienced when he offered it strictly as a friend?"

I ran my hands through my hair, dislodging the

combs that held the loosely curling ends behind my ears.

"Admittedly, I had him helping mostly out of my own self-interest, but it also went through my mind that doing the kind of work he used to do might make him see how much he missed it."

Freeze was silent a minute. He stepped back and leaned against the wall behind him.

"You really think he believes that scar down his face will spook people out of talking to him?"

"Yeah, I do. Maybe not spook them, but make them uncomfortable. For some of them — a few of them — it could be true. Mostly I think he's still getting used to what he sees in the mirror."

He rubbed his chin.

"I'm sorry, Freeze. I really am. For letting Hashimoto get away, but also for botching things up between you and Boike, if I did. The blame's on me, not him. He pushed me to notify you before I went up to that apartment, but I was sure my way was better."

"You think Laura Gray's telling the truth that she doesn't have any idea where he might have gone or who might help him?" he asked abruptly.

"Yes. Is she tucked up in a cell somewhere? She's not answering her phone or the door either."

"She's at work. At the printing place."

"What?"

"We worked on her until about two this morning.

When it became clear we weren't getting anywhere, we sent her home. Today when we got to the printing place, there she was at her desk, making squiggles in the margins of things."

I dipped a toe into what might be quicksand, given the mood he'd been in initially.

"I saw the police cars in front of the place and didn't want to get in your way. I hoped I might pick up some gossip in the front office on what was happening, but the girl at the counter told me in no uncertain terms that I'm not allowed on the premises and no one is allowed to tell me anything."

"Imagine. Could it be you rubbed one of the company bigwigs the wrong way?" He started a cigarette.

"No confessions, no bringing anybody in for a chat if that's what you're wondering. That blonde's a piece of work. Acts like only a fool would expect her to do anything or talk about anything she didn't want to. She claims she never made a call to Hashimoto and doesn't know anything about it. So do the other two. Spooner's secretary got so worked up I worried she'd keel over."

"And Phyllis Chapman? Kirby's secretary?"

"Drew herself up and gave me a look that could have turned me to ice."

"Spooner, of course, did his wounded indignation routine, interspersed with pally little chuckles to show you he's a swell guy."

"You're right about the indignation part. He practically stamped his feet denying he got Hashimoto there that night. He figured out early on that I wasn't interested in how swell he was or wasn't."

"I just learned a couple of interesting things about the Spooners from a kid who works next door to their building.

The detective glanced at his watch.

"Make it fast."

I did. We both knew it didn't necessarily mean anything, let alone prove it. He acknowledged, though, that it was handy to know.

"Hey, Freeze," I called as he started off down the sidewalk. "Did you happen to ask the older proofreader if she made that phone call?"

He turned back.

"The giggler? No, why?"

"Just a thought. I haven't been looking at her, but she always seems keen to get on Spooner's good side. I can't decide whether she has a crush on him or she's buttering up the boss. Has what I did made trouble for you? My finding Hashimoto and him getting away again?"

"Nothing that I can't handle," he said over his shoulder. "But it's nice to have somebody ask."

CHAPTER FORTY-FOUR

Since Freeze and his men hadn't asked Velma whether she'd made the phone call that lured Tosh in the night of the fire, or if she'd heard anything about such a call, it seemed like the smart thing to do. Not while she was at work, though. Not only was I *persona non grata* at Kirby Printing, but despite Spooner's jolly ways, employees seemed less inclined to talk when he was around.

Velma was a chatty sort. If I could get her started on one of her favorite subjects, Spooner, she might spill more than she intended.

I'd found trolleys made a swell spot to keep someone confined and responding to questions when they didn't want to, even if those responses were 'I'm not going to answer.' When Laura left work the previous day, she and Velma had boarded the same trolley. I stationed myself in front of a store a few steps away from the bus stop. As soon as Velma's iron-gray curls bobbed into view, I fell into line half a dozen spaces behind her. There was no sign of Laura.

The trolley arrived. We mashed up the stairs. All the

seats were occupied, as I had expected. Velma went two-thirds of the way before giving up her hunt. She grabbed a dangling hand strap as the trolley pulled away. Far enough away that she wouldn't notice me unless she looked, I did the same. Then I surveyed the seated passengers and selected my hapless victim. He was, at most, ten years younger than Velma and sat two rows behind where she stood, with his nose buried protectively in the evening paper.

I let the trolley make one more stop and worked my way a few spaces closer to both of them.

"Shame on you," I said in a clear voice. "Sitting there while a woman old enough to be your mother stands after working all day."

He rooted deeper into his paper.

"I'll bet you call yourself a gentleman, too."

People were starting to look. The man's face reddened. He stood and muttered to Velma and they changed places. She twisted to look in my direction.

"Thank you…Oh. It's you."

I waggled my fingers and smiled. Trading hand straps with a couple of people, I wormed my way closer to chat.

"If you're following me because you think I'll tell you something, I won't," Velma said before I could open my mouth. "We've been warned not to say anything to the press, or to you. You won't get a thing out of me."

She made a grand, zipping gesture across her lips and folded her hands on the purse lying on her knees.

"Gee, no, I wouldn't think of putting you in a spot like that. One of the detectives who was there this morning told me how they'd put you all through the ringer. Although…I am dying to know…" I leaned closer. "What color was it today?"

She'd been staring primly ahead. Now she wavered just enough to let curiosity sway her.

"Color?"

"Mr. Spooner's necktie."

It did the trick. She tucked her head and giggled.

"I guess it won't hurt to tell you *that*. Before the…Well, you already know they were there, so I guess I might as well say it…before the police came, he was planning to go to one of his men's lunches. Rotary, I think it was.

"When he's attending one of those, he wears his dull gray. That's what he calls it, his 'dull gray,' but it's not really dull at all. It's very attractive. Dark gray suit, lovely gray silk tie with tiny red stripes, and of course his harlequin cufflinks. I'll bet you didn't know he matches his cufflinks to his ties. Not that they actually match — it's more like they harmonize.…"

Ye gods, did the woman have every outfit Spooner wore memorized? How was I going to move her beyond his sartorial cleverness to what I wanted to ask?

"...of course, the harlequins aren't really gray, they're black-and-white enamel — that's what makes me think of harlequins. I think they're my very favorites. He wasn't wearing those today, though. How peculiar. I wonder why. Not that the new ones aren't nice — onyx, I think — but..."

Her words flowed unabated, but I'd stopped listening. My attention had latched onto one thing: black-and-white enamel.

***

Unlike other things in war, the ration of lies a detective hears from suspects is unlimited. Even decent people are allotted a few to tell themselves. That something doesn't matter to them when it does; that they're doing something for someone else when they're doing it for themselves. The lesser lies that keep us all going. Maybe Spooner had started with the lesser kind, but when he'd run out of that supply, it looked more and more as if he'd crossed over. He'd started a fire, then concocted a story from the same well of lies used remorselessly by people like Mitzi. Now I needed to prove it.

***

The fire investigator was gone by the time I got there. Not surprising since it was after quitting hours for most people, but that wasn't the reason.

"He's picking through the ashes from a fire up north," a clerk informed me. "It'll be a couple of hours, at least, before he's back. Could be midnight."

"I need to see the evidence from the fire at Kirby Printing three weeks ago."

More than that, I needed to talk to the man presently unavailable to me. Only his expertise, and his alone, could confirm whether the small lump of metal with a black streak on it found by the back stairs after the fire once could have been a cufflink. Meanwhile, a peek at it with my own eyes could reassure me I was on to something, or suggest I was skipping merrily in the wrong direction.

The clerk, however, told me no one was there with authority to let a civilian like me look at evidence from a fire scene. There was nothing to do except come back tomorrow. I went home and ate supper with Seamus.

"They buried Kathleen Connelly today," he said as we sat on the back steps afterward with our coffee. "Just Mick and the kids and the priest. It's how Mick wanted it. For the kids' sake, mostly, but for him too. There's too much awkwardness. Over how she died, and what's come to light since."

"About the sister who's really just a cousin?"

His mouth worked in and out as he considered. For one of the rare times I could remember there was anger in his features.

"It's telling tales out of school, but you've a right to know if anyone does. The baby she was carrying wasn't Mick's most likely. He didn't say anything until the neighbor lady came forward and told the police a man had visited Kathleen most Thursdays, when Brigid was at her Scouts meeting and a mother up the street had Owen at her house to play with her little boy.

"After that and some other came out, Mick admitted to me that he'd had doubts. He'd slept down on the couch for months, but Kathleen claimed he was drunk one night and forced himself on her. So, let go of some of that guilt you've had over pushing Mick into her arms. She was looking to get her hooks into a man who'd provide for her, and she did. Pure and simple."

***

Between what I'd learned from Velma and what Seamus had told me, I spent the night tossing and turning. Mostly my half-waking thoughts were of Connelly's step-daughter, Brigid, a bright little girl, a curious kid. I liked her. According to Seamus, the priest had denied Kathleen burial in the churchyard proper. People would whisper. Those whispers would filter down to their children. I knew how cruel schoolmates could be. It was a relief to get up early to catch the fire investigator.

"A cufflink."

He squinted his eyes a couple of times as he studied the lump of melted metal he'd removed from the evidence box and set on the desk in front of him. It wasn't eight o'clock yet.

"It could be, yes. I'd need to see another one like it, or have dimensions or something to be sure." He put it back in the box.

"Will you tell Freeze," I asked, "or should I?"

"You can if you want. Like I said, I'd want something to compare it to before I could say definitively."

CHAPTER FORTY-FIVE

I found myself out on the street with a whole day ahead of me, and not much to fill it. I headed for Market House. Freeze wasn't in. As the day crawled on, he didn't return my phone calls either.

By noontime, I'd finished every routine task that entered my mind, and I felt increasingly frustrated. I had a good idea how to prove not only that the lump of metal found at the fire was a cufflink, but who had been wearing it. Freeze was in the best position to do that. Why couldn't I reach him?

He wasn't at his desk when I paid another in-person visit. I crossed the street and had a sandwich at the Arcade. When I tried the detective squad room again, and he still was nowhere to be found, I left him a note. It gave the high points of what Velma had told me, and that the fire investigator believed my idea about the metal might be valid.

Thoughts about the cufflink connection were my only company once I got back to the office. Prove that, and not only could it get Tosh off the hook, it would point overwhelmingly at Spooner as the one who started the fire that killed two men. Establishing that would mean he also had a motive to want Seth Rowe silenced, by murder if necessary.

In order to prove any of that, I needed the mate to the one that the fire reduced to a misshapen lump. Spooner might have gotten rid of it by now. He'd had plenty of time. That assumed he recognized the need, which in turn hinged on realizing when and where he'd lost it.

Otherwise, some human impulse to shove stray jewelry items to the back of a drawer or toss them into a box with wearable things was stronger than the logic that said to throw them away. I had three earrings without mates, and a pretty lapel pin I never wore because one of the fake stones in it was missing. There'd been two orphan cufflinks in my dad's things when I went through them after his death. Spooner might still have the cufflink.

I tried Freeze again.

"He's still not here," said a put-upon clerk. "He's talking to a sheriff's deputy out around Phillipsburg. Quit calling every five minutes, okay?"

Phillipsburg was in the northwest corner of the county in a rural area that was just about as far from Dayton as you could get. It was out of Freeze's jurisdiction. The only thing I could imagine taking Freeze that far afield was a reported sighting of Tosh Hashimoto. Maybe the Sheriff had nabbed Tosh.

Or was I way off base? Was Freeze thinking of trading his police badge for one bestowed by the county? He'd made some dissatisfied sounds this past year, but they'd had to do with being short staffed because of the war. The Sheriff's Department had to be feeling those same effects.

Either way meant Freeze was out of reach, and without the information in the note I'd left him. He wouldn't be leaning on Spooner for hours, if then. And he wouldn't be looking for cufflinks.

I got up and paced.

Spooner was at work, presumably. So was his son. It presented a dandy time for me to have a look through their apartment to see what I could find.

It was also a bad idea.

If I let myself in via crochet hook, anything I did find would be tainted. Freeze was the one who needed to do it, or to send some of his men. He had the authority.

Resisting the urge to try calling Freeze again, I told myself that patience was a virtue. The argument grew weaker as the urge to let myself into Spooner's apartment intensified. I bought an afternoon paper and didn't remember a thing I'd read by the time I finished it. By five o'clock I had proven myself extremely virtuous.

I hadn't accomplished anything since my early morning confab with the fire investigator, but the afternoon had given me plenty of time to stew over a couple of things I suspected Tosh's belligerent roommate and coworker Zenzo could explain. I doubted it would shed any light on who had framed Tosh, or why, but answers would make me feel better. And I was in exactly the right mood to make sure I got them.

***

I was leaning against my car, waiting, when Zenzo and half a dozen other young men came up the drive to the house where they lived. Those who knew me stopped when they saw me. The others slowed.

"The cops have already hammered at us for two days. We don't know where Tosh is, or who might have helped him. Hand to heaven," Zenzo snapped.

"That's not why I'm here. I have a different bone to pick with you. Away from your friends.

"I promise not to hurt him," I added to the others.

There were uncertain chuckles.

"Fine. There." He indicated a patch of grass toward the back of the house. "Tell Mrs. Morita I'll be in for dinner," he said to Kensuke. The young man I'd given a ride to the library was now free of bandages. Angry red railroad tracks showed where his hand had been stitched.

I let Zenzo lead the way to the grass. He threw himself down. His edge of defiance was still in place, but worn thin. He lay back in the grass.

"If you're not here to grill me about who could be helping Tosh like the cops did, why are you here?"

I didn't sit down. I crossed my arms.

"Because I want an explanation of why you tried to strangle me in the alley. Why you hit me in the side of the neck outside that bar, and did the same thing to Detective Boike night before last. What kind of threat do you think I am? What do you think I'm going to do?"

Like a wooden Jumping Jack whose various parts moved as the string was pulled, he sat up and thrust his hands out in a single movement.

"Stop. No. That hitting the neck wasn't me. Yeah, I grabbed you when you were sitting there in your car, but I wouldn't have strangled you. I just wanted to scare you. I never expected you to fight back. The other, that was somebody else. And none of it had to do with you. It was about Daisy."

"Daisy!"

I sat down. "Start talking. No BS. I'm in a lousy mood."

"Oh, man." He put his head between his hands. "It's going to sound…That guy in back of where Tosh was staying was a cop?"

"Up to the day he was drafted. They just sent him home on a medical discharge, so he's free to be one again." Lovely how truth could work for you if you were creative. "What did you mean it was all about Daisy? If you're not the one who punched Boike and me and put us to sleep, who did?"

His throat constricted. He looked weary, and young and old at the same time.

"I told you at the beginning that I didn't like Tosh much, and I didn't. But he was decent, you know? After the fire, I got thinking how he'd worried about his sister. That in California she'd been used to going wherever she wanted and insisting on answers if somebody gave her the runaround, but if she did it here, she'd get in trouble.

"So, I talked to this other guy who knows Tosh—"

"Who?"

"You don't need to know. We thought if we kept an eye on Daisy, it would be like doing something for him and his family. We didn't know she'd be such a handful."

I smiled, but he didn't see.

"The other guy watches her from when she gets out of school until half past seven, then gets picked up for his ride to work. By then I'm free to take over the next four hours. We decided if she goes anywhere after half past eleven, well, we're doing as much as we can.

"That night in the alley, I didn't know what you were up to. I thought you were watching her, sitting there after she went in. So, I tried to scare you."

"But it's this other good-hearted pal who whacks

people in the side of the neck?" I made no effort to hide my skepticism.

"Hey, I didn't know he'd do that!"

"It was way past seven-thirty that night he knocked me cold."

"Yeah, there was some training thing where he works so he had the night off. He was just supposed to rough you up — get you to stop asking questions. We still didn't trust you. Hitting someone in the neck like that, it's stupid. Dangerous if you do it too hard. He promised not to do it again."

But he had.

What followed was a tale of good intentions gone amok.

On the afternoon Daisy hid in my trunk, her would-be protector grew alarmed when she didn't leave school as usual. When she wasn't at my office, where he'd followed her a few times, he'd gone to the printing plant to talk to Zenzo when he got off work. Instead, he'd spotted my car, and me "acting funny" following a woman. At Laura's building, seeing me talk to Boike and the two of us split up, Zenzo's pal leaped to the conclusion we'd nabbed Daisy and had her somewhere inside to wring information from her.

He followed Boike around to the back. After a few minutes Boike started inside, reaching for what the bodyguard thought was a gun.

"It was a flashlight," I said.

Zenzo groaned.

The bodyguard jumped Boike. They scuffled. The bodyguard gave him a whack on the neck, then fled in a panic. When Daisy came barreling out the front door, he assumed it was me and knocked her down to slow pursuit.

"We've given it up. Watching her," Zenzo said in a small voice.

I gave him a long, long look.

"That night I dropped Daisy off in the alley, there was a gray car parked across the street, watching the house."

"The cop car? It's been out there every night since I started watching. Several nights ago — before you found Tosh — it quit showing up."

"It wasn't the cops. It was the War Department, FBI, someone like that."

Zenzo sucked in his breath.

"Since you and your pal started keeping an eye on Daisy, has anything unusual happened? Anything that bothered you? Think, Zenzo."

"No. That is...I didn't see this; the other guy told me. One afternoon when she got out of school, a delivery truck followed her. Three, four blocks till she got on a bus. He said all that time, the truck didn't make a delivery. It was dawdling so much a car behind it finally honked and it went on."

***

Seamus had a meeting and wouldn't be home, so I went to Finn's and caught up. In between conversation with Rose, I thought about what Zenzo had told me.

A delivery truck that didn't stop for deliveries had followed Daisy.

Spooner's son drove a delivery truck.

Spooner, though he glossed it over, nursed at least a grain of resentment that Japanese-American workers had been hired for jobs his son wanted.

Had he transferred that resentment to his son? Or did Roger Spooner already harbor plenty on his own?

The first thing I did when I got to my office the next morning was call Freeze.

"He's been in, but he's out again," reported the clerk.

"Is Dots there?"

"No."

"Do you happen to know whether Freeze read the note I left him yesterday?"

"No idea. Sorry."

I hung up and leaned back in my chair in frustration. Why was he ducking my calls?

To ensure he didn't have another chance, I picked up my purse and went to sit in the chair in front of his desk and wait.

CHAPTER FORTY-SIX

I sat in front of Freeze's desk swinging my leg for ninety minutes. When he finally arrived, with Dots trailing, he paused at sight of me. Continuing toward his desk, he ripped off his jacket and loosened his tie.

"Don't start."

"Did you read that note I left you?"

"Yesterday after wasting half the day driving out to Miamisburg because the Sheriff's office had gotten reports of a man who looked Japanese and the rest of the day driving up to Phillipsburg for the same reason? Both of them dead ends probably meant to keep us chasing our tails while Hashimoto went in a different direction. Sure, it was top of my list."

He threw his hat on the desk. He looked beat.

"And if you're wondering why I was traipsing around where I didn't have jurisdiction, it was because I was told to. So to answer your question, yes, I read the note. Skimmed it anyway. Something about Spooner's cufflinks and how they connect to the fire. I'll give you a call when I've had a chance to read it in detail. Now beat it. I've got things to do."

I didn't budge except to move forward.

"Freeze, you need to read it now."

He'd lifted the receiver of the phone at his elbow. He banged it back without dialing.

"Didn't I just tell you I had other things to deal with?"

"Freeze, listen to me. There was a wad of metal found at the fire with black-and-white enamel on it. Hoolihan at the fire department says it could be a cufflink. He says if he could see a similar cufflink intact, he could be sure."

"So?"

I expelled a gust of breath that could turn a windmill.

"If you'd read the note…Spooner owns cufflinks with black-and-white enamel. He was wearing them the day of the fire. Velma, the giggly proofreader, told me he always matches his cufflinks to his bow ties. Two days ago, when she told me about it, she was all upset and went on and on about how he wasn't wearing the right ones — the black-and-white ones — that day. He had new ones."

Boike came in and paused, observing our altercation.

"Freeze, you need to get a search warrant, and a team into Spooner's apartment to find that other cufflink. It's proof who started the fire and killed two innocent men — three, if you count Seth Rowe."

"It may not even be there. Assuming you're right

about any of this, if he's smart — which he is — he may have ditched it already."

"And he may not have! He may not even realize where he lost it. He may just as well have tossed the one he still has in the back of a drawer somewhere."

"Let me read through it and give it some thought. It's not strong enough to thrill a judge. And that story Hashimoto spun about getting a phone call could be a lie. He could still be the one guilty."

"You can't seriously...With that new account from the neighbor of how he came by whistling? With an eyewitness inside the building whose description of where Tosh was standing and how he was facing contradicts Spooner's, and another witness who contradicted it dead? I've learned something else, too. About his son."

"I said I'll consider it."

A haze of anger engulfed me, obscuring everything in the room except Freeze and me.

"And meanwhile, Velma asks Spooner why he's quit wearing her favorite cufflinks and he ditches the evidence? Meanwhile sheriff's departments from here to Timbuktu are watching for Tosh Hashimoto with orders to do God-knows-what if they spot him, now that he's run a second time?"

His jaw shifted. He avoided my eyes.

"Don't tell me how to do my job." He glanced at Boike. "What?"

"I couldn't find those magazines." He turned to go.

"Come back in twenty minutes," Freeze called.

Boike didn't respond. He kept on walking.

Tired of smashing my nose on a wall when I tried reasoning with Freeze, I smacked my feet on the ground and rose.

"All day yesterday I sat on my thumbs when we both know I could have gotten into that apartment and looked for that cufflink myself. I didn't. I waited for you to read a note summarizing new information, and you to take action because I wanted everything to be by the book. I'm not going to stand by while an innocent man pays the consequences for something he didn't do."

I turned and put distance between us as fast as possible.

"You could be wrong, you know!" Freeze yelled as I left.

***

On Main Street, women left the Arcade carrying shopping bags of canvas or cloth that held items destined for that night's dinner, or maybe tomorrow's. Three young women laughed their way out of a beauty shop while one of them pretended to pat her curls and flutter her eyes. I strode past the pleasant scenes almost blindly.

Freeze was an idiot. No, not an idiot. Pigheaded. At

least he hadn't dismissed my belief in the cufflink's importance outright. There had been a time when he had dismissed leads I thought should be followed but couldn't yet prove as whispered to me by leprechauns. Nevertheless, his refusal to act promptly now could result in disaster, for Tosh Hashimoto at least. That same lack of action would let a killer go free if Velma asked Spooner about his change of accessories, which, once it occurred to me, I was increasingly concerned she might.

After two blocks, some of my anger had dissipated. As I came to the intersection of Third and St. Clair, I saw Boike on the cross street, headed away from me. The set of his shoulders suggested he wasn't much happier than I was. It would be a miracle if Freeze lured him back to work.

I had no doubt at all what my next move should be as I climbed the stairs to my office. Once my fanny hit my chair, I pulled the phone book over and found the listing for the cleaning supply company that employed Roger Spooner.

"Is Roger Spooner there?" I asked the receptionist. "This is his Aunt Edith. I thought I was supposed to go with him to his doctor's appointment, but he's not at home."

It took her a moment to check.

"He's here, but he's out driving his route. Would you like to leave a message?"

"No, that's all right. I'll straighten it out. Thank you."

Roger was occupied for the day. Now to check on his father. That was going to be trickier, since the front-desk people at Kirby Printing had been told not to talk to me, specifically, and might be leery of anyone they didn't know. In the last half block of my walk from Market House, I'd hatched a plan. It hinged on my having earned a shred of trust I wasn't sure I could count on, and the woman I wanted to speak to being as fast on her feet as I thought she was.

Dialing Kirby Printing, I pitched my voice a few notes higher and held my index finger under my nose.

"Could I please speak to Laura Gray? This is Daisy and it's a family matter and it's kind of important. Oh, she's a proofreader."

"Just a minute. I'll see if she can be interrupted."

I leaned against my desk and closed my eyes and waited. After a minute, Laura answered.

"Daisy?" she said cautiously. Her voice was muted.

"Actually, it's Maggie Sullivan. Don't hang up. Please. I need to know if Spooner's there."

"Yes. Yes, he is. What—?"

"Thanks."

I hung up and put on my holster. Settling my Smith & Wesson under my jacket, I set out to look for a cufflink.

CHAPTER FORTY-SEVEN

It was getting on toward noontime when I parked up the street from Spooner's apartment building. I did a quick check of the parking lot behind it. Spooner's car wasn't there.

With steps that pretended confidence in case I met anyone, I went up the stairs to the third floor, and then down the hall. My fingers were crossed against having the woman at the end of the hall pop out again. The set that wasn't crossed clutched my crochet hook.

Silence echoed around me. Pressing my ear against Spooner's door, I heard more of the same on the other side. I knocked softly. Nothing. A glance toward where the less-than-friendly neighbor lived, and I chanced knocking more loudly.

Still no response.

Turning so my back would hide what I did next from the eagle-eyed neighbor in case she did come out, I took a breath to steady my nerves and inserted the shiny little Boyle in Spooner's lock. There was an odd exhilaration about sliding the thin crochet hook into unknown territory. I experienced it now. Those first endless seconds of wondering whether it — whether I — would identify the right tumblers; wondering if someone would come up the stairs and see what I was doing. Then I felt the lovely, small shiftings I couldn't see, and the doorknob turned silently under my hand. The hallway was still deserted, except for me. I dropped the crochet hook into my purse and went in.

"Hello? Is anyone here?"

No one called out they were, but people who know their crimes could catch up with them have been known to hide. I took out my gun. The curtains were open. The only activity in the apartment appeared to be dust settling, motes sliding down a shaft of light that the overhead sun of noon allowed to make its way past neighboring buildings.

I stood in a living room almost painfully devoid of decoration. A few framed photographs of father and son topped a console table. Heavy brass andirons stood at either end of a fireplace so clean I wondered if it had ever been used. A big wingback chair with its back to the fireplace made up a conversational grouping with a plump sofa and a Boston rocker.

The kitchen was empty and tidy, with two cereal bowls stacked in the sink. No one waited to pounce in the hall closet, or in the bathroom. I turned my attention to the two bedrooms.

The first belonged to Roger. A golf trophy from

some local tournament held solitary court on a shelf. A government propaganda poster depicting the enemy, a leering Japanese soldier, hung on one wall with darts embedded in it. One of the darts had sunk halfway up its wooden shaft.

Sickened by the hate I saw there, I turned away and opened the attractive louvered doors of the closet. It revealed only everyday items plus a bag of golf clubs and togs for the game. On the floor of the closet, on top of the shoes, a suitcase was tossed haphazardly on its side. A quick peek showed it was empty, but its very presence made me wonder if the Spooners were planning a trip.

I entered Spooner Senior's room with a new sense of urgency. On the bed, a suitcase lay open and half packed with a couple of shirts lying next to it. All at once I suspected I'd interrupted someone's packing.

With no place to shield myself, I took a shooting stance and aimed at the closet.

"Come out or I shoot. I won't miss."

The doors to the closet swung open. Mitzi Fitzgerald stepped out. The pistol she held pressed into the soft flesh under Roger's chin.

"Put the gun down or I fix that useless tongue of his with a bullet."

CHAPTER FORTY-EIGHT

Smug satisfaction bathed her face. Beside her, the larger, taller Roger made whimpering sounds.

"Do it!" snapped the blonde. The gun she was gouging into Roger's skin was a short .38 not unlike the one I carried.

"Yeah. Okay." I placed my Smith & Wesson on the bed, keeping most of it behind the suitcase where I might get a chance to grab it.

"Where I can see it," said Mitzi.

"Picky, aren't you?" I obeyed. "Do you even know how to use that one you're holding?"

Her smile was pure malice.

"You better believe I do. My mother was a bootlegger's girlfriend. Wore furs and a diamond bracelet till the gang he was with got in a shootout and he popped a cop. And there she was, expecting me. Kept her from testifying, though. She taught me plenty."

Lowering the gun she'd held against Roger's chin, she aimed it at me. She gave the man beside her a shove.

"Put her gun in the drawer of the night stand where she can't grab it. As soon as we get to the living room, find some rope to tie her up."

He moved without delay, and with no trace of fear. She smiled her ugly smile at me again.

"We gulled you. Now move."

I'd already called myself every kind of idiot for walking into a trap like this. I began to run a scorecard of things to even with her when I got out of it. If I did.

"Oh, I'd already figured you and Spooner and Roger were a threesome," I said as I turned toward the living room in response to the gun against my back. "I just hadn't figured which one of them was your lover — or if it was both."

"I wouldn't let that freak touch me for a million dollars!"

"But you let his old man do it for a whole lot less."

"Shut up!"

If I could goad her into pushing me, maybe I could fake a fall and take her down with me. I could try and wrestle the gun away. But before I could think of anything else to needle her with, we reached the living room.

"Stand over there until he finds something to tie you with." She gave me a shove and moved to stand in front of the wingback chair, facing me. She was as cold as the fireplace behind her.

"How did you know we were here?"

"Lucky guess."

"You're lying." Her eyes narrowed.

I smiled.

The longer I could keep her in the dark about why I'd shown up, the more rattled she'd be. People who were rattled made missteps.

"I figured father and son might be taking a trip." I looked pointedly around. "Doesn't look like you're included, though. I don't see a suitcase."

Mitzi smirked.

"It's in the car. I put it there last night." Her voice took on an irritated tone as Roger appeared from the kitchen, empty handed. "Where's the rope?"

He shook his head.

"Does that mean you couldn't find any? Bring clothesline rope, moron. You must have that. Get something to stuff in her mouth, too."

He glared at her and growled.

A key rattled the hallway door. I looked around in time to see Spooner enter.

"Is everything…?" The words froze on his lips at sight of me. He gave the door behind him a push. "What's she doing here?"

"Nothing to worry about. She'd be tied up in a closet out of the way already, but your moron son couldn't even find clothesline rope."

"Don't call him that," Spooner begged.

"He's smart enough to know they don't need a clothesline since they don't do their own laundry." It was my turn to smirk.

Spooner made a semi-circle around me, staring as if struggling to decipher what was happening. He came to a stop on my right. Alarm flickered in his features.

"What do you *mean*, nothing to worry about? How did she——?" For the first time, he noticed the gun his girlfriend was holding. "Mitzi, what are you doing with that? Put it down."

"Only if you want to spend the rest of your life in jail — and that's if you're lucky. Do you have the tickets?"

"Yes."

"Do you have the cash?"

"Yes."

"And you left twenty bucks in your savings account so the bank wouldn't get suspicious?"

"Just the way you said." He waggled an admonishing finger and attempted a chuckle. "But you haven't answered my question yet. Why is she here?"

Mitzi switched her approach.

"You know I hate it when you do that Silly Boss thing, sugar," she pouted. "I'm not sure, but I think she came here to look for something. She spent just enough time in the other rooms to see if anyone was here — and for us to hide. Then she came straight to your room. I don't know how she knew about it, but she was probably after this."

Dipping her free hand into her bra, she brought out what even from five feet away I could see was a small square divided diagonally into black-and-white triangles.

"My cufflink!" Spooner was struck almost speechless.

"You didn't even realize where you'd lost the other one, did you? The next time you wanted to wear them, you thought you'd dropped it somewhere in the apartment and the cleaning lady would find it. But I knew as soon as you started grumbling that one was missing. I remembered your shirt sleeve flapping when you got here after the fire. You kept babbling how when you tossed the match, your sleeve ignited, and snagged on the wood of the stair railing."

"You knew I was hunting it, and you didn't tell me!"

"It seemed smarter for me to have it."

She tucked it back where she'd gotten it. Spooner, not looking jolly at all, held out his hand.

"Give it here."

"No."

Roger grabbed her from behind, his right arm pinning her shoulders, his left around her neck. One move and he could snap it. Her forearms could still move, though.

"Let me go or I'll shoot your old man," she choked as the gun in her hand shifted toward Spooner.

Halfway through seizing the moment to rush her, I stopped. There was too great a chance Spooner might get shot. The cops were more likely to get him to talk than they were Mitzi.

"Don't! Roger—" His hand thrust out in a desperate plea. To his son? To Mitzi? I wasn't sure.

With an inarticulate sound I took for frustration, Roger flung his arms clear of the blonde, taking care not to jostle her. Roger was smart, just as his father had said. Retreating behind the wingback chair, he curled his fists on the top of it and glared at the back of Mitzi's head.

"There, now. That's better." Mitzi pulled the cloak of phony sweetness back over her. With her .38 once again marking me as the enemy, she blew Spooner a kiss. "Don't worry, sugar. Mitzi will take good care of your cufflink. And as long as you don't make her too cross, she won't give it to anyone else or tell anyone how Roger killed that old man."

"It was an accident! You know that. He was only supposed to give him a knot on the head so nobody else believed his talk about what he saw that night." Spooner flung me an angry look.

Mitzi shushed him.

"We're wasting time, sugar. Throw those shirts that are on the bed in your suitcase and leave everything else. We've got to get going, and we've got to make one small change of plan. Since we can't tie this meddler up, Roger will have to put her in a closet and make sure she stays in there for, what, four hours? We should be far enough away by then that the cops can't catch up, even if they believe anything she tells them since she doesn't have evidence."

Spooner looked dumbfounded.

"Leave Roger? Is that what you're suggesting? Leave Roger?"

"I know you love him, but you just saw how unpredictable he can be. Grabbing me for no reason. We can't risk that, him attracting attention somewhere."

"But—"

"It's for the best, sugar. He's got a job here, and friends. And he's jealous of us. You know he is…how he sulks when he sees us together."

Roger's eyes jumped to his father's, seeking reassurance. Spooner's gaze wavered between his son and Mitzi.

"I can't…"

Mitzi threw me a glance to tell me she wasn't forgetting me for a minute. Her faintly swaying hips recaptured Spooner's attention.

"You've put him first all these years," she crooned. "You deserve a life of your own now, sweetheart."

Spooner moistened his lips. Behind the chair Roger dropped to his knees with a howl of anguish.

"Get the suitcase," Mitzi prompted.

I balanced on the balls of my feet. With Roger consumed by his sorrows, when Spooner moved, I'd have the best chance I was likely to get to rush Mitzi. Then I saw movement behind her. Roger surged up, left hand brandishing one of the heavy brass andirons.

"Roger, no!" his father screamed.

"Look out!" I shouted.

Uncertain which of us was trying to pull a fast one, Mitzi wavered. The andiron had reached the top of its arc. I lunged at her knees.

CHAPTER FORTY-NINE

The gunshot roared in my ears. Momentum threw me against Mitzi's shins and she fell on top of me. If the shot had hit me, it wasn't bad. At least I couldn't feel any effects. My muscles worked well enough to try to wrestle the .38 from Mitzi's hand. She fought like a hellcat.

Mitzi started to rake her fingernails into my cheek. I gave her an awkward sideways sock in the jaw. It startled her enough to loosen her grip on the gun, but not enough for me to pull it free. Ducking her renewed efforts to scratch my eyes out, I threw one leg across hers and straddled her.

The upright position gave me distance enough to put more force behind another imperfect punch, this time an uppercut. It dazed her more than the first. While I still couldn't pry the gun away, it bought me precious seconds to think.

Leaving myself with no way to block her attacks, I brought my left hand down, now gripping her hand between both of mine in the fight for the gun. Her single focus was to bring it up and in enough to shoot me. For half a second I ceased resisting. The sudden change allowed her hand, and mine, to lurch in her intended direction. But then, just as suddenly, my two hands shoved it down toward her thigh. I jammed my finger in on top of hers on the trigger and squeezed.

Mitzi shrieked. Her grip loosened, then tightened again, but too slowly. I ripped the gun away. Blood seeped out of the hole I'd put in her skirt. With her still kicking at me with her uninjured leg, I pushed out of her reach.

For a moment, I lay as close to the floor as I could, suppressing my urge to pant while I listened. Where were the others? I rolled quickly onto my back, but Roger wasn't looming, waiting to bash me. In between Mitzi's moans and curses, I heard someone sobbing.

Had Mitzi's shot hit Spooner? Was he sobbing from pain and betrayal? Or had she missed? Was one of the Spooners weeping because the other had run and abandoned him, thanks to the rupture the woman who now lay bleeding had caused between them?

With Mitzi's gun at the ready I sat up. A broad-shouldered man stood over a figure that lay by the wingback chair. His revolver hung listlessly by his side.

"Boike?" I croaked. "Did you follow me here?"

"Not exactly. I went back to have it out with Freeze. He was on his way to see a judge about a search warrant. He told me to get to your place and make sure you didn't launch out on your own, but you weren't in your office. You okay?"

"Yeah, fine."

I got slowly to my feet. Roger Spooner lay sprawled on his back with the andiron on the floor beside him. His father knelt over him, stroking his cheek and sobbing.

Boike had saved the life of a woman who didn't deserve to be saved. He'd put an end to a man who had killed once and was about to kill again. Yet I found myself feeling sorry for Roger Spooner as I stood in the midst of the sad tableau while Mitzi spewed curses and Spooner Senior keened his grief.

Roger had been misjudged and jeered at all his life just because he was different, and different in the eyes of society meant flawed. The one person who had loved him and bragged about him, and resented slights to Roger more than Roger himself had was his father. Then a woman who cared about no one but herself came between them, a serpent slithering into the imperfect Eden father and son had made for themselves.

"Daddy's here, Roger. It's going to be okay, Roger. Daddy's here…" Spooner was crooning.

His tenderness, his remorse, came too late. Red saturated the front of Roger's shirt and the pool beneath him was large.

Boike was on the phone calling the ambulance.

"How bad is she?" he asked nodding at Mitzi as he hung up.

"Not as bad as she deserves. Her days of swaying her backside are probably over, but she'll make it."

"Police!" yelled a voice at the door.

It was Freeze. His eyes swept the scene and he let out a long breath.

"The blonde's got the cufflink stuffed down her blouse," said Boike. "You'll want my weapon."

"And mine," I said.

"Wait," snapped Freeze.

In the hall outside there were sounds of other policemen arriving. Freeze slapped a detective badge and identification card into Boike's hand.

"You rushed out so fast you must have forgotten to ask me for these. Put them back in your pocket and save us all a lot of trouble."

CHAPTER FIFTY

It was a gorgeous day. I had my office windows open and the rumble of carts bumping over bricks drifted in from the produce market as I waited for Daisy. She had made an appointment, and she walked in right on the dot.

"I've come to say goodbye, and thanks."

She looked very different today from the girl who'd entered my office less than a month ago. Today she was a young woman, poised and polished in suit and heels, with pearls in her ears. I shook the hand she offered.

"It's final, then? You're all returning to the camp in Wyoming?"

"Heart Mountain. Yes. After what we've been through, my parents think the whole family should be together. I had some last bits of business to wind up first."

In the ten days since things came to a head in Spooner's apartment, Tosh had made his way back to the War Relocation field office in Cincinnati. Several Japanese-American lawyers who had found jobs in that city quickly arranged with a local legal team to protect his interests. Since Spooner had made a full confession, it appeared Tosh would be completely cleared. He professed not to know the names of the people who helped him reach safety, and maybe he didn't.

"Grandma asked me to tell you money alone can't express our gratitude," Daisy said. "She made you this." A wide, radiant, in-on-a-secret smile spread over her face. "Grandma says you're the sparrow."

Unfurling a scroll tucked under her arm, she displayed a Japanese painting. Its delicate strokes depicted a small bird attacking a hawk.

The End

READ ALL THE MAGGIE SULLIVAN MYSTERIES

No Game for a Dame

When a stranger who threatened her and wrecked her office winds up dead, 1940s private eye Maggie Sullivan finds herself facing a crime boss.

Tough Cookie

A high stakes swindler Maggie is hunting is found floating in the river. Now someone wants to silence her – and the corpse is strangely active.

Don't Dare a Dame

A 25-year-old murder jeopardizes Maggie's future as a private eye as well as her life when it points toward people with political connections.

Shamus in a Skirt

Murder and theft at a posh hotel pits Maggie against well-heeled suspects fleeing the war in Europe.

Maximum Moxie

Kidnapping, murder and a child's plea draw Maggie into a new case days before the attack on Pearl Harbor.

Dames Fight Harder

Maggie becomes the last hope for a friend accused of murder.

Uncivil Defense

To save innocent lives, Maggie must learn who killed a newly released convict during a blackout drill.

ABOUT THE AUTHOR

M. Ruth Myers received a Shamus Award from Private Eye Writers of America for the third book in her Maggie Sullivan mysteries series. She is the author of more than a dozen books in assorted genres, some written under the name Mary Ruth Myers. If you shine a bright light in her eyes, she'll admit to one husband, one daughter, one son-in-law, one grandson and one cat – all of whom she adores. She lives in Ohio.

CPSIA information can be obtained
at www.ICGtesting.com
Printed in the USA
LVHW011022130620
657889LV00010B/2050